I0673751

MAGIC OF THE VOID

Winslow Witch Chronicles
Book the First

Lena Mae Hill

Copyright © 2017 Lena Mae Hill
Second Edition

All rights reserved. No part of this book may be reproduced or
transmitted in any form or by any means, electronic or
mechanical, including photocopying, recording, or by any
information storage and retrieval system, without the express
written permission of the publisher, except in cases of reviewer
quoting brief passages in a review.
This book is a work of fiction. Names, characters, places, and
incidents are used factiously. Any resemblance to actual persons,
living or dead, business establishments, and events are entirely
coincidental. Use of any copyrighted, trademarked, or brand
names in this work of fiction does not imply endorsement of
that brand.
Published in the United States by Lena Mae Hill and Speak
Now.
www.lenamaehill.com

This edition
ISBN-13: 978-1-945780-32-5

In memory of author Edna Walters, whose magic left this world too soon.

ACKNOWLEDGMENTS

I'd love to thank all the awesome people who made this book possible and helped along the way. First off, a huge thank you with chocolate frosting for my beta readers—Jennifer G., Jennifer R., Meagon C.W., and Jill M. Y'all helped me so much I can't even begin to tell you.

As always, the GRITS group for all the moral support and hot tub therapy.

And last but definitely not least, my family for their endless support. Couldn't have done without any of the above. Thank you!

ONE

Winslow, Arkansas,
1987

Sagely peeked at the sunset lighting up the sky over the low, lush hills of the Ozark Mountains. It was that perfect time of evening, when the air itself seemed a cool blue, and a gentle breeze rippled over the short grass in the park.

"Look out!" Annie yelled.

Sagely spun towards the Frisbee, her Tae Kwon Do training kicking in as she executed a perfect turn. Unfortunately, martial arts hadn't taught her to catch a Frisbee flying by just out of reach. She dove for it with outstretched fingers. Too late, she caught sight of the figure jogging across her path. She had just enough time to see that he was totally ace before she slammed into him so hard they both went sprawling. Or rather, she went sprawling...right on top of him.

While she was trying to decide whether to jump up and run away in humiliation or enjoy the moment, he smiled up at her. The corners of his green eyes crinkled.

Definitely enjoy.

He had an appealing amount of stubble on his square jaw and dark blonde hair pulled back in a knot at the nape of his neck. Under her, she could feel the heat of his skin and the hard, solid muscle of his bare chest. She couldn't believe her tiny frame, which barely cleared five feet, could knock him flat. Her t-shirt had had ridden up a few inches when she fell, and his skin against hers sent a rain of sparkles through her body.

"Hey there, Little Red," he said, his voice deep and smooth, without a hint of gravel. His strong hands rested gently on her upper arms, warming her entire body.

"Hi," she breathed.

A teasing curl tugged at the corner of his lips, and she knew he'd caught the appreciation in her voice.

As their eyes met, a jolt rocked through her, like a quick pulse of electrical current. She gasped.

The smiled melted from his lips. "I better get back to my run."

"Oh, right!" she said, scrambling off him and reaching up to tighten her bright-red side ponytail. "Sorry. Are you okay?"

She offered a hand to help him up, but he leapt to his feet in one nimble, graceful motion. Before she could say another word—or ask for his number—he sprinted away down the path through the park.

Well, he *was* jogging before she bowled him over, she reminded herself. Still, she'd never made a guy literally run in terror.

"You'll have to show me that trick," her roommate said behind her. Sagely had planned today's outing to the state park in an attempt to create a bonding experience with her roommate. They didn't have much in common, and after a couple weeks of sharing an apartment, she'd almost given up hope of being more than casual acquaintances with her roommate. But she was nothing if not determined.

While she'd talked to the guy, she'd forgotten all about Annie and the Frisbee. She could still feel the heat of his hands on her skin. Damn, she was getting desperate if she could fantasize about a random guy in the park. For all she knew, he could be a total creep. She probably needed to start thinking about losing her v-card.

"Oh, bite me," she said. But she didn't want Annie to think she was really mad, so she smiled and added, "Trust me, that was not intentional."

"It was a little obvious," Annie admitted. "You ready to go? I hate driving on these curvy roads in the dark."

After a fruitless search for the Frisbee in the gathering dusk, they gave up and headed to their cars.

"I have to stop for gas," Sagely said. "Would you feed Rizzo if you get home before me?"

She hadn't seen her beloved cat since morning, as she'd come straight from Tae Kwon Do after changing into a t-shirt knotted at the side, jean shorts, and her treasured red python cowboy boots. She and Annie had driven separately, so she climbed into her hatchback Cavalier and slipped Madonna's new cassette in the tape deck.

As she pulled out onto the two-lane road that led away from the park, she couldn't stop going back to the moment her eyes locked with the guy's, when that weird bolt of electricity passed between them. So, she might've been a little distracted as she wound along the steep blacktop road leading back to Fayetteville, the tiny college town where she went to school.

A pair of headlights coming in the opposite direction brought her full attention. She slammed her foot on the brake, waiting for the truck to pass. Instead, she was rocketed forward. Her head slammed into the steering wheel, and she felt a sickening crunch as her nose broke. The lights from the other vehicle blazed into her eyes, blinding her completely.

Instead of stopping, the truck pushed forward, forcing her car towards the drop-off at the edge of the road. She grabbed the wheel and wrenched it in the other direction, away from the steep incline. Before she could get off the road, the truck backed up, away from her. Finally.

Still stunned, she sighed in relief, barely aware of the blood dripping down her face. But then the truck roared straight at her again, crushing into the front of her car for the second time. Glass showered across her and the seat.

Her head bounced off the steering wheel and then slammed back against the headrest. The back end of her car careened into the ditch next to a sheer wall of rock where they'd cut into the mountain to make the road. Groping blindly, she found the door handle and kicked open the door, only then feeling the pain in her leg. She tried to stand, but her knee buckled with a screaming pain, and she collapsed onto the blacktop road. Tears blurred her vision, and she only realized she was not alone when strong hands gripped her shoulders and flipped her onto her back.

She tried to stifle her sobs, fury boiling inside her.

She wanted to scream at the asshole who'd run head-on into her car—twice. But just as she sucked in a breath to cuss him out, a boot stomped on her abdomen.

The foot seemed to belong to a stone statue, crushing the air and life out of her. She raised her elbow to bring it down on his shin and splinter it just like the boards she broke in Tae Kwon Do competitions, but before she could, an iron grip clamped down on her forearm.

She could just make out the shape looming over her, impossibly dark against the twilight behind him, as if he were a man-shaped black hole, absorbing all light and air from the world. Faintly, as she began to pass out from lack of oxygen, she heard the crunching of her bone when he twisted her arm all the way around. She opened her mouth, but she didn't hear a scream. A scream required breath, and she had none.

The man leaned over her. She smelled burnt hair, and something damp and musty like a basement. The man wore a black hat and cloak. *Like the devil in an old movie,* she thought crazily as she ebbed away on a tidal wave of pain.

"Give me what's mine," he rasped. A light glinted in his hand, and a blade sliced across her throat.

Just before she passed out, light washed over them as a car drove past. Her last thought was that at least Annie would be home to feed Rizzo.

TWO

Sagely woke to see a man leaning over her. She jerked to sit up, but he placed a gentle hand on her chest and pushed her back, murmuring kind words in his smooth voice. She knew that voice from…somewhere. She couldn't tell if she was dreaming, or hallucinating, or if she was dead and having an after-life vision.

She tried to open her mouth, to speak, but a searing pain sliced across her throat. She remembered the blade sliding through her flesh. The memory hurt almost more than the pain now consuming her body.

She couldn't formulate a sentence even if she could've spoken. The pain turned off everything in her brain, so that all she could do was feel instead of think. Warm, sticky liquid trickled down her neck, and an itching sensation found its way through the pain. She twitched, searching for a word for how ridiculous it was to notice that when she was dying. Or already dead.

6

The man spoke again, his words soothing. But his hands came for her throat, a ball of white-blue light cupped between his palms. Sagely tried to turn away, to scream, but she was trapped, paralyzed, as his hands sank to her skin. A bolt of cauterizing heat split open the wound on her throat, and she slipped from consciousness again.

When she woke next, she could immediately feel that something was different. Something was wrong. She was only halfway conscious, but she could feel something moving inside her. That ball of lightning he touched to her slit throat had somehow crawled into her belly. She could feel a foreign and dark presence stirring inside her like a parasite.

He'd shoved it down her throat, and now she was the host.

She tried to cough, to choke it out, but her body refused to cooperate. For a second, she wondered if she was still paralyzed. Her limbs were as heavy as the earth itself, and she felt like she was moving through thick mud.

"Close your eyes," the guy whispered. The guy from the park. That's where she'd heard his voice. His hand brushed tenderly but firmly over her eyelids, sweeping them closed as if he were closing the eyes of a loved one on her death bed. She was going to die now.

The next time she woke, the sun was shining in her window. For one split second, she forgot the darkest night of her life. For one split second, she was in her apartment, waking up on a Sunday morning with the sun slanting in through the blinds. Served her right for putting her bed next to the window.

But then it came rushing back. The previous night.

More like nightmare.

She sat up, and her head swam with dizziness. She had to lie back. While she struggled to remember, she took in the room. It wasn't the dorm room she'd left a few weeks ago, but it looked like any dorm room anywhere—cream-colored cinderblock walls, a window with Venetian blinds, generic furniture.

But there were no decorations, no bulletin boards pinned with shots of sunburned spring-breakers or photos of parents from back home, no Bon Jovi or Richard Marx posters on the wall. No carefully chosen duvet that had to match that of a roommate or cute décor indicating someone else's personality.

Am I in jail?

A dorm room without personalization looked an awful lot like a jail cell, after all…

She hung her head over the edge of the bed, and her red hair tumbled forward. Someone had taken out her ponytail and pulled off her boots. With a flash of panic, she searched the room until she found them sitting neatly in a corner. Those boots were her most prized possession, the one indulgence she'd allowed herself…pretty much ever.

She breathed a sigh of relief when she saw that the rest of her clothes were still on, and that the bed was not bolted to the floor. But she winced at the slightly painful tugging sensation when she twisted to see the floor. Throwing back the covers, she gasped when she saw the blood-encrusted t-shirt clinging to her flesh. Not sure that she actually wanted to see her wounds, she braced herself before looking. The blood had dried, sealing her shirt to her belly, and the same stinging sensation came when she pulled it away.

In shock, she stared down at her abdomen. Smears of dried blood streaked her skin. Her hand flew to her throat when she remembered the black silhouette standing over her, and the slash of his blade through her neck.

Wherever I am, they must have access to one hell of a medicine cabinet.

But there was no bandage. No wound at all. Her skin was as smooth as it had been the previous morning. Her arm was not broken, though she'd clearly felt it splinter. And her nose wasn't even swollen. If it wasn't for the blood-soaked shirt still hugging her body, she could've convinced herself it was a dream.

A shudder wracked her body when she remembered the blinding, earth-defying pain of the fireball being forced down her throat.

She'd been dying, practically dead. Then someone shoved a ball of white-hot fire down her spurting windpipe, and it cauterized her wound. Not just cauterized it, but healed it. She had no idea how it could be true, but it was. She was perfectly healthy and healed.

But whatever he'd put inside her... It was still there.

THREE

Something was buzzing inside Sagely like a swarm of microscopic bees. Or flies. Or something else that she probably didn't want inside her.

But like it or not, it was there, waiting, like some kind of beast that might spring out at any moment. If she was a beast, that buzzing might be the prickle of fur about to sprout all over her body. She was gonna need a serious supply of Nair if that were the case.

Before she could contemplate whether she needed a shave or an exorcism, a tap sounded at the door and a boy stuck his head in. The tingling inside her ratcheted up a notch. The boy was about five years younger than she was, somewhere in his mid-teens. He had a fringe of red hair hanging just above his blue eyes, and a spattering of freckles across his turned-up nose.

"Good morning, sunshine," he said with a grin, stepping into the room when he saw that she was decent.

Even though he didn't look familiar, somehow he *felt* familiar. It was like meeting a little brother she'd forgotten since childhood. Except she'd never actually had a little brother. She remembered her childhood all too well, even the parts she'd rather forget.

"I guess you're wondering what's going on," the boy said.

Hello, understatement.

He loped over to the bed, where he sat down beside her. It would've been presumptuous for a strange man to waltz in and sit on the bed when she was still in it, but this was a boy, not a man. She could tell it was totally innocent, and that it never crossed his mind that it might be inappropriate.

"I'm Eli, by the way," he said before she could speak. "I'm here to unofficially welcome you to the coven. The others will welcome you officially later. So. What do you want to know?"

"I do have a few questions," she admitted.

Understatement of the century.

"Ask away," he said. "I'll do my best to fill in the blanks and explain what your new life will be like."

New life? She swallowed hard. "Was I…abducted?"

Eli laughed. "Of course not."

"Okay, good," she said, relaxing a little. "Then first off, where are we? And when can I go home? I don't seem to be injured anymore, and I'm definitely not looking to start a new life. Sorry."

He dropped his gaze and twisted the wide band he was wearing on his little finger, some kind of dull metal that looked like iron with tiny symbols etched all around it. "You can't just *leave*," he said. "That would be dangerous."

"Great. I'm a hostage."

"It's only for your safety that you need to stay." He paused a long moment, frowning down at his ring. Finally he asked, "Do you remember what happened to you last night?"

"How could I forget," she said, her heartbeat speeding. "Some psycho ran me off the road and tried to kill me."

"That's good. That you remember, I mean, not that someone tried to kill you. Of course that's bad." He rushed through the words, his face turning pink under his freckles.

"Who tried to kill me? You said it's not safe to leave, but I'd never even met that guy, so I don't think he'll be looking for me in particular. I'm just lucky enough to chance on a murderous psychopath. Lucky, lucky me."

"You are lucky," Eli said earnestly. "Lucky that Quill got there in time to save your life. He was leaving the park when he saw someone had been in an accident. He said the other guy took off when he drove up."

"Okay, let's call that lucky," Sagely said. "But I'm not in any danger. I'd never seen that guy before in my life. Trust me, I'd remember." She shuddered thinking of him, but she wasn't afraid to go home. He'd obviously run off before searching her glove box for her insurance cards, so he didn't even know her name. It wasn't like he could look her up in phonebook.

"When you've had some time to clean up, I'll take you in to meet the whole gang," Eli said. "Quill sent me in first to answer any questions, because I'm not intimidating like some of the others." He didn't say this like it was a bad thing, but like he was stating a simple fact.

Sagely was a bit offended on his behalf, though it was true. This Quill person had gotten one thing right—this kid was not a bit intimidating. Even if she was still injured, she could fell him with one good roundhouse kick. But everything else he said was wrong. She could take care of herself. She was a blackbelt for a reason.

Her head swam with questions, though, and she wanted answers before she left. She didn't know what to ask first. Finally, she settled on the most pressing questions. "Who are the others? And who is Quill? And why do I need to meet them?"

"Quill is our highest-level student, almost fully vested in his magic, and the guy who saved your life. And the others are...the other students of magic," Eli finished with a shrug. "And you'll need to meet them because you'll be staying here while you learn to use your new magic."

The guy who saved her life. The blond guy she'd bowled over at the park. Heat crept into her cheeks, but she pushed away thoughts of that hard body under hers and focused on the present.

"Magic." She gave Eli her best no-bullshit look, the one she usually reserved for the Tae Kwon Do students she taught at the studio.

"That's what healed you," he said. "You must know people don't heal from that kind of injury. If it wasn't for Quill, you'd be dead right now. You said you remembered last night."

"I do," she said, trying to keep the defensive edge from her voice. She didn't like being called a liar. She took a breath. She had no better explanation for why she had no marks from last night. "Magic. Okay. I'll play along. Is that what that...fireball...was?"

"Exactly," he said, his face lighting up like now they were on the same page. "That was Quill's magic. Not everyone has enough to save someone from death like that. Not if they want to keep some for themselves." His eyes shone with admiration.

"Um, okay, right."

"Quill has some of the strongest magic the Majoris have ever seen. He's totally boss."

"Majoris?"

"Those are our teachers," he explained. "Quill is the highest-level student. He was born with an enormous capacity for magic. Some people have magic in their bloodline, and it gets passed on to the next generation, but it's been diluted through time. Not Quill's, though. He's strong enough to protect pretty much the entire coven."

"But I'm not…magical," Sagely said, unable to think of a better word. "Why would he protect me?"

"He gifted you some of his magic," Eli said, lowering his voice. "You probably feel it right now. That tingling sensation? That's the magic. It should have just healed you, but it stuck around."

So this feeling would never go away? She was stuck with internal pins-and-needles for the rest of her life, like a scar no one could see? She hadn't asked for this. She hadn't asked for any of this. She was a regular college student, independent and driven, ready to graduate college in a year. Not some crazy chick with magical…blood? She didn't even believe in magic.

She started breathing hard. It didn't make sense. Someone had tried to kill her the previous night, and now she was stuck here because someone else shoved fire down her throat and it might be dangerous for her to leave. She was so ready to wake up from this nightmare.

"Yeah, but why?" she asked, gripping the edge of the bed to steady herself.

Eli shrugged. "I told you. He saw the accident, and he found you on the road and did what anyone would do. He tried to save you. He didn't know the magic would stay inside you like it has."

"Great. I can't leave because he gave me his magic?"

"Would you rather be dead?"

"No," she admitted.

"You're lucky," he said. "Magic is the most precious gift in the universe. The most precious energy. You should feel honored. Most witches are born with just a trace, or given just enough to feel a pull when someone else with magic is nearby. They spend most of their lives gathering it from the world around them and learning to harness it. To save your life like he did...depending on your condition and your capacity for magic, he could have given you a lot. You could have all kinds of powers. You might be even stronger than some of the witches here."

Sagely blinked. "Witches?"

She pictured Halloween witches, the kind with green warty faces, hunched over cauldrons stirring bubbling brews with broomsticks. Or weird girls playing with Ouija boards and having seances. Oh shit. He'd said something about a coven earlier. She was pretty sure her high school had warned her about devil worshipping cults. Was that what this was?

I will not freak out, I will not freak out. I. Will. Not. Freak. Out.

"Witches?" she squeaked again, her voice rising.

"You don't have to call yourself that," Eli said

quickly. "I don't call myself a warlock, though that's what I am, I guess. But since I'm only fifteen, and I'm still learning to use my magic... It doesn't kick in until..."

He broke off and turned a strange shade of magenta. "Puberty," he finished, his voice cracking like he'd reverted back to that awkward age.

The moment she saw him blushing and flustered, an instinct kicked in to protect him just like she would a kid who got embarrassed in class. If this was what witches were like, they were just like anyone else. And if she was freaking out, she couldn't very well reassure him. She took a deep breath. No use panicking before she saw what it was all about.

"I'm Sagely," she said, smiling to show him it didn't embarrass her, hoping to ease his mind. "And I'm already twenty-one. And I guess I better learn to use this magic stuff Quill gave me so I can get home. My cat is probably freaking out right now."

He gave her a grateful smile, but quickly looked away, obviously not over his embarrassment. "It might depend on how much magic you have. I don't have much. But anyone who has usable magic has to be trained in how to use it. Otherwise you could hurt yourself or someone else."

"How long does training take?" she asked, already calculating how long summer break lasted. She could double up on classes, call it summer school, and be back by fall at the latest. She was nothing if not ambitious.

"Again, that depends on the person," Eli said. "It sounds like I've answered all the easy questions. You're probably ready to meet the others."

"In this?" she asked, gesturing to her crusty shirt.

"Oh, right," he said, jumping to his feet. "I'll get you something. I'll be right back." He seemed relieved at the excuse to leave.

Damn. Way to screw up your first introduction, she thought as Eli slipped out the door. She jumped up and paced the room. Outside the window, she saw a small yard, and beyond that, a forest of lush green trees. Eli hadn't told her where they were, but it didn't look much different from Fayetteville. Maybe they weren't too far. She could go back to teach classes and continue training for her fourth-degree black belt, and come here to train in magic a few days a week.

It couldn't be harder than Tae Kwon Do. She'd work her way up and graduate by the end of summer, a master of her newfound abilities. As excitement began to build inside her, the buzzing intensified. This time, she relished it. Her magic. Who wouldn't want magical powers?

She wondered what she could do.

She'd start by tracking down the asshole who attacked her and punching his teeth down his throat.

FOUR

A few minutes later, Eli returned with a stack of folded clothes. Sagely wriggled out of her t-shirt, glad to dump it in the trash can in the corner. She'd just about kill for a shower, but there was no bathroom off the bedroom, so she made a mental note to ask about that when she got a chance. After pulling on a pair of skin-tight jeans and a hot pink t-shirt and her own boots, she stepped out of the bedroom into the hall where Eli was waiting.

The house was furnished more like a cozy cottage than a dorm. It was small but clean, with wooden floorboards and walls, and crowded but homey furniture. In the main room three fat, comfy sofas sat facing each other like three sides of a square. The front door stood open, the entrance covered by a screen door. Through it, Sagely could see more familiar forest swaying gently in the midday sun. Before she had time to wonder too much about the oddity of this cute little house having one cinderblock room, Eli opened the door to a basement.

"Oh, hell no," Sagely said, stepping back. "I'm not going down in your basement. I've read Stephen King. I watch the news. I'm not stupid."

"It's okay," he said. "I promise."

"Um…yeah, no. That's not making me feel better. First off, no one knows where I am. *I* don't even know where I am. And even if there was a cop standing by to protect me, I wouldn't do it."

"We're right by Boxley Valley," Eli said.

Not too far from home, as she suspected. She'd never been to Boxley Valley, but she'd heard of the historic cabins there. The Buffalo National River ran nearby, and tourists came to canoe, hike, and camp. But no matter how idyllic the setting, she was still not going into a basement with a stranger.

Suddenly, the wall beyond the doorway began to emit an eerie glow, and the buzzing in her blood intensified. A deep, resonate voice commanded, "Come."

She gasped, struggling against the urge to shoot off a rude answer. Did the wall just speak to her? She was losing her freaking mind.

"It's okay, really," Eli said again, touching her elbow. "You share the magic of the coven now. We'd die before we'd let anything hurt you."

Sagely herself was dying of curiosity about how they got the wall to speak. After a second, she stepped forward. She knew how to defend herself. She could probably take down a dozen of them before they hurt her. If they had weapons, she knew how to get one and turn it back on her attacker.

She quelled the tiny voice asking why she wasn't able

to overpower her would-be murderer. Stepping forward, she passed through the door. The walls continued to glow, as if not made of regular sandstone but a giant, flat, phosphorescent pearl. She couldn't help herself. She reached out and touched the wall. As her skin tingled with magic, the hairs stood up all along her arm. The swirling glow immediately began to move towards her fingers, which rested against the cool, smooth surface. It collected under her hand until a bright spot rested under her palm. When she moved her hand, it followed, as if magnetized.

She noticed Eli grinning, proud to show off his awesome home. Pulling her hand back, she continued down the stairs, her fears forgotten in the face of such wonder. She couldn't wait to see what else they had down there. Turned out, magic was pretty cool.

At the bottom of the stairs, they stepped into a chamber made of ordinary brown sandstone, with wall sconces set around the cavernous room. Stalactites and stalagmites lined the cavern, with a few randomly placed in the center of the chamber. Around the base of a stalagmite towards the back of the cavern, a tiny trickle of water flowed, lit up with a flickering golden glow, a reflection of the light from the sconces. The trickle continued towards the back of the chamber, where it disappeared into darkness.

In the chamber, a group of teens and a few adults stood facing her. Waiting. Here was her chance to make an entrance. But she was overwhelmed with the sudden intensity of the magic buzzing in her blood. It was deafening, drowning her in waves.

Get a grip, Sagely.

She took a steadying breath and surveyed the group.

Not a single hooded black robe among them, no one holding a broomstick or wearing a pointy hat. No one in ripped fishnets with black lipstick, either, and hardly a hippie skirt among them.

They didn't look like witches at all. They were just wearing regular clothes like her. She started to relax. Then she spotted Quill standing at the edge of the group, his hands clasped in front of him, his broad shoulders squared and his chin tilted up just slightly, a hint of a smile on his wide, red lips.

Damn, I just want to bite those lips!

As if he had read her mind, his smile turned into a smirk. A jolt went through her when his eyes locked on hers, and she gasped at the exquisite sensation of it, almost painful, like an invisible bolt of electricity was dancing along their connected gazes. She tore her eyes from his and staggered forward a step before recovering her dignity.

What the hell, Sagely? Total airhead is not the impression you want to make.

She straightened up and stepped forward with more purpose, letting her eyes move over the others while she ignored the vibration of magic inside her. It was as if someone was holding an electric razor to the nape of her neck. How the hell did anyone concentrate enough to learn anything with this feeling running through them all the time?

Unsure how to proceed, she faltered again when she was a few paces from the group. She didn't know who to greet. No one stepped forward to extend a hand, and she didn't know who the leader was. She knew Quill was powerful, but it seemed so forward, so obvious, to choose him first.

So she thrust out her hand towards the group in general, avoiding his eyes. That was when she noticed all the others' expressions. Most looked curious, but some looked wary, or excited, and one blonde girl was glaring at Sagely like she'd rather set her on fire than shake her hand. Weirdly, the magic inside her began to vibrate at a higher frequency when their eyes met. She pulled her gaze away and addressed the group as a whole.

"Hi," she said. "I'm Sagely. I'm told that I'm now in possession of some magic, and I need to learn how to use it before I go home."

A couple kids who looked about Eli's age exchanged glances. An older man took her hand and gave it a polite, quick squeeze before letting go.

"Welcome to the Winslow Witch Coven. I'm Ory. I'm the Majori for the entry level, when people are just coming into their magic."

"Thanks," she said. "But I'm just here to learn what to do about this magic stuff I supposedly possess."

After an awkward pause, Quill stepped away from the group and stood beside her, facing the others. "Winslow Witches, this is your new sister," he said, addressing the group. He put an arm around her shoulders and gave her a reassuring squeeze. She went rigid as that simple gesture made her magic explode like he'd thrown a lit match into a warehouse full of fireworks. The magic sparkled and popped and spun inside her until she was breathless, nearly choking on it. Was he feeling this? If so, how did he continue to speak?

"We're each anxious to know which class you'll be joining after your initiation, so maybe we should go ahead and measure your capacity for magic before anyone gets too attached."

Too attached? Um, no. She was leaving. No one should be getting attached to her.

"Whoa there," she said, holding up her hands. "But I'm not joining any coven. I have a life at home."

Quill dropped his arm from her shoulders. "You don't have to join," he said. "But it would be best to save that decision until we know if it's safe to let you walk out of here without training. Untrained magic can be very dangerous to both the user and those around them."

Sagely thought it over and then nodded. Now she understood. They weren't worried about her being attacked again. They were worried about her being dangerous. "Then let's do this," she said.

Quill clapped Eli on the back. "Did you answer all her questions?"

"I did my best," Eli said, smiling up at Quill with reverence.

"I'm sure you were rad," Quill said, squeezing Eli's shoulder before turning to Sagely. He grinned, excitement flickering in his eyes as if challenging her to a sparring match. "Ready to measure your magic against ours?"

FIVE

Was she? She wasn't sure if she even wanted this magical "gift." It seemed as much curse as gift. Maybe she could fake it, lose on purpose, so they'd think she didn't get enough to be a danger to anyone. Then they wouldn't have any reason to keep her there.

"Don't be scared," Quill said in a low voice, so only she could hear.

"I'm not scared."

She wasn't. Uncertain, yes. If she gave it her all, and turned out to have only a tiny sliver of magic, would she be disappointed? Would they let her leave, or make her stay anyway? If she wasn't very powerful, would they look down on her? If she was super magical, would they be jealous? And more importantly, would it take years to learn to control it enough to go home to her Tae Kwon Do studio and Rizzo?

Quill looked doubtful, but he stepped away from her

without arguing. Majori Ory stepped forward. "I'll be the proctor for your first magical exam. Call it a pop quiz, if you like."

She answered his smile with her own. Though the magic was still buzzing inside her, he had a calming presence, and she was immediately at ease with him. She hoped she'd get him for a teacher, even if it meant she didn't have enough magic to do anything cool. He was a short guy with a little pot belly, skinny legs, and a head as bald as a cue-ball. He wore black shoes and slacks, and a pale blue striped shirt with suspenders and a bow tie. Compared to the Majori standing behind him, a tree of a man who was glaring with thunderous eyebrows drawn together, he was about as unimposing as a person could be.

"Come along," Ory said, holding out an arm in a grand gesture, ushering her towards the back of the cavern. She expected to step into the tunnel that the water trickled into, and she wondered if the walls there would light up, too. But Ory stopped about halfway across the cavern. A grove of stalagmites had been cut off at stool level and polished to a smooth surface.

The stools were clustered around a large, flat stone table. Ory gestured for her to sit on one of them, and he took his place on the one across from her.

"How do you decide who tests me?" she asked. "Shouldn't I be meeting with your leader or something?"

"We don't have a leader," he said with a smile. "We govern ourselves according to the laws of magic. Within that, we're allowed anything."

She wondered what "allowed anything" entailed, but he went on before she could ask.

"As to your other question, we all test you." He set his hands on the table, and as she watched, the surface began to glow gently, with a slight concentration around the ring he wore. "Think of this as an entrance exam where we test what you already know. Except today, we're not only measuring how much magic you possess, but also how much you are capable of containing at once. Your magical capacity tells us what training you need. You may not have much now, but if your capacity is high, you'll need to learn to control not only what you currently possess, but also your magic when it's at full capacity."

"So I could get more than I have now?" Sagely asked, trying to ignore the buzzing in her hands.

"Magic, like any energy, varies. Depending on a witch's activities, and even her latest exercises in class, her magic will fluctuate daily. What we want to measure is less variable, though your current magic does show up in the test as well. So if you're trying to upstage me, you can call on your magic." He gave her a wink to show he was joking. "But you'll be using it if you do that, and since you haven't been trained how to do so safely, we recommend you just relax and let it measure your capacity without expending anything."

"So it's not like a magical arm-wrestling match?"

Ory smiled. "No, it's not a competition against the others. No one here has any more authority or status than anyone else. We are all equals. Everyone is allowed to follow his or her own interests and passions. The Majoris don't make rules. We are here to instruct only. We offer guidance, having practiced magic longer than someone whose magic has only just awakened."

As he spoke, the glow became brighter and brighter,

until it was swirling and pulsing across the table, like a video she'd once seen of the surface of the sun, except this table was glowing blue instead of orange.

"If I have Quill's magic, shouldn't it already be awakened?"

It sure felt plenty lively and awake.

"It's been a long time since I trained gifted magic," Ory said. "Usually, witches are born with all the magic they are capable of containing at once. But it stays dormant throughout childhood. When it awakens, we train them to control their abilities. A witch who is gifted magic, and is able to retain it, is rare."

"Eli said anyone who has magic used on them gets some magic."

"That's true," he said. "But usually when someone receives magic, it is only a trace amount, and they spend it without awareness. That feeling you get when you have a premonition? That's a trace of magical energy. When the magic sends you that signal, it is usually spent. Most people who get a trace of magic never even know. But you got more than a trace. And the fact that you retained it means you have the flame inside you."

"I'm a little lost. What's this flame?"

"Think of it like…a pilot light on the stove. It keeps burning quietly, though you never pay it any mind. From that, the flame on a burner can be lit. When Quill gave you a healthy dose of magic, it didn't burn you up. It stayed inside you. Which means that you had that flame all your life. You just needed him to come along and light the more obvious fire."

He'd definitely lit some kind of fire inside her.

"Witches have this spark of magic always within, that

they must protect, even if they were to exhaust all their other magic."

With that, he stood and smiled. "This is the easiest test you'll ever take. Just place your palms on the table, as I did."

When he stepped aside, Eli took his place. "I already know you have more magic than I do," he said. "I saw you touching the wall in the stairwell."

She remembered that delighted look on his face. Was he happy that she was more powerful than him? Did having more magical capacity automatically make her more powerful? And why wasn't he jealous?

After a second, the light began to glow brighter under her hands. Under his, there was only a slight glow, barely a discernible difference between that and the rest of the table. He stood and smiled.

"Congratulations," he said, then dropped his voice to a whisper. "Beat Majori Romero for me." With a dopey grin, he walked away, and a skinny, mousy witch sat across from Sagely. Her hands were shaking when she set them on the table, and within seconds, it was apparent she had almost no magic.

It was super cool watching the witches parade by, getting to take in each one, even though they only made a bit of small talk. They all wore rings similar to Eli's, with symbols etched around them, though some were silver, copper, or gold. Some witches introduced themselves, some just looked curious, and some concentrated, as if willing the magic to come to their side of the table. But one by one, they got up and left, the glow on their side never equaling that under her palms.

A black girl with the most flawless complexion Sagely

had ever seen sat down across from her. Her skin looked as if it was made of silk, and her long hair was done in braids that reached her hips, with feathers and beads and ribbons woven into a few braids here and there. With her petite figure, big eyes, and light-weight orange sundress, she looked more like a fairie than a witch.

Like most of the others, as soon as Sagely examined her face, it was as if she'd always known her. Her magic called out to Sagely's.

"Shaneesha," the girl said, tossing her braids back. "Ready for this?"

"As I'll ever be."

"You're strong," she said. "Quill must have dosed you up, and you lived through it. You beat almost all the students already."

"I thought it wasn't a competition."

Shaneesha smirked and set her hands on the table. "You aren't summoning your magic?"

"Okay, maybe I'm concentrating a little," Sagely admitted with a grin.

Shaneesha smiled back. "At least you don't lie about it."

"What can I say, I'm competitive."

"Good," Shaneesha said. "You'll need it here."

A shiver went through Sagely, and she glanced up at the blonde girl, one of the five waiting to take their turn. She was still glaring daggers. "Ory made it sound like everyone's equal, and it doesn't matter how much magic you have."

Shaneesha snorted, staring at her hands. The pulsing light began to brighten under them. Sagely turned her concentration back on her own hands, which brightened the slightest bit. She was starting to sweat.

"Oh, yeah, we are," Shaneesha said. "But there's definitely a little bit of a social order."

"Great," Sagely said. "It's like high school all over again."

Shaneesha smiled. "Nah, it's not so bad. It's just human nature, especially at a school that teaches mastery of a skill. You said yourself that you're competitive. Don't you strive to better your opponent even if it's a friendly competition?"

Sagely thought of all the Tae Kwon Do tournaments she'd entered. She did it for fun and for the learning experience. But she also did it to win. "Okay, you got me."

"Yeah, I did," Shaneesha said. "Beat ya."

With a dazzling grin, she stood. Sagely started to protest. The girl had distracted her with all that talking. Surely that was cheating. A bunch of the others were clapping, and some of them were laughing. Not in a mean way, though, like they were glad she'd lost. Rather, they laughed like they'd laugh after a friendly arm-wrestling match between two friends.

"You've got more magic," Shaneesha said. "Just showing you how easy it is to lose your concentration when you're using magic."

"Does that count?"

"You decide," Shaneesha said. "I know that'll drive you crazy, not knowing if you won or lost." Obviously, she was not going to end Sagely's misery. She glared after her, but Shaneesha just tossed a grin back at her before joining the others.

Next, the huge, fierce-looking Majori sat down across from her. He was so big she'd swear she heard the stone stool creak under his weight. She wanted to pull her hands off the table, to wipe them on her jeans. But she licked her lips and focused on the tingling in her fingers, like her palms were connected by invisible energy to the table. The magic in her blood pulsed with the magic in the stone. She would not be duped again.

After a minute or so, the Majori's scowl deepened, and his massive eyebrows knitted together to form the unibrow to end all unibrows. Seriously, it looked like a fox tail was pinned across his giant forehead. Beads of sweat broke out on his ruddy cheeks, and he jumped up from the table and stomped away muttering curses. The spot where his hands had lain was bright blue...but not as bright as Sagely's. She'd already beaten Ory and now Majori Romero.

She started to get nervous. What if, somehow, she had more magic than any of them? What then? Did that make her, like, Queen of the Witches? The coven may not have leaders and pretend all students were the same, but they weren't. Even if the school didn't sanction cliques, status happened.

She glanced up at the next witch, the last Majori. She was a Hispanic woman with a round face, dark lipstick, and her eyebrows completely drawn on with eyebrow pencil. She sat and smiled warmly at Sagely without a trace of nervousness. "It's wonderful to have you here," she said. "I'm Yordine. We rarely get a sister who was gifted enough magic to join us."

"Who else here wasn't born with magic?" Sagely asked, keeping most of her attention on her hands.

"All of us here today were born with the gift, although we get more along the way." She moved her hands a little, and the magic swirled to her side of the table. "I'm the highest level Majori," she said. "Your benefactor is my top student."

At the mention of Quill, Sagely's heart raced, but she knew that was not the reason for Yordine's win. She got her, fair and square. Sagely sat back in her seat, defeated yet relieved. Her competitive side had wanted the win, but her rational side was definitely glad that she wasn't harboring a freakish amount of magic that would make everyone hate her.

She beat the next two witches, although one of them was so gorgeous it was hard to concentrate, and she had to look at her hands to remember what she was doing.

What the hell? I'm not attracted to girls!

Then the snooty blonde sat across from her. She had a thin face and thick, glossy hair pulled into a ponytail and draping forward over one shoulder. She stared Sagely down, her hands hovering just above the surface of the table.

Sagely could feel her magic sparking through her, like static electricity crackling against her palms and up her arms.

"I'm Raina," the girl said. "You'll want to remember my name."

She didn't toy with Sagely or play games. Magic flared under her hands, bright as a sunburst. In a matter of seconds, she'd quite literally outshone Sagely. With a satisfied smirk at her win, Raina rose and swept off to join the group.

As Sagely turned back from the witches, now buzzing with excitement, Quill took his seat across from her. He was the last one. She swallowed hard.

"They're wondering if I gave you so much of myself that I'm no longer stronger than them," he said with an easy smile. "I'm sure Ory told you that this measures both capacity and your current level of magic. We're mostly at full capacity, since we haven't trained today. I'm the only one who's depleted."

"Because you saved my life." Her eyes moved to his lips, and he smirked again, his eyebrow lifted in a cocky arch.

God, he was hot as hell on a Sunday. Just looking at those lips made her squirm in her seat. She imagined just how soft they would be against hers, just how good it would feel to touch them…

He licked his lips, and she felt her face flush at the thought of that tongue touching her skin.

"Now that you have my magic, I can pick up on your emotions," he said, lowering his voice so only she could hear. Without dropping his gaze, he set his hands on the table. The surface throbbed a blinding blue-white like the fireball he'd shoved down her throat last night. A jolt of magic shot up her arms. She gasped, but she didn't pull her hands away.

"Great," she muttered, her face burning. "A mind-reader. I better learn to control my thoughts along with my magic."

"Not a mind reader," he said with a grin, like he was seeing her naked right now and not ashamed of how much he enjoyed it. "Better. You can protect your thoughts, block someone out of your head. You can't block shared magic from calling out to its likeness. Since I gave you my magic, I can read it inside you." As he smirked at her, her face flushed hotter. So, he knew exactly how attractive she found him. Fantastic.

"What am I feeling right now?" she challenged, refusing to drop her eyes from his.

"Kind of embarrassed. Frustrated," he said with that same broad grin. He dropped his voice and leaned forward, his eyes locked on hers. "A little excited."

Dammit. She'd hoped he was bluffing.

"So can I read your emotions, too?" she asked.

He shrugged. "Yes. It goes both ways, but it's in proportion to the amount of shared magic you possess. Since I have more magic, I can sense yours more easily."

"That hardly seems fair. You already have the advantage in everything else."

"Don't be upset," he said. "It also means I can sense when you're in danger, protect you as I'd protect myself and my magic. You have a part of me inside you, Sagely." His eyes went serious, almost vulnerable.

"Great," she whispered. At long last, her gaze dropped to the table. A dense blue glow remained under her hands, as it had all along. Compared to his, it was like pea soup. She'd need sunglasses to look directly at the magic pulsing under his hands. It was so intense that his hands themselves had begun to glow with a soft, pulsing blue light, and his ring was as bright as a white-hot sun.

He arched an eyebrow at her again. "Call it a draw?"

She laughed before standing and bowing to him. "I invoke the mercy rule. Voluntary forfeiture."

SIX

After the test, the atmosphere in the cavern relaxed, but the buzz of excitement remained. Everyone was talking and murmuring at once. Majori Yordine approached and placed a closed fist over her heart. "Welcome to the Winslow Coven's training section," she said. "You'll need to stay and master your magic. I'll be honored to be your Majori when you reach my level. I have no doubt you will move up quickly."

"Thanks," Sagely said, not wanting to offend her by showing how pleased she was to start with Ory. He was obviously the easy teacher. She was not looking forward to the middle level, when she'd have to train under Romero the Giant.

This was all so new, she wasn't sure where to go now, what to do. But she didn't want to stand around looking awkward and alone, either. Just as she was starting to panic, Quill's head swung around, and their eyes locked.

He was talking to a group of witches who were hanging on his every word. Sagely remembered the intensity of his gaze when he said she was part of him, and a tremor traveled through her, making her thighs weak.

Quill said something to the group and ducked over to her. "Sorry I left you like that," he said. "I forget what it's like to be new somewhere. Come on, I'll take you to your room."

He rested a hand on her back, and she jumped a mile. Would she ever get used to the charge of their shared magic?

"You'll get used to it," he said.

Or his ability to practically read her mind?

She laughed nervously as he stepped into the dark tunnel. Her mind flashed to that man last night—could it be only last night?—who seemed to absorb light like a black hole. That was how the cave was, and she drew a little closer to Quill.

"Don't be afraid," he said, reaching out to run his fingers along the wall, leaving a streak of light behind. All around them, the walls began to glow a faint yellow, growing brighter with each step they took.

"Magic is just an energy source that most people aren't privy to," he said. "Once you get it, you can see a dimension of the world that others are oblivious to. It's like a sixth sense awakening."

She watched, transfixed, as his long fingers trailed along the wall, leaving tracers in their wake, as if shooting stars were falling from his fingertips. She wondered if they'd do that to her if he ran them over her body.

"Are you, like, the most powerful witch in the world?" she asked when he grinned sideways at her, obviously catching that fleeting thought from her. It was getting pretty damn annoying, actually. "Or whatever you call yourself. Wizard? Magician?"

He laughed. "Want me to pull a rabbit out of my hat for you?"

"Just tell me," she said, elbowing him as they made their way down the corridor. "Mage?"

"Warlock," he said.

"Oh, right. Eli told me that. So, how much magic do you have? Because I admit, I was feeling pretty smug about mine, and then you just…blew me clear out of the water. So, for real. Are you the most powerful warlock in the world?"

"Maybe someday."

They made their way along the softly glowing sandstone tunnel. The tiny stream trickled beside them as they walked.

"But no," he said, shaking his head. "I'm only the most powerful in the coven. Unfortunately, the most powerful warlock in the world practices dark magic."

Great. More things she didn't know. And it wasn't like she could go look this stuff up in the encyclopedia. She remembered the man from the night before, how his shadow swallowed the night. She shivered. "I take it you're not a dark warlock?"

"Of course not," he said, looking deeply wounded.

"Sorry," she said, feeling the wave of indignation rolling off him like it was her own. So that's what he felt from her, but stronger, because he had much more magic.

They stepped into another chamber, this one smaller than the one at the entrance. It was as big as a living room and smelled a little like eggs. Sagely heard water gurgling and bubbling somewhere, and what sounded like birds chirping, though they were deep underground. Quill stepped up to a half-circle inscribed on the wall like a rainbow. The apex was about seven feet tall, and it was bisected by a line straight down the middle.

"Magic responds to magic," he said. "With so many of us here, the place absorbs our magic, and in turn, replenishes us. Only those with magic can open our doors." He placed a hand next to the vertical line running down the half-circle, and the stone itself gave way, like it was a curtain instead of a solid rock face.

"Doesn't that use up your magic?" she asked. "You said you could spend it, right?"

"Magic is energy," he said with a grin. "It can't be created or destroyed. It can only be absorbed, given, transferred, passed from one to another."

"So how much did you give me?" she asked as they stepped into yet another passageway, this one lined by strange carvings that lit up as they passed and blinked off as soon as they stepped beyond them. Moons, suns, stars, comets, constellations...

He shrugged. "Enough to save your life. It's not something you can easily measure, like I gave you ten percent, or this many amps."

She sighed, frustrated by the vague answers. She wanted to know for sure how much she had. Why couldn't their table have a gauge for magic decibels or whatever? That would make this whole thing so much easier to comprehend. Her brain couldn't make sense of undefinable things that, until yesterday, were fairy tales.

Quill stopped beside a constellation that looked like a *W* tipped on its side. The scant light from the few stars cast his face in shadow, and she had to swallow hard as her eyes moved over his strong profile and those gorgeous lips. "I know this is a lot to take in," he said, his eyes earnest. "But don't feel like you have to know anything already. If you have a question, you can ask anyone. If they don't know the answer, chances are, they'll know who does. You share the magic of the Winslow Coven. Even if you're not a member, we're all here for you."

She thought of the blonde, Raina, who had out-magicked her, but she didn't bring that up. Raina was not a threat to her, not competition.

Quill took her hand, and the magic that swirled between them was slower now, though just as intense. His fingers slid along hers, lighting every nerve ending in her body on fire. Slowly, he raised her hand to the constellation. With his fingers over hers, he traced her fingertips along the path of stars. The heat of his body next to hers made her want to pool, weak-kneed, onto the floor.

"You're safe here, Sagely," he said. "Safer than you've ever been, probably. That's the important thing." When her fingertips grazed over the last star, they sank into the stone itself. It felt cold against her skin, as if a cool breeze was brushing over it. She pressed harder and watched in wonder as her whole hand and then her arm disappeared. Quill stepped closer, his body brushing hers. Heat exploded along her skin and she gasped.

"Step through," he whispered. "It's safe."

She took a breath and plunged through, halfway expecting her forehead to bounce off the sandstone. Instead, she slipped through the curtain of cool air into a small, neat bedroom. Wall sconces lit this one, which looked more like somewhere a hobbit would live than a witch. The walls were made of stone. A small, round table made of a section of tree trunk sat in one corner, flanked by two square stone seats. On top of the table sat some kind of salt crystal lamp and a potted plant.

Against the other wall, a large canopy bed was made up neatly with a quaint, patchwork quilt.

"I hope you're not claustrophobic," Quill said.

"Nope." Something brushed against her leg, and she jumped away, ready to defend herself. But it was only a cat. "Shit. That scared me. Come here, kitty." She picked up the cat, only to remember Rizzo was at home. Of course, her roommate would have fed her, but she'd be missing Sagely, wondering where she was. What was Sagely thinking? Was she really going to stay?

"I'll let you get settled in," Quill said, backing up to the wall where they entered, which looked completely solid again.

"Sure," she said. "I do have one more question. Where's the shower?"

"Oh, of course. You probably need to relax, too. We have great mud baths. I'll show you. It's exactly what you need right now."

Sagely bristled. She didn't need some stranger telling her what she needed, not even one who was sexy as hell and made her blood sing. "I'd like to get clean. So just a shower will be fine."

"Did I say something wrong?"

She sighed. This emotion-reading was getting really old. She wondered if it wore off after a while. "Just show me to the shower, please."

"Alright," he said, holding up one hand. "It's just

down the hall in the Orion room. Towels are in the cabinet."

"Thank you."

"If you want a cat, you can get one," he said, nodding at the cat she was cradling in her arms. He stepped out into the hall. "That one is Yordine's. Once you move to level two, you can choose a familiar, although a witch who was gifted magic doesn't need one."

"I have a cat," she told him. "Which is all the more reason I need to train my magic and get home."

"We can talk about that," he said. "Go get your shower and join us whenever you want. Remember your way back?"

They stopped at the rock face where Orion's belt was etched into the stone. "Not all women are hopeless at directions," she said with a toss of her hair.

"Sure you don't want company?" he offered with a wink.

Do I ever. Her eyes roamed from his smiling mouth to his broad shoulders, down his well-defined chest and torso, and her snippiness melted away as quickly as it arose. She knew he was making a peace offering, but she was not that easy.

"Ha," she said, unable to keep herself from smiling. She didn't even care if he caught her checking him out. "Nice try."

"We seem to have gotten on the wrong foot somewhere. Don't you think we should remedy that as soon as possible?"

"I'm going to go in now," she said, tracing the stars in the constellation like he had on her bedroom door.

"Yeah, you're probably right," he said. "You're all

tired and vulnerable. That would give me an unfair advantage."

"In what?" she asked, giving him her most innocent look.

He was still smiling, that wide smile that seemed to stretch beyond the reach of his full lips. "Rain check? Offer still stands, you know, for next time. Just make sure you're well rested so you can keep up."

She liked the sound of that challenge, but she didn't want to show him how seriously she was contemplating it, because she couldn't tell if he was completely kidding. If he was, she got the feeling he would change his mind in a hurry if she said yes.

"I'll remember that," she said, shaking her head like she thought he was ridiculous, rather than sinfully sexy. Like she was not actually considering his offer before she even knew his last name, or how old he was, or what he did for a living. She couldn't help wondering just how well rested she'd need to be. She'd never imagined sleeping with a warlock. It seemed like magic might have some advantages she hadn't previously considered.

SEVEN

After twenty minutes in her bedroom, she was bored. It was cute and quaint but not exactly a thrill ride. She left her room and headed back the way she came, down the hall and out into the cavern. As she started for the next tunnel, the pale light coming from the walls began to dim. She reached out her hand and touched the wall, trying to relight it the way Quill had. But instead of a calming yellow glow, the light turned a pale, sickly shade. The colors swirled together, making a nauseating, sulfuric hue. It perfectly matched the lovely egg smell.

Not quite as breathtaking as the stars that came from Quill's fingers.

In another minute, the light went from yellow to entirely gray, and she could hardly see a foot in front of her. She glanced around for other witches, but she didn't see any. Hoping to reach the main room before the light went out entirely, she picked up her pace.

No such luck. Just then, the light dulled to a murky shade of grayish yellow that made her stomach curdle. Her magic was doing something strange, too, answering the call with a flickering of its own. Her heart beat faster, and her breath came quicker.

When she heard a commotion from the cavern ahead, she began to run. A shout echoed down the tunnel towards her, and a rock crashed somewhere beyond that. Running blindly through the murky gray, she pushed herself forward. Her foot slipped into the stream, soaking her boot, but she didn't slow her pace. She raced for the chamber, for the accident, though she didn't know if it was a cave in, gas leak, or something else entirely.

She knew one thing for sure. She was not about to die in a gas-filled witch chamber. Not when her cat was at home worrying about her. Right then she decided she was not staying in this deathtrap. She just had to find a way to tell Quill she was leaving with whatever magical abilities he'd given her. She'd just have to figure them out on her own.

At last, she burst into the huge cavern. The murky grey emanated from the walls there, too, although the sconces gave off enough light for her to see what was happening.

At first, she thought it must be some of the witches fighting over some witchy thing. Maybe even over whether to welcome her to the coven or somehow suck the magic back out of her, if that was even possible.

Instead, a dozen witches were skirmishing, along with shrieking and scuffling animals. Earlier, Quill had mentioned familiars, and now she was seeing them for herself. She spotted a fox, wriggling and crying while Eli held it trapped on the cave's floor with some kind of invisible magic. A hideous possum was hissing and bearing its sharp teeth at Shaneesha.

A giant vulture turned towards Sagely. When it blinked its translucent inner eyelid, its eyes appeared whitish, like a spoiled egg. It screamed, its giant beak opening wide to reveal a long red tongue, and flew at her. Fighting the urge to shriek, she dropped into a fighting stance. She'd never drop-kicked a vulture, but she wasn't above it.

"Take that, Big Bird," she said, doing a spinning sidekick and delivering a punishing blow to its scaly reptilian head. Its head snapped so far around that surely its neck was broken, and it thudded to the floor. A cry came from somewhere in the cave, and a foreign witch shot up from where she was wrestling with Yordine. Sagely could tell she was not from their coven and did not share their magic. Hers was different, strong and foreboding.

The witch leapt towards Sagely, only to be taken down by a bear-hug from Quill.

For real. These witches were in dire need of some cooler moves. Maybe she could get a job teaching them Tae Kwon Do.

The bird slowly lifted its head from the stone floor, murder in its pink eyes. She readied herself to take it out with one well-aimed knife-hand-strike to its scaly neck. But just as it began to flap its black wings, a witch from the invading coven hurtled towards her.

Raina cut her off, dug in her heels, and slid to a stop, thrusting out her hand to deliver a perfect palm-heel strike to the incoming witch's face. Except her hand stopped short of touching the woman, and instead, when her palm got to the end of her reach, a ball of fire shot from her hand and hit the witch in the eye.

Sagely remembered exactly how much that fireball hurt when Quill shoved it down her throat, so she was not surprised that the woman let out a piercing shriek. She began to stagger away, but before Sagely could jump in to help Raina, her own magic pulsed painfully.

And then it began to turn. She felt the coldness as if black, snake-like fingers had reached down her throat, begun to poison her magic from within. She grasped at her throat, her eyes searching the chaos for what was defiling her new power. At last she spotted it.

A rail-thin warlock in a black cloak, with bone-white skin and stringy black hair leapt at Quill and sliced his arm with a blade. Quill slammed his forearm up into the man's chin, and the man stumbled backwards. For a second, Sagely was reminded of the man who had attacked her. But this man was smaller, almost waifish, with long dark hair, and unlike her attacker, he had substance. And then she realized why they struck her as similar. This man had the same black emptiness in his eyes that had made up her attacker's entire form.

Cursing, Quill threw out a hand to fireball the guy, but before he could, the guy dropped to the ground and rolled at Quill, knocking his legs from under him. As he fell, Quill landed a punch to the guy's face, and blood sprayed from his nose.

He leapt onto Quill and kneeled on him, his fingers gripping Quill's throat. Quill strained so hard against his attacker that Sagely was surprised his bones didn't snap. Quill's strong fingers dug what looked like inches into the flesh of the man's upper arms. His muscles were taut inside his shirt, his biceps bulging against the fabric. But the man straddling him refused to release his grip on Quill's neck. His bony knuckles pointed out like shards of glass against his skin.

The dark feeling swept over Sagely again. Quill's face reddened and his eyes narrowed. She frantically searched the crowd for someone to help, but the other witches were engaged in combat. Raina was grappling an invading witch. She raised her hand, lifting the other witch off the ground by the throat without actually touching her. Holding the other woman in the grip of her power, she lifted her higher, until she was hovering a foot above the ground, grasping at her neck and gasping for breath. Then Raina abruptly chopped her hand through the air. The witch's body was slammed to the stone floor at Raina's feet next to the injured bird. The witch screamed and writhed, grasping the back of her head.

Raina was fast—she'd be a good Tae Kwon Do opponent if she could be trusted not to stage an accident where she knocked out all her opponent's teeth.

Sagely couldn't tell her coven from the other by sight, but after a second, she reached out and felt the familiarity of their magic.

It was as if she was suddenly seeing auras, except she couldn't actually see them. Like Quill said, it was a sixth sense that could feel them when she focused on two of the combatants. Her magic sung at the same frequency as the witches from her coven.

A few of the witches she recognized were grouped in a huddle staring at Quill like they were willing the man on top of him to burst into flame. Sagely wanted to shake them and scream at them to do something instead of standing there holding hands like they were about to sing an angry, metalhead version of Kumbaya. This was why she didn't want to join a coven—all this good-witch nonsense. There was no point in getting pissed if you couldn't use it to defeat your opponent.

She turned back to Quill. If they wouldn't stop this asshole, she would.

She leapt towards the man straddling Quill. She didn't know how much longer Quill had left. Her entire body buzzed with the urge to get the creeps out of there, out of the cavern, out of her coven, her head, her body.

The man's fingernails dug into Quill's flesh, tearing through the skin, as if he intended to rip out his jugular with his nasty, overgrown fingernails. Rivulets of blood trickled down Quill's neck.

Rage exploded inside Sagely as she grabbed the foreign warlock's dark head. Touching his hair was like grabbing a handful of damp, oily snakes, but she refused to let go. His crooked nails were crimson with blood that ran thick with Quill's magic. *Her* magic.

Blinding fury flashed through her like a surge of electricity, and she wrenched his head back.

His head…exploded.

A shriek sounded somewhere in the cavern. Sagely's first dazed thought, as if it were coming to her via telepathy instead of her own mind, was that at least she wasn't the girl who shrieked first. Several of the witches who did not share her magic were frozen, their faces masks of horror. When her eyes moved to the witches from the Winslow Coven, she saw the exact same expression.

Oops.

One of the invading witches leapt to her feet with another deafening shriek. She ripped a dagger from her belt and bolted toward Sagely, blade held high, gleaming in the golden light of the sconces. Her face twisted into a mask of killing rage.

Sagely was ready, despite the shock of what she'd just done. She delivered a knife-hand strike to the woman's forearm. Bones cracked like the boards she broke in her Tae Kwon Do practice.

The witch shrieked again and boxed Sagely in the ear with her other hand. Sagely wasn't expecting an ambidextrous fighter. Her head reeling, she stumbled back, barely blocking the next blow.

The woman bared her teeth, her eyes narrowed in unadulterated hatred. As she charged, Sagely raised her arm to block the next blow. The woman rocked forward and clamped her teeth into Sagely's forearm.

Sagely stumbled back in horror, trying to shake the witch loose. While she was distracted by the revulsion of the woman's teeth in her arm, the woman thrust a fist into Sagely's face. Sagely ducked at the last second, but the witch's ring tore across her lower lip, splitting it wide open. With a scream of her own, Sagely delivered a punch directly to the witch's ear. Let her see how it felt.

The witch didn't release her grip, so Sagely raised her knee, slamming it into her gut as hard as she could. With a grunt, the witch's teeth loosened. Only then could Sagely wrench her arm away and deliver a swift left hook. Though her left hand was not her strong one, she managed to knock her sideways. The witch knelt on the floor, breathing hard.

Sagely was about to finish her off when Quill sat

upright. His hand shot out and wrapped around Sagely's calf.

"Don't." His voice was low but firm.

A horrifying thought entered Sagely's mind. What if she'd interrupted a sparring match between her coven and their friends, one of whom she'd just murdered?

EIGHT

When Sagely saw the psycho witch going for her dagger again, she knew she was no friend of theirs. Quill held out a hand, and the dagger lifted off the floor and shot to his hand as if it was a magnet. His fingers closed around the handle, but she couldn't tell if he was holding it to protect himself from the crazy witch...or her.

"You need to leave." The voice came from the far side of the cavern, where Majori Romero was holding a young witch in a headlock. Whatever voodoo magic he was doing to her did not look pleasant. Her face had gone the white of curdled milk instead of red, so he couldn't be squeezing too hard. But her mouth was open in a silent scream, and tears streamed down her face, dripping over the burly arm that circled her neck.

"I'm binding her magic," Romero said, as if hearing Sagely's confusion. His eyes were trained on the psycho witch, though. "You have two minutes to get out of here before I bind yours, too."

The invading witches scrambled to their feet. Sagely turned, already thinking they'd won. But just then, a giant lizard ran at her, jaws open to reveal needle-sharp fangs. The ruff on his neck was extended in a huge, leathery fan. She lifted her boot and brought it down hard, trying to crush its head. But the lizard darted forward, and her heel landed on its tail. It sank its teeth into her other foot.

Her snakeskin boot was now full of holes. With a cry of fury, Sagely reached down and punched the creature in the back. Her knuckles stung from the scaly skin and the row of barbs along its spine that dragged a deep scrape across her knuckles. It released its hold on her foot, opened its big red mouth, hissed, and wiggled ferociously. After a moment, it scrabbled away, leaving its tail squished under her foot.

"Control your familiars," Yordine ordered, her commanding voice echoing through the cavern like thunder.

Romero waited until most of the invading witches had collected their familiars and climbed the stairs before he released the young witch from his hold. Just as she stumbled towards the door, Sagely spotted a rat the size of Rizzo huddled in the middle of the floor, eating chunks of something grey. That was when she remembered that she'd exploded someone's head.

Sagely gagged, fighting back waves of nausea. When she saw a tuft of human hair trailing from the corner of the rat's mouth, she couldn't hold it back. She turned away and got sick.

When she turned back, the witch who had attacked her was the only one left. She slowly clambered to her feet, her hair still hanging in her face. Her eyes were cold, blank as death. Her pupils had overtaken her entire irises, and with a shudder of revulsion, Sagely recognized that blackness. The absolutely featureless sheen, the all-consuming shadow. She gasped, stepping back. A tremor of fear traveled through her.

The woman's lips pulled back from her teeth. "We'll get you yet." She said the words slowly, annunciating each one as if Sagely were stupid or deaf. But she heard her all right.

"I don't think so. And if you don't get out of here you never will. I'm giving you three seconds before I explode your head, too."

With a groan, the witch stood and shook back her auburn hair. A bit of gray matter stuck to the end of a strand that must have brushed the floor when her head was bowed. Again, Sagely had to swallow hard to keep from vomiting.

The witch took one staggering step towards the stairs. Sagely's shoulders began to relax, and she turned to spit blood from the cut across her lip. Suddenly, the witch spun around with a level of speed and agility that would've made Master Zuchowski proud. She whipped a ball of magic through the air, aiming straight for Sagely's head.

Sagely threw herself to the floor, knowing she wasn't quick enough.

But Quill was.

His hand shot out, and a stream of electricity bolted from his palm. The ball of energy hung mere inches from Sagely's eyes.

With a cry of anger, the witch spun and raced up the stairs. That's when Sagely noticed the owl that had sat by and watched, blending in to the cavern's walls. It flew out behind the witch, its wingtips brushing the doorframe. For a second, they all stood frozen, staring at the majestic beauty of the grey owl. Sagely had never seen an owl so close, and they had a certain dignity that inspired awe. It was the perfect closure to the surreal attack they'd just survived.

When Sagely turned away, she found Quill staring at her.

"What?" she asked.

"I think we should go over some rules," said Majori Yordine.

Sagely figured now would not be the time to remind the coven that they'd told her there were no rules, and that the Majoris didn't have power over the students.

"We don't use dark magic," Quill said. He was still sitting on the floor, a black cloak crumpled beside him. Inside the cloak was a body. A body Sagely had killed.

Suddenly she was shaking all over. She'd killed someone. She'd taken someone's life. She hadn't even needed to, she was just trying to get him off Quill. How was she supposed to know that her abilities included blowing up heads? No one had told her that.

She'd been thinking more along the lines of levitation, maybe some flying or a little bit of fortune-telling. It might be cool to turn off lights from across the room or ignite a candle with willpower alone. How was she supposed to know that if she wrapped her hands around someone's head, his skull would detonate like a bomb was inside it?

"I didn't know," she said, hating the defensive edge in her voice.

"I know," Quill said. "It's my fault. I should've explained more. But...don't use any more magic until you're trained."

Before this moment, she'd been thinking she needed to go home, that she could control these powers. All she needed was a few lessons, and she'd be out of there. She'd been thinking that she'd live in her apartment, come back a time or two every week for the rest of summer. But now she faltered. What if she accidentally hurt her roommate next time she was mad at her? What if she hurt Rizzo?

"Okay," she said, taking in a shuddering breath. "Okay, I'll study with Majori Ory." She tried not to giggle at the unintentional rhyme, but though she covered her mouth with her fingers, laughter burst from behind them. Even when she pulled her fingers away and saw that they were covered with blood, and that she was smearing it across her mouth, she giggled until tears were running down her face.

Everyone was staring at her with their sober expressions, and the frown on Romero's face could frighten a tiger. Quill's face was a mask of bland, expressionlessness that she'd never seen before. Until then, he'd looked at her in a teasing, appreciative way so she knew that whatever was between them was more than the magic he gave her.

But now he only watched and waited for her to finish hysterically giggling. When at last she got it under control, she wiped her tears, smearing blood across her face. For a moment, she could only stare at her gory hands. She'd never meant to kill someone, never thought she would, even if he deserved it. But she had.

NINE

No one spoke as she helped Quill to his feet. They moved aside as she passed, casting wary glances her way. Even Eli dropped his gaze when she smiled at him, and the unearthly gorgeous witch stepped behind him as if to hide.

"What, they've never seen someone die?" she asked when they were out of earshot of the chamber.

"Not often," Quill said with a grimace. "Sagely, we hold all human life as sacred, even that of a dark witch. If we killed as easily as they did, we'd be no better. Our magic is for creation, not destruction."

"But he was going to kill you," she pointed out. "Can't you fight for your own life, since it's so sacred and all?"

"Of course," he said. "But we prefer more peaceful ways of subduing them than...exploding their heads."

"I didn't mean to," she said, throwing her hands up.

"I know," he said, taking her hand. The magic that

usually exploded through her at his nearness, at his touch, sizzled briefly, but it was tied up with something else now, something dark and strangling, choking their magic.

She pulled her hand away, and he turned to her, his eyes wide. He'd felt it, too.

"Are you okay?" he asked.

"I'm fine," she said. "It's you. He hurt you." Her voice came out more accusatory than she intended.

He took a deep, shuddering breath, and that was when she felt it. She could read the depth of his pain, how much it was hurting him. With a shiver, she thought how glad she was that she didn't experience his pain firsthand, too. She didn't think she could handle it as well as he was.

"You're hurt," she said again, this time softer.

He paused a moment before answering. His eyes searched hers, vulnerability building as he held her gaze. "Yes," he admitted at last, his strong shoulders slumping. "I didn't want the others to see how easily those witches weakened me. They'd be terrified." He leaned against the wall as he spoke, as if he didn't have the energy to stand and speak at the same time.

"Maybe they should be terrified," Sagely said fiercely. "And whoever they were, if they could do this to you... Is he the warlock you told me about? The most powerful in the world?"

He shook his head miserably. "No, it wasn't Viziri. But perhaps he was controlling them. Did you see their eyes?"

Sagely nodded, coldness creeping up her arms.

"I'm sorry, Sagely. I want to talk more, but I think...I should lie down."

"Let me help you," she said, stepping beside him. She

draped his arm over her shoulder, and, ignoring his protests, pulled him away from the wall.

"I can walk myself," he growled.

"Maybe I'm just trying to get close to you," she teased.

He grunted in response, but he let her help him down the corridor, which worried her even more. When they reached the tunnel with the constellations, she was relieved to learn that his room was the first on the left. Her shoulder ached from supporting his weight, which had steadily increased as they walked. His fingers skimmed across his constellation without even looking at it, and they stepped through.

"Only witches can enter," he mumbled. "When they're invited."

"Does that mean you want me here?" she asked, suddenly feeling shy for the first time since they'd met. "Or do you want me to leave?"

"I don't like you seeing me like this," he said with a scowl as he sank onto the bed. "But you can feel how much of my magic he took, whether I invite you or not. Can't you?" He glared like that was her fault.

"I didn't ask for your magic," she reminded him. "I didn't wring it from your unwilling throat. In case you forgot, I stopped that guy from taking all of it, or worse, your life."

"I know," he said, sinking back. "I'm sorry. I'm being a jerk."

"Yes," she said. "You are. Now let me help you."

He sighed. "Do I have a choice?"

"Nope. Right now, I'm stronger than you, and I have every intention of taking advantage of that."

"You do, huh?" He smiled and tugged at her hand, giving her his best puppy dog eyes. She clambered onto the bed, though her cautious side was wondering what the hell she thought she was doing, hopping in bed with some guy she'd just met. Another part of her didn't care a lick, and it won out this time.

Her moment of shyness forgotten, she lay down beside Quill.

"Okay, but no funny business," she said firmly.

"Is this funny business?" he asked, trailing his fingers up her arm. It was exactly as she'd imagined in the tunnel, like comets threading their way over her skin.

"Yes," she said, taking his hand in hers so he couldn't make her want to do something she'd regret. "So, if you lost some of your magic, and I have some of your magic, can't I just give it back to you?"

"You don't want your magic?" he asked, looking mortally wounded by the idea.

"I don't know," she said. "So far, it hasn't been all that useful except for killing a guy, and you said I'm not supposed to do that."

"We'll teach you how," he assured her, his eyelids drooping. "But if you don't want it…I could try to take it back. No one is going to force you to be one of us, Sagely."

She thought about it for a minute. They had said she should learn to control her magic before she left. But now, she had a choice to make. She could give it back and leave right now. Tomorrow, she'd wake up in her apartment in Fayetteville, with her roommate she hardly knew and her cat. She could go back to the life she'd always known.

How freaking dull.

After being here just a day, she already knew that wasn't going to work anymore. She didn't want to give her magic back. She wanted to use it. And if that black-hole guy came after her again, she might need it. She couldn't leave now, not when she had this power, when it could destroy someone. Maybe someday she'd leave, but not yet.

Taking Quill's hand, she laced her fingers through his and squeezed. His ring was white-gold, with little rune-like symbols etched in it. "I'm in it for the long haul," she said. "So, tell me what to do."

"Good," Quill said with a weak smile. "After seeing you work today, I don't think I'd want to be on the receiving end of your magic. You might, you know, blow up my entire body."

"Shut up," she said, punching him lightly. "Seriously, though. If that guy stole your magic, and I killed him, where is it now?"

"You should be able to find it better than anyone."

She remembered his words from earlier. *Like attracts like.* Did that mean she could find his magic and absorb it? "So, someone could just find it lying around, absorb it, and be more powerful than you?" she asked.

His eyelids had fallen halfway closed, but now they snapped open again. Their eyes met, and she had another flash of his emotion. His eyes pooled with that same vulnerability tinged with fear that came through their shared magic before. He knew what she was thinking, that she could take his power away. "Theoretically," he said after a long moment.

She knew then that he'd given her something more precious than his magic. He'd given her his trust.

"I won't," she whispered, her heart beating hard

suddenly.

"You better not," he said, smoothing her hair behind her ear. One corner of his mouth quirked up the slightest bit, but his eyes remained serious, searching hers.

"I promise." She took his hand and placed it on her pounding heart. Their eyes caught, held. His gaze moved over hers, down her face to her lips.

She leaned in, brushing her lips over his.

Electricity exploded through her body, and she gasped against his mouth. In one motion, he rolled over onto her, pressing her down into the soft bed. His lips claimed hers, hard and then soft, soft and then hard. He sucked her lower lip between his teeth and bit down gently, his tongue teasing the tear in her flesh.

She gasped again, arching up against him, but he pulled away.

"I want you, Sagely," he murmured, his voice hoarse with longing. "But when I can do it right. Not when I'm weak. You deserve more."

"It better stop raining soon so we can use all these rain checks," she said, smiling and rolling over onto him. She pressed her body along his and gave him a quick kiss. "Now you need to rest while I go find your magic."

"So I can't tell you what you need, but you get to tell me?"

"Exactly," she said lightly, sitting up. "Now. How do I find it?"

"It's tricky," he said. "Like a leprechaun. It might hide. But it will be in something important to me, hiding until someone finds it."

"And if I find it, I should bring it to you?"

"Yes," he whispered, his eyes tinged with fear again.

"Or bring me to it."

"I promised," she said. "I don't take that lightly, Quill. I'm not going to steal your magic."

"Then don't tell anyone," he said, closing his eyes. "Unless you're certain you can trust them."

"Who?" she asked.

But his eyes had already closed.

She jumped up, but just as she started for the door, he muttered something. She turned back. "What?"

"I'm sorry," he said, his eyes still closed. "This is my fault."

"You did bring me into this," she admitted. "But like you said, it was better than the alternative. You could have let me die last night."

"No, it's my fault...that he attacked you."

"What do you mean?" she whispered, her stomach tightening with dread. When he didn't answer, she poked him in the shoulder.

He grimaced, but after a moment, he answered. "I think...he was looking for me. Winslow is the coven's place of origin. That's how we got our name. There's power in a name..."

He stopped and took a moment to just breathe before going on. "We sometimes go there to cleanse or refresh our magic. That's why I was there. I think that warlock must have followed me there, and when you left... Maybe he got our cars mixed up, or..."

"Or what?"

He didn't answer, and his pale, drawn face told her that he'd slipped into unconsciousness. She could be pissed at him later, when he was better. So she'd better make sure he got better.

TEN

Sagely raced out of the room, only pausing a second to marvel that she'd just run through a solid rock face. She was getting used to this already. Her foot crunched on a piece of gravel, and she started to despair as to how she would ever find something important to Quill. For all she knew, his magic was hiding in the pebble she'd just stepped on. Or the table where they'd measured their magical strength. The mud baths he loved so much. It could be anywhere.

She shook the questions from her mind. She had to try. She had to find it. The magic inside her pushed her onwards, pulsing with need to heal her healer, to save her savior. He'd shared his magic with her. If only she were skilled enough to return the favor, to heal him with her magic. But she was scared to go near her magic after what she'd done to that warlock.

She'd killed a man. Taken his life. This wasn't a crazy

63

dream, as much as it felt that way. She had blood on her hands. Literal, not metaphorical, blood. She swallowed her bout of nausea and hurried along the corridor. When she stepped into the big chamber, all eyes turned her way. Silence fell.

At last, Raina spoke. "You did this." Her voice was deadly, cut through with actual hatred. Sagely had never been hated before. Not this real, this deep. It shook her, and for a second, she thought Raina was talking about Quill. Had she already found his magic and realized that he'd lost it?

But then she saw that Raina was holding the enormous vulture by the neck. Its body dangled limply from her grasp.

"This is your fault," she growled, thrusting the dead thing in Sagely's direction. "We haven't been attacked in years, and then you come along, and the next day, the dark witches show up. You led them here!"

"Me?" Sagely asked. "I don't have anything to do with it. Two days ago, I didn't even know witches existed outside of story books."

Raina curled her lip in a snarl and stalked away. Looking uncomfortable, others shifted and studied the walls or their shoes.

Sagely caught Eli's eye at last and gestured for him to join her. With a guilty glance at the others, he shuffled to her side. "I need to find something," she said. "Can they hear me if I tell you here?"

"Let's talk in the tunnel."

They stepped into the tunnel, and she quickly filled him in. "And I killed the warlock attacking him, so it must have spilled in here somewhere," she finished.

"We need to get him his familiar," Eli said without a second's hesitation. He turned and raced down the tunnel, with Sagely following at a jog. She should have thought of this. Quill must have known where his magic had gone, but he'd been testing her. She'd obviously failed that one. How was she supposed to know that his escaped magic receptacle was his pet? Or spirit animal, or whatever.

Familiar, she reminded herself as they entered the damp chamber with the sulfur scent. Eli placed his hand on another half-circle cut into the wall. The door swung open, and sunlight flooded over them. She had to squint for a second, her eyes having grown accustomed to the underground light.

A horrible, high, whining noise was coming from some kind of animal racing around the room so fast she couldn't make out what it was. From far above, sunlight filtered down. Vines hung from the circular opening, and the walls were covered in thick green moss. It was like looking up from the bottom of a well. Above them, birds chirped and fluttered up and down the depth of the "well."

A pool of the clearest water Sagely had ever seen beckoned before them, glimmering with light from within. She spotted huge koi fish circling in the pool, around which, assorted animals lazed. When she noticed a hyena among them, she shrank back. She'd hate to be the person who fell into this well from above.

She stepped towards the serene pool, but Eli held out a hand to stop her. "Some of the familiars are pretty fierce," he said, then looked up to where the shrieking animal was running in circles around the circumference of the opening. "Some of them are fish and water creatures. Quite deadly."

He caught her expression and turned his attention to the shrieking thing. With a little coaxing and some magic, he got it down, though it continued keening pitifully all the while. It seemed to be some kind of glossy, chocolate-colored weasel. Holding it firmly around the middle, Eli started back along the passageway towards Quill's room. Sagely followed.

"What's your familiar?" she asked. "Is it deadly?"

"I have a bat," he said, looking quite pleased. "It's in my pocket."

When they reached Quill's room, Sagely entered before turning to see that Eli was not with her. She remembered Quill saying that he had to want someone to come in before they could enter. Stepping back out, she took the animal, which was now writhing and shrieking. Its little claws scraped trenches in her skin as she gripped it firmly. She hurried to the bed, barely able to contain it as it wriggled and lashed out in her grasp.

Let's hope it doesn't eat his face off, she thought as she released it onto Quill's sleeping chest. The moment she let it go, it darted for his throat.

ELEVEN

Sagely snatched at the weasel, but it was too late. It dove into the nook between Quill's shoulder and neck, tunneling under him. He opened his eyes sleepily and smiled, shifting his position as the thing burrowed under his back.

"Thank you," he said, looking relieved.

"Is that it? That's where your magic went? Why didn't you just tell me?"

"I wasn't sure it would make it that far," he said. "If we'd known about the attack, I'd have had her with me. A warlock never goes anywhere important without his familiar."

"What if your familiar is a fish?"

"Then you find a way to convey water," he said with a grin. "Most of us are earth workers, though. Hence the underground." His smile faded and he sat, reaching behind him to retrieve his familiar.

"Earth workers. So you influence the elements?"

"We're very in touch with the natural world, yes," he said. "Witches always have been. We draw our energy from the earth, and yes, we worship Mother Nature."

"Great. You really are hippies," she said, sinking onto the edge of the bed.

He didn't smile at her joke. "We originally came down here for protection," he said. "Today...well, that used to happen often."

"You were attacked by dark witches a lot?"

He cradled his familiar in his hands, stroking its shiny fur. It made her miss Rizzo, though she had a feeling her cat might try to eat his weasel.

"Over the centuries, witches were not protective of our magic, and we let it be diluted by entering the mainstream population and marrying common people. When we realized what was happening, that almost no one had potent enough magic to actually do anything, we started to form covens again. We wanted to save the witches we had left, to train them to the fullest of their abilities and procreate with the intent to strengthen the magic in our children."

"Covens are actually breeding programs? Sounds lovely."

He shook his head, holding out an arm to let the weasel run up his bicep and leap onto his head. "Not at all. But they recognized we were losing a sacred art. Not everyone was happy to see witches honoring our culture. And some people saw an opportunity." He frowned down at a blood splatter on his arm. "Let's just say the children with the highest capacity for magic often disappeared before they reached adulthood."

A shiver went through Sagely as a memory surfaced, unbidden, of her own childhood, shuffled from one foster family to another, dragging her one bag of possessions with her everywhere she went, not wanting it to be left if she was suddenly moved to a new placement without notice. "They were kidnapped by the dark witches?"

"Dark witches, fae, and goblins," he said, his forehead knitting with concern. "Are you okay? Is this upsetting for you?"

"I—I had a rough childhood," she said, then added quickly, "But I wasn't kidnapped. Nothing compared to that."

He reached out and placed a gentle hand on her arm. "What happened?"

"Oh, you know, nothing special," she said, trying to sound light. "Foster kid."

"I'm sorry."

"Not a big deal," she said. "I'm all grown up now, and it doesn't matter. So, tell me more about these dark witches. They kidnapped kids and turned them on to dark magic?"

"Remember when I told you the strongest witch in the world was a dark warlock? He appeared on the scene about twenty years ago. He goes by the name Viziri. No one really knows where he came from or who he is. But he started taking children, unlocking their magic before it was ready and twisting it into something dark. He and his people use them like child soldiers. It got worse around the time when I was coming into my magic. Kids started disappearing almost every day. That's when we started training underground."

"They built all this to protect you? Wow, you really

are their star quarterback."

Quill looked at her blankly, then shook his head. "The coven wanted to protect me, yes, but also they knew how devastating it could be if I turned against them. The amount of magic I possess was a danger to them. If it turned dark, I could probably wipe out the entire coven. We moved underground to keep the kids safe and hidden from the world, but also to protect the coven. And to hide our training, so no one sneaking around the forest could see our abilities."

Sagely nodded, remembering the feeling of the dark magic invading the cave, invading her. "So you're supposed to be safe down here. But the dark witches found us anyway."

"The rest of the coven lives outside," he said. "It's not impossible to find us. Just takes a little more planning."

"You didn't know the dark witches who attacked today?"

"No, but if they're Viziri's, they could be from anywhere in the world. He seems to attack somewhere new almost every day."

"I thought you said he took a lot of kids from here."

"When I was growing up, we didn't know as much about him. He'd only been around for six or seven years when he focused on our coven. After a few years, he disappeared again. Since then, he shows up every now and then, attacking random covens around the world and stealing children and magic."

"How do we know if the attack today was by his people?"

"We don't," Quill said. "They were definitely being…

controlled by something. But any witch can go dark, just like any person can do evil. We all have both good and evil inside us, the potential to be either. That's how magic is, too. If you feed the darkness, it grows. It needs more food. Only more darkness satisfies it."

"That makes all too much sense," she said. "I've had my own periods of darkness."

"Imagine that, but with the added power of magic. It's a gift, but also a burden. If you're angry and you lash out as a common human, you hurt someone's feelings. If you lash out with magic…"

"You might kill someone," she said softly, dropping her eyes to her hands, blood dried in the creases of her palms like a sinister prophecy.

"It's not your fault," he said, his eyes boring into hers, almost glowing green in the golden light of his bedroom. He waited a long moment, until she didn't know if he was talking about today, or…

But he couldn't know about her childhood. He couldn't read her mind.

She stood abruptly. "Let's get out of here. I need some air. I can't live down here all the time. I'm not a kid who's going to get snatched, and I'm not a mole."

"You could have a mole familiar," he teased, standing and letting his weasel hop off his head to crouch on his shoulder. "That would be sexy."

Sagely returned his smile, grateful he wasn't going to pry into something she obviously didn't want to talk about. But she caught his look and understood that even as he let her off for now, he knew there was more. But it was her past, not something she wanted to share with a guy she barely knew. She'd already told him more than she told most people in a year.

"You're healed," she said as they stepped out of his room. "That was fast."

"She takes good care of me," he said, reaching up to stroke the weasel's head.

She was not jealous of a weasel. She was totally not.

She noticed the wound on his arm, where the dark warlock cut him, had already scabbed over. She was still splattered with blood, but she tried not to dwell on it. A lifetime of practice helped with avoidance of ugly topics.

As they stepped out into the main corridor, Quill's hand brushed her back. The magic crackled between them, back to full strength. "So, your little weasel there," she said. "What's its name?"

"Okay, first of all, she's not an *it*." He took the familiar off his shoulder and cradled her along his forearm. "All familiars are the opposite sex of their owner. It's about balance. And her name is Maude."

"You named her that on purpose?"

"You'll find that witches have a sense of humor when it comes to naming their familiars," Quill said with a smile.

"Poor weasel," Sagely said. "I bet all the other weasels make fun of her."

Quill drew up tall and puffed out his chest. "She's not a weasel, she's a mink."

"Like the thing they make coats out of?"

He let out an exaggerated gasp and covered Maude's little ears with a thumb and forefinger. "Earmuffs," he hissed, holding her away from Sagely, as if she'd threatened to make Maude into said coat.

She laughed as he returned the mink to his neck. "Where are we going now?"

He grinned sideways at her, his green eyes shining. "To the Enchanted Forest."

TWELVE

After a quick lunch of ham and cheese sandwiches, which she found immensely comforting in this crazy new world, they headed out. When they stepped into the cabin above all that hidden wonder, she had to blink a few times. She'd forgotten all about the little building where she awoke.

"This place makes you feel comfortable," Quill said. "It takes on the features that you find familiar and safe. Did you feel at home when you woke up?"

"If my home was a prison, maybe," she said with a laugh. "But seriously, I wouldn't know. I spent the last three years in a dorm room, though, so I guess it did feel like home. But your magical house has a severe lack of decorating skills."

Quill opened the screen door, motioning for her to follow. They stepped outside into the warm June sunshine. A gust of wind sighed through the trees, swaying the greenery of the jungle-like forest. Sagely inhaled the fresh, nature-scented air.

Quill grinned. "Are you ready for this?"

"If by *enchanted,* you mean the Ozark National Forest, then I'm already used to the Enchanted Forest."

"To quote Bachman-Turner Overdrive, baby, you ain't seen nothing yet."

She laughed at Quill's lame joke and stepped off the porch after him. They made their way down a small dirt trail into the woods. Suddenly, a grapevine as thick as her forearm fell from a tree, swinging across their path. Startled, she glanced at Quill, who was grinning his fool head off. "After you, milady," he said, gesturing grandly at the grapevine hanging in their way.

She gave him a look. "Am I supposed to click my heels together and wish I was home?"

"The forest is inviting us to play." Quill grabbed onto the vine with both hands and gave her a wink. "I guess your first ride will be with me."

She stepped forward and wrapped her hands around the vine below his. Quill slipped an arm around her waist, gripping the vine in front of her while keeping his other hand above hers. Then he muttered something in a language that was definitely not English.

Before she could ask, the vine swung away from the trail, down and out from the mountain. She stifled a shriek of surprise, but Quill had no such reservations. He let out a loud, joyous whoop as they swung between trees. The vine lowered them to the ground about fifty feet from where they started.

Still laughing, Quill reached up without even looking. A branch bent down and twisted lovingly around his hand. With his other arm still around her waist, he jumped up, and the branch lifted them aloft. It delivered them only ten feet from where they began, not quite as thrilling as the vine but still awe-inspiring. They made their way down the entire mountain that way, each tree branch bending to cradle them in its thick quilt of leaves or grasp them with its supple branch. But the vines were the most fun.

At last, they reached the bottom of the mountain, out of breath and laughing, their hair tangled and their faces shining with excitement. Sagely had never met someone like Quill, a guy so unconcerned with looking cool. He simply enjoyed himself—a rare adult who had not forgotten pure and simple joy.

For a moment she was envious. She didn't know if she'd ever been like that, even as a child. Definitely not since her parents had died in a freak hiking accident.

Quill's smile melted, and his eyes moved to her lips, but a frown creased his brow. Damn it. He'd sensed her lapse into gloom. She didn't want to be the thing that took the smile off his face.

"Well, what are we waiting for?" she asked. "Is that all you got?"

"That's just the beginning." Quill motioned for her to follow as he jogged down a narrow dirt path. They emerged next to a sparkling stream. For a few minutes, they followed its course in silence, taking in the peaceful gurgle of the clear water as it trickled over the mossy stones. At last she heard roaring ahead. They stepped from behind a boulder and into view of a cascade of water pouring into an emerald green pool.

Quill grinned at her and reached for her hand. "Ready for a swim?"

"I didn't bring a swimsuit."

He darted a look at her, a challenge in his eyes. "Who needs a swimsuit?"

"I just met you," she said, laughing. "But nice try."

"Remember how you were afraid that we were all hippies?" Quill asked. "Well, I don't think there's a bathing suit among us. We swim here all the time, Sagely. But if you're uncomfortable with nudity, wear your underthings."

"I'm not uncomfortable with nudity," she said. "I have nothing to be ashamed of."

Quill's eyes moved slowly down her body, almost painful in their scrutiny. She waited, her heartbeat coming fast. She'd been checked out before, but never quite so thoroughly. Quill's eyes finally made it back to her face, and she was surprised by the hunger she saw pooling there.

"Maybe a bathing suit would be a good idea for you," he said.

"I don't know how this shared magic thing works," she said when she found her voice. "How do I know if this is the magic, or if it's real?"

She wasn't used to being so open with guys, but Quill was so open that it was hard not to be the same way with him. It was nearly impossible to play games with someone who so obviously refused to play along.

"Magic is real, Sagely. If this is our shared magic, or if it would've happened without it… either way, it's happening, and it's real."

After a second, she had to look away. He was so intense, and he was offering so much, so fast. But she didn't get emancipated at age sixteen, graduate high school a year early, and put herself through college on academic scholarships by studying her ass off to keep her grades up, just to wind up getting carried away by lust. If she didn't get a grip on herself, she'd wind up a pregnant housewife. Or house witch, or whatever they called it.

"Quill, listen. Maybe this is real." She broke off and swallowed hard before forcing herself to go on. "If it's real, I'm not going to run away from it. I'm not afraid of intimacy. At least not deathly afraid." When she smiled, Quill smiled back at her, but he didn't interrupt. He waited for her to go on, knowing there was more. After a moment, she did.

"I need you to let me take the lead on this. I know you're the most powerful warlock, and I can tell by the way the others treat you that you usually get your way. But I need to control how fast or slow this goes. And you need to let me."

Quill's eyes flashed with a brief stubbornness at the challenge, and she could tell he wasn't used to taking orders. But after searching her eyes for a moment, he must've felt how determined she was, and he relented. "I can do that. But it won't be easy for me when you start adding to your collective. It won't be easy for me to see you swim naked." He glanced at the pool and cracked a small smile, but his eyes remained serious.

"Adding to my collective? What's that?"

"When you marry other guys."

"What the hell, Quill," she said, drawing back. "You think I'm some kind of man-eater?"

"Witches are polyamorous," he said. "Women get to do that."

"You're polygamists? With the sister-wives and everything?"

Quill shook his head. "Not sister-wives. In covens, women have that luxury, not men. Our society is matriarchal."

"Oh." She tried not to let her curiosity show. "So only witches have more than one partner? Not warlocks?"

"Yes," he said, a frown creasing his brow. "We hold life as the most sacred gift the universe gave us. So, it follows that women, who bring new life into the world, are precious to us. Collectively, a group of warlocks protect their witch. That's why it's called your collective. Every coven does it at a different time, but in the Winslow Coven, you'll be expected to start finding partners for your collective after you finish your training."

"Damn, if I'd known that, I would have joined a coven a long time ago."

Her attempt at a joke worked, and Quill smiled. "It might sound like a dream come true, but believe me, there is plenty of bickering and some fighting. But once things are ironed out, it moves smoothly. There are bound to be jealousies, especially for a jealous man like me." He circled her waist with his muscular arm and nuzzled her neck.

She rather liked how he openly admitted his jealousy instead of hiding it. She liked the way his green eyes flashed when he thought of her with another man. But she couldn't pretend she wasn't also intrigued by the idea. "So, you only get one girl, but I get multiple guys?"

"Right. A warlock never marries more than one witch. But if she'd like to share one of her husbands with another witch, usually because they're friends or because they would make a child of stronger magic, then yes, you may share him. Usually, she waits until they're no longer enjoying each other's company, and they part ways amicably. Everything is done very respectfully and consensually."

"Sounds peaceful enough."

"Usually it is," he said. "Our practice is to marry as long as it makes both people happy and makes sense for the couple. We try to maintain peaceful unions and breakups. Our marriages are more than legal—they're magically influenced. Members of a collective share magic and communicate through a magical bond."

"Like telepathy?"

"In a way," he said. "We can ask for protection and exchange magic psychically instead of having to push it into you as I did before. And unlike in your society, there's no shame about dissolving a marriage that doesn't work. That doesn't make sense. Why stay when you're miserable? Our vows are to love each other fully and respect each other's dignity. We live long lives. People change. Forever doesn't make sense for us."

"And you don't belong to anyone's collective yet?"

He grinned, obviously pleased that she was scoping his eligibility. After a long, torturous minute, he shook his head. "No."

She thought this over, not sure how it was possible. But then she remembered he'd said witches had to finish their training first. Maybe that explained Raina's ill temper towards her.

"Let's swim," he said, stripping his shirt off over his head.

Sagely tried not to ogle his bare chest, sculpted muscles that made her want to run her fingers over his shoulders and pecs, over his tight abs to the tiny trail of hair that led from his bellybutton to the waistband of his shorts.

Tried, and failed.

She tore her eyes away from him and peeled off her own shirt. Her magic increased tempo as their clothes disappeared, bringing them closer and closer, layer by layer. When she was at last undressed, she glanced up, expecting Quill to be doing a cannonball into the water. Instead, he was watching her, his eyes tortured as he drank in every inch of her skin.

Her magic leapt to the surface, tingling over her skin as if she could feel the weight of his gaze moving over her body. In that moment, she knew that what he said was true. It was going to be as difficult for her to take this slow as it was for him. All she wanted to do was to fling herself at him, rejoin her magic to his and let it fit where it belonged. She'd never felt anything close to this before, as if he were her *home*. As if she was a missing part of him, as if she belonged to him. The feeling was so intense that she could hardly stand to look at him.

At last she tore her eyes away. "Last one in owes another rain check."

With that, she sprinted for the pool and dove in, realizing as she plunged beneath the cool, clear surface that she hadn't asked if any deadly familiars might be lurking in the serene, emerald water. She surfaced with a quickness. By the grin on Quill's face, she could tell that she was safe. A moment later, he ran and dove in, too. He swam closer, the water buzzing with electricity. Sagely's skin prickled with chill bumps, her nipples contracting under the frigid water's surface.

Quill stopped a few feet away and treaded water. The waterfall cascaded beside them, sending sheets of spray across the surface every time a breeze blew. She'd woken from a nightmare into a paradise. Already, she was growing a new appreciation for the world around her, for the nature and beauty of this place that she'd known most of her life without really noticing.

Maybe it was all the hippie magic, or maybe it was the fact that for the first time in fifteen years, she was not driving herself relentlessly. She allowed herself to relax as she lay back and floated on the surface of the water. The white torrent rushed down the falls, green leaves waved in the wind above them, and above that, the crystal blue of the summer sky stretched out lazily towards evening. Despite all the craziness around her, she felt comfortable. Almost safe. Like she could let her guard down at last.

THIRTEEN

After a time, Quill swam closer. Sagely could feel the energy conducted through the water, so even as she floated with her eyes closed, she knew exactly where he was. When he drew near, her blood began to sing at the same frequency as his, drawing her closer and closer, until his shoulder brushed hers.

"We're naked," she pointed out.

"I know."

"Should we really be this close?"

"It's your call, remember?"

A battle raged inside Sagely. Her mind, her heart, her body, her magic, all of it was in chaos. Her mind said she didn't even know this guy's birthday, or where he was from, or if he liked chocolate gravy or regular. She didn't know how he treated his mother, if he preferred Led Zeppelin or Debbie Gibson, or if he chewed with his mouth closed. They'd never gone on a date or met each other's friends.

But the rest of her said, so what? She'd done all that with other boyfriends, and they were history now. They hadn't lasted. So why not wrap her legs around Quill and pull him close, right there in the water? She wanted him, he wanted her, and she sure as hell had never felt this way before. As if she'd known him all her life, and yet, everything about him was new and fascinating and irresistible. So why not?

"Are you thinking what I'm thinking?" he asked.

"I don't know," she said, rolling over in the water and smiling at him. "What are you thinking?"

"That we should test your magic while you're out here where you can't accidentally light innocent bystanders on fire."

"That's totally what I was thinking!"

"Really?" he asked, his head popping up from the water. He swam upright, grinning at her with his gorgeous smile, his hair plastered down against his tan skin, and his eyes squinting against the bright sun. Her stomach did a lazy flip when his toes brushed her shin beneath the water's surface.

"No, not really," she said. "But let's do it. Does everyone have a special gift, or do we all do the same things in the same order, like school?"

He began to do a lazy crawl towards the shore, and after one last look at the rushing waterfall, she turned to follow. They clambered out of the water, and she tried not to completely ogle his muscular body as he stood, water streaming from his skin, his nipples hard from the chill of the pool. Again, *try* was the operative word.

But he didn't seem to be having much more success

than she was. She caught him gazing at her tan skin with a warm and possessive hunger that made her want to preen in front of him. Instead, she picked up her clothes, forcing herself not to respond to the weight of his gaze.

"So," she said, pulling on her shorts and stepping into her red cowboy boots. "What are you going to teach me first?"

He tore his eyes away from the water droplets clinging to her wet body. "Technically, I'm not supposed to teach anyone until my training is over and I've mastered all four types of elemental magic. I can't give you a proper lesson like a Majori could. We'll just see what you can do. I'll guide you a little as you test it, play around with it. Experiment."

He smiled at her, this one different from his carefree, playful grin. This one was slow and languorous, appreciative. She didn't shy away from his hungry eyes this time. She stood facing him, letting him take her in. She could tell he liked what he saw, that he was admiring her. She let herself enjoy it. As his eyes worked her over, something deep within her warmed like she was a creature emerging into the sun after a long winter of cold hibernation. Something sparkled inside her that had nothing to do with magic. Her blood felt carbonated, fizzy as the first drink from a freshly opened bottle of champagne.

She swallowed hard and, when she could trust her voice, asked, "What's all this about elemental magic? And I thought you didn't have any rules."

"Once you complete your training, you are an adult witch or warlock, with full mastery of your own element and a decent mastery of the remaining three elements. You can continue learning the others all your life, and other spells and binds, things like that. But you'll never master another element like your own." As he spoke, they finished dressing without looking at each other.

Okay, maybe she peeked a few times.

"What exactly are the rules of magic?" she asked. "Like, why can't you master other elements?"

Quill sat on a boulder and let his feet dangle into the stream that emptied out of the pool. Patting the seat beside him, he went on. "That's one of the rules. It's like a law of nature, though, not something some old witch decided a century ago. It's more like…gravity. Magic is energy. It attracts like magic. It can be blocked, like all energies. It can be mastered, but you've never learned all there is to learn. You can't change the essential makeup of an object or creature, can't change its element. For instance, you couldn't change stone to water, but you can change stone to iron."

"Could you turn stone to diamond?"

Can't blame a girl for asking.

"Sure," he said. "How do you think we get money?"

"So, you could make a million diamonds right now? You could make the entire shore of this pool into diamond?"

"What would I do with them?" he asked with a smug smile. "You can't go to a store with a handful of diamonds, unless you want to be arrested."

"Huh. Then it's not as cool." She took a seat beside him and tossed a tiny pebble from a crevice in the lichen-covered boulder into the water. The sun warmed her back after the cold water, and she closed her eyes.

After a second, he nudged her, and she opened her

eyes. He held out a fist towards her, a blue swirl of magic drifting off his ring like mist. When she didn't respond, he grinned, his green eyes sparkling like the water behind him. He opened his hand, palm up. There, in the center, was a diamond the size of a marble.

"Oh my God," Sagely said, covering her mouth. "Is that real?"

"Of course it's real," he said, looking slightly offended. "Would I give you a fake diamond?"

"You're not giving that thing to me," she said, shrinking away as if he'd made it by dark magic.

"I thought you wanted a diamond."

"Yeah, like a...I don't know. I'm not taking a diamond from you, Quill. We just met. Diamonds are forever."

"Oh, I forgot they symbolize that for commoners."

"Commoners? That's what you call nonmagical people?"

He smirked. "What did you want me to call them?"

"I don't know, not that." She closed his fingers over the diamond and pushed it away. "I can't take that, Quill. It's too much. That's probably worth a million dollars."

His smile vanished, and he took her hand. For a second, she thought he was going to propose. She couldn't breathe. "It feels like I've known you my whole life," he said. "You're a part of me now, Sagely. You always will be. There's nothing I wouldn't give you. Nothing is too much."

She swallowed hard. "That is."

"You're worth a hell of a lot more than a million dollars to me."

"Well, thanks. But I'm still not taking a diamond

from you."

"Suit yourself," he said, and slipped it into his pocket.

FOURTEEN

"You saw what I can do," Quill said a few minutes later. "What can you do?"

Sagely laughed, glad the tension stemming from his inappropriate gift had eased. "I have no idea. Let's see if I can make diamonds from pebbles, too. I'll be set for life."

"You are set for life," he said with a smile. He placed a tiny pebble on her open palm.

"How do you actually *do* magic?" she asked, staring at the pebble, wondering if it would explode like that warlock's head. A wave of nausea passed over her when she thought of him again. She wondered if that would ever go away. Probably not. She'd killed a man. That was a human being, no matter how evil. She'd taken his life in a gruesome way. Using freaking dark magic she didn't even know she had. She couldn't just turn him into a frog like a normal witch.

"I usually squeeze it, since a diamond is created under

pres——." Quill broke off and stared.

Sagely looked down at her palm. Great. *Now* she had turned something into a frog, when it was just a stupid, unfeeling rock. As a frog, it was the cutest thing ever, though. She leaned closer to peer at the tiny thing, no bigger than the pebble it came from, about the size of a dime in her palm. Its skin was cool and soft against hers.

"That's not possible," Quill said, taking her hand and pulling it closer. He leaned down, studying the frog for a long moment. When he poked it gently, it sprang away in one giant hop, onto the boulder near their feet. With another leap, it was gone forever, lost in the leaves and rocks and water of the forest.

"Okay, it wasn't a diamond, but that was pretty cool," Sagely admitted, grinning at Quill. She felt as proud as if she had made a diamond.

But a frown creased his forehead. He was still staring into her palm like he expected another frog to materialize there. She concentrated as hard as she could, straining to remember every detail of the little critter—its bumpy grey skin that matched the tree bark of the trees around them, the tiny round eyes, the blunted snout with nostrils no bigger than pinpricks. The damp cool of its belly, the movement in its delicate sides when it breathed.

Nothing happened.

Of course not. When she wanted the magic, it wasn't there. When she didn't want it, she made frogs where she wanted diamonds and blew up people's heads when she wanted…what? She'd just wanted a fair fight. She was not a killer. But try telling that to the coven, who stared at her like she was some kind of black magic woman. How was she supposed to know she had dark magic? She thought she had the same kind as they did. And then that witch, Raina, saying it was her fault. She'd like to turn Raina into a frog—an especially warty one.

A slight, cool pressure on her palm drew her attention. She'd done it! She'd made another adorable baby frog. Ha. That figured. The key to her magic was getting pissed.

"It's not possible," Quill whispered to the frog sitting right in front of his face, just inches away.

"Now you know how I felt when you made a big-ass diamond," she said. "Except, you know, this frog isn't worth a cool mil."

"No, it's not possible to make something out of nothing," he said, straightening and releasing her hand. "That's not how magic works. You can't make a frog out of a rock. You can make a frog out of a person, or change the shape and mineral makeup of a rock. But you can't make something living out of something non-living. That's…"

He broke off and, though he tried to hide it, drew away from her a little.

"That's what?"

After a pause, he shook his head and took her hand, seeming to relax again. Her pulse sped then slowed to sync with his. "Necromancy. That's bringing the dead back to life. That's the darkest magic. But you didn't do that. You made a frog out of thin air." His voice filled with wonder, and a wave of pride went through her. Apparently, she had some awesome power that no one else had—and it was not dark magic.

"What's that called?" she asked.

He shook his head again. "Unbelievably amazing?"

He laughed and squeezed her hand, and her heart skipped a beat. "But seriously, Sagely. I've never seen anything like that. It's not called anything—that I know of. It shouldn't be possible."

"Obviously if I can do it, it is."

"Let's go back," he said, pulling his hand from hers and hopping off the rock. It was weird, because she'd never been a hand-holder or overly affectionate with guys. But now her hand felt cold without his, as if something were missing. He held out a hand to help her down, and her pulse settled when his warm hand closed around hers again.

"Are you scared of me?" she asked in a teasing voice, but a little part of her was afraid he actually was.

"In awe," he corrected. "We'll have to go consult the Wise One."

"Who's that?"

"It's this ancient tree," he said. "The oldest in the forest."

"Great. I'm some kind of freak witch, and now I have to go talk to a tree? Am I going to have to pass a test before it speaks to me?"

"I was kidding," he said. "The Wise One is our oldest witch."

"You jerk," she said, pulling her hand away and punching him in the shoulder.

"You pack a punch," he said, looking impressed as he rubbed his shoulder.

"You're lucky I didn't do Tae Kwon Do on you. Speaking of which…" She trailed off as they reached the head of the trail and he reached up for a grapevine. He wound his arm around it but didn't take off yet.

"What?" he asked.

"I need to go home," she said, scuffing the toe of her boot in the leaves. She might as well get this over with now, before things went any further. "I have a job. I have to at least put in my notice if I'm taking off a few months. I don't want to quit and sit around making diamonds when I need money. It feels like cheating."

"We do plenty of work," he said.

"I need to teach," she said, willing him to understand. "There are kids there counting on me. I can't just abandon them."

He searched her eyes, and after a moment, he grasped the importance to her, if not the reason. "Okay. I'll talk to the coven." He held out an arm to her, but she shook her head.

"I want to try it myself this time."

"Are you sure? What if you fall? I can't let you get hurt."

"I'm not going to get hurt." She reached for a vine, but he held out a hand to stop her.

"That one's not friendly."

"How do you know?"

"They'll come to you if they want to play or help. Send them a message."

Feeling incredibly witchy, she tried to telepathically communicate with the trees.

Nothing happened.

"Try asking out loud," he said with a grin.

"You said I didn't have to talk to a tree." She gave him a doubtful look, but turned back to the trees. "I need a ride, please."

A vine swung towards her, and Quill laughed. "Just

kidding. You don't have to say it out loud. I summoned that one for you."

"You bastard," she said, reaching to punch him again.

This time he ducked, swinging away on his vine, laughing all the while. She wrapped her hands around her vine and jumped, sure it was going to drop her on her ass. But it obeyed her intent, conveying her along after Quill. He whooped like Tarzan, holding on with one hand and one foot, leaning out from his vine as it swung. And he was afraid *she'd* get hurt.

After she got the hang of swinging solo, she let go with one hand, too, and held her arm out like she was flying. It was not a broomstick, but who wanted a hard stick of wood for a seat anyway?

By the time they got back, she'd decided she was never taking any other mode of transport again if she could help it.

FIFTEEN

When they stepped through the door into the basement, the familiar smooth wall where she first saw her power reflected lit the way for them. At the bottom of the stairs, the cavern waited, just as she had first seen it. The coven was all gathered, including a hunched old woman she hadn't seen before.

"How'd she know we were coming?" she whispered to Quill. "Is she telepathic?"

"Maybe a little," he said with a smirk. "She can also speak into your mind."

Great. She was probably going to hate Sagely when she saw what was in her head. As she approached, she couldn't help but think the old woman looked a little like an ancient tree, with her hair hanging down in wisps like Spanish moss, and her millions of wrinkles like the bark on a tree. The way she sat over the others, perfectly still, waiting for them to join her at the table was a bit tree-like, too.

Crap. Stop thinking! She can read your mind.

"Come, little sister," the Wise One said, not moving a muscle.

"Hi. It's an honor to meet you."

The Wise One's eyes were rheumy and clouded white, and Sagely realized she couldn't see her. But her eyes crinkled at the corners with a kind smile when Sagely sat before her. Blind or not, she definitely sensed Sagely's presence.

Her hands rested on the table, palms up. With an almost imperceptible nod, she said, "Put your hands in mine."

Quill rested a large, comforting hand on Sagely's shoulder and gave her a nod of encouragement. She swallowed hard and rested her hands in the gnarled claws in front of her. With lightning speed, the Wise One's wrinkled hands snapped shut on Sagely's. Startled, Sagely tried to pull away, but the older woman's hands clamped down like they were made of iron instead of brittle old bones. Magic zinged up and down Sagely's arms as the Wise One dragged her towards her until the edge of the table dug into her belly.

She leaned down, examining Sagely's squished palms the same way Quill had done by the waterfall. Sagely wondered what she was looking for with those cataract-eclipsed eyes. Suddenly, she pictured the white film over the vulture's eyes, and she shuddered.

The Wise One didn't seem to notice. "Fascinating," she muttered. "Your magic...I remember your magic."

"I don't think that's possible," Sagely said with a nervous laugh. "I didn't have magic until a few days ago."

"Ah," the Wise One said, lifting her head and raising one hand to shake a finger at Sagely. "But your magic has existed since the beginning of time."

"Right," Sagely said, letting out a breath of relief that the old woman had released one of her hands from her death grip. "Magic can't be created or destroyed."

Quill gave her shoulder a reassuring squeeze.

"Exactly right," the Wise One croaked, sounding pleased. "And your magic...I have not seen this type since I was a little girl." She sat back, her milky eyes going somewhere far away. "They said it was all gone. That all the void magic was bound and given to the fae to hide where it would never be found."

"Fae? As in faeries?"

"The very same."

Sagely took a moment to process that, but she decided it was not her main concern just now. "But I have Quill's magic," she reminded the Wise One.

"Yes, there is that, too," the Wise One said with a mischievous smile deepening her wrinkles. "And no small amount of it. It's no wonder you are so smitten with each other. It makes for quite a bonding experience. Among other...benefits."

Sagely's face flushed hot.

"What about her ability to create something from thin air?" Quill asked.

"Ah, yes," the Wise One said, smoothing Sagely's crushed palm out in her hand like a crumpled note. "Our magic is always creative or destructive. As is yours. But you, my child, have magic that is not of this world."

Sagely shook her head. "No, that's not possible."

"And yet, it is so."

"I've never had magic before. If it didn't come from Quill, where did it come from?"

"Have you had strange coincidences?" Raina asked from behind her, as if she was coaxing Sagely to give the right answer. "Something you wanted that happened seemingly by magic? Are you lucky beyond normal odds?"

"No," Sagely said, shaking her head. "Nothing. Believe me, I could have used some luck in my life."

The Wise One leaned down to study her captive palm again. "Your magic, it is the stuff of legends. We called it *void magic*. It is the magic of nothing, not of any element. The magic between stars, of the silence between music notes that makes the song, of the spaces between atoms." She traced the lines in Sagely's palm with a long, yellowed fingernail.

"Long ago, it was confused with dark magic, because much destruction and chaos came about when it was used. But like all magic, it has the potential to be used for either destruction or creation."

"But where did it come from?" Sagely insisted. A memory slammed into her, jarring her teeth together. That man standing over her, like… a black hole.

The space between atoms. The void between stars.

"It came from that man who attacked me, isn't it? He did something to me."

"No," the Wise One said, patting her hand. "Bound magic cannot be used. It must be unbound first. Until then, it is trapped within, magically contained as a small parcel that is passed from one generation to the next."

Sagely swallowed hard. "So it came from…my parents?"

"Yes, that must be it," the Wise One said, nodding

slowly. Her bones creaked and popped at the slight movement.

"Okay," Sagely said. "Okay. Let me get this straight. Some weird kind of magic that was mostly used for evil was bound up into parcels and stuck in a few random people, including one of my ancestors, and it was passed down every time one of them had children."

"Not random people," Quill said, his voice deep with emotion. "Faeries."

"Great. Lovely. Two days ago, I was just a regular person. A commoner, as you so snootily put it. And now I'm some kind of witch-faery hybrid and the ancestor of one of the lucky faeries who was given this scary magic. This is a lot to take in."

"The faerie blood is faint within you," the Wise One said. "That has been diluted. But the magic, it is bound in one parcel. You have the same magic as the first faery who was gifted with it. It passes from first born to first born."

"My mother, then," Sagely murmured, a memory rising. Her mother lying in bed with her, reading her fairytales over and over until she fell asleep. Sagely never reached the argumentative or rebellious teen years with her mother, so their relationship would always remain as it was when her mother died—sweet, simple. As a child, she'd thought her mother as beautiful as a queen, the fairest of them all, with her auburn hair falling against her pillow in the warm lamplight, and her voice that never ran out no matter how many times she read *Rumpelstiltskin*.

The Wise One smiled and released her aching hand at last. "Tell me about this man who attacked you."

Sagely quickly filled her in on the attack that she'd thought was random. The attack that still might have been, or it might have been someone trying to find Quill, trying to steal his magic.

"No," the Wise One said, shaking her head. "Trying to steal *your* magic."

For an instant, Sagely was too startled to speak. Then she remembered. The old woman could read her mind.

"Why would anyone want my magic? You said it can't be used."

"I said *bound* magic can't be used," the Wise One said, shaking her finger at Sagely, her wrinkles creasing even deeper with her smile. Little pouches of skin hung above and below her milky eyes, almost obscuring them when she smiled. "Void magic, however, can be used like any other once it is unbound."

"So, you're saying that wasn't an accident? Someone didn't just run me off the road because my car was the one that passed at that particular moment? And it wasn't someone after Quill. It was someone who wanted the void magic. But if I didn't even know I had it, how did he?"

A weighted silence hung over the coven for a long minute. Finally, Yordine spoke. "Like calls to like," she said. "Only someone with void magic could sense yours."

"So…a fairy?" Sagely asked. She'd assumed it had been a warlock.

Her head swam with a million questions, thoughts, furies. For some reason, knowing that the man had run her off the road intentionally, that he'd slit her throat as part of a premeditated plan, made it so much worse than if she was just a random girl who got attacked on a dark road at night. It was worse than being killed senselessly, as a mistake, because someone stopped her car and not Quill's.

It wasn't a mistake. It wasn't random. He knew

exactly who she was. And he'd slit her throat like she was nothing more than a hog at a slaughter.

This shit just got personal.

"Be careful," the Wise One said. "Anger is a fuel that more often burns the host than the intended victim."

"I thought I was the intended victim here," Sagely reminded her. "I'd be dead if it weren't for Quill."

"He's a good one, isn't he?" the Wise One asked, the crinkles at the corners of her eyes deepening further when she smiled. "He'll be a fine addition to anyone's collective."

"Okay, that's probably enough for now," Quill said. "You both need rest, and I'm sure you need time to process all this, Sagely."

"For sure," Sagely said. All she wanted was to crawl into bed and curl up with Rizzo and take a long nap. To wake up and find that there wasn't some psycho out there trying to kill her for some bundle of magic she didn't even know she possessed. "But first, I need to get my cat."

SIXTEEN

After breakfast the next morning, they all gathered in the main cavern, and Sagely addressed the coven. "I admit, I was unsure about staying here. I like my life back home. But now that I know that guy was trying to kill me, I accept that I probably do need to stay here. Not because I can do crazy magic stuff, but because this guy is still out there."

"And now he's going to come here," Raina muttered. Majori Yordine gave her the evil eye, and she shut up, though Sagely could see she did it grudgingly.

"But I do need to go home and get my stuff," Sagely went on. "I'm not trying to escape. I'm honored that you've all welcomed me to your coven, and I accept."

Quill gave her his thigh-weakening grin, but she would not be distracted. She tore her eyes from his and went on. "I need to say goodbye to my Tae Kwon Do students, give notice to the studio, get my clothes, pay out the rest of my rental contract on my apartment. I can't just waltz off and join a coven like I don't have responsibilities back in the real world."

"Out of the question," Quill said. "I'll go and take care of those things. You can't leave here, Sagely. Not two days after a dark warlock basically murdered you for your magic."

A couple of the other witches nodded.

"I need to do this myself," Sagely said. "I'm not passing off my obligations to someone else. Whoever he was, he's not going to jump me the second I leave this burrow. Obviously, since we left yesterday."

"That's different," he said. "We're all here. We can protect you. Now that we know you have a lost magic, we have a duty to protect you."

"We do," agreed Majori Yordine.

"I can protect myself." She stared Quill hard in the eye, but he didn't back down.

"No," he growled. "I'm going. And you're staying here."

"Like hell," she said. "I have an obligation to those kids. I'm already leaving them. The least I owe them is an explanation and a goodbye. And besides, my cat won't come with a stranger."

"I'm sure I can manage a cat."

They stared each other down. Sagely was not used to this side of Quill, so commanding and domineering, but on her behalf. He was scared for her welfare, she realized as she caught the strains of their magic flowing between them. She softened a little when she felt the concern and protectiveness coming off him.

"You can come with me," she said. "That's as far as

I'll relent."

"That's fair," Majori Ory said.

"No," Quill shouted, slamming his fist down on the stone table. Sparks exploded from the blow. "She's not safe out there. If I hadn't come along at just that second…" He stopped and drew a shaky breath. "What if I can't protect her?" His voice was low now, so low they could hardly hear the question, which he'd directed at the Majoris.

"Then no one can," Majori Yordine said evenly.

"I'll go in her place," Quill said, his eyes locked on Yordine's. "There's no reason she needs to risk her life just to sign a couple forms and pay some bills."

They glared at each other, a silent communication seeming to pass between them. A flare of jealousy lit up within Sagely. She didn't want someone else having a psychic link to Quill that she didn't have.

"My cat," Sagely said, thinking quickly. "She's basically my familiar. That's how important she is to me. I need her, and she needs me. And I'm not going to let someone who's a stranger to her put a sleeping spell on her. I'll pack up and take care of my business. You can come to protect me, or you can stay here. Those are your choices."

Of course, he had other choices. He was stronger than her in every way. He could bind her magic, or her body, or put a sleeping spell on *her*. He could probably overpower her in a hundred ways.

But the fight seemed to go out of Quill then. She felt bad for him, but she wasn't going to let this coven run her life just because she was new at this whole magic thing. She refused to let anyone dictate who she saw and said goodbye to. But she had to admit, it was hot seeing him get so passionate at the thought of harm coming to her.

"If you're afraid you can't protect her on your own, take a few others for backup," Majori Yordine said quietly.

"I can protect her," Quill growled. But after a second, he said, "Raina and Shaneesha? Are you up for a field trip?"

Raina? Was he serious? If the man in black showed up, Raina would probably throw her in his path and stand back laughing while he rid the coven of her questionable magic.

SEVENTEEN

The next morning, they headed out. The four of them squeezed into the cab of Quill's Datsun pickup truck, leaving the bed empty for Sagely's stuff. She'd never been overly attached to her things, probably because she wasn't able to take them with her while moving from one foster home to the next. But she would like to have her clothes and her cat at the very least.

When they'd loaded up that morning, Raina had raced to grab the front seat next to Quill, so Sagely was stuck in the tiny back seat like a kid. At least Shaneesha was friendly, making small talk and asking about Sagely's life in Fayetteville.

After Sagely told her she was terrified of snakes, Shaneesha put away her shiny green familiar. They spent most of the trip in comfortable silence, listening to the radio and dozing after the first part of the drive, when Sagely memorized each turn so that she could make it back when she needed to.

Halfway there, her magic suddenly began to tingle, on high alert. Raina's familiar, a baby seal with big adorable eyes, made a honking noise. Sagely sat forward and looked around.

"No magic," Quill said, frowning at her, his own familiar slipping from his shoulder to stare out the window.

"What was that?" she asked.

"We passed someone with magic, that's all," Quill assured her, reaching up to pat her hand, which was resting on the top of the front seat. "Don't worry. If anything happens while we're there, let us take care of it. That's what we're here for—to protect you."

Again, she glanced at Raina doubtfully. She wished Quill had chosen someone else, even if they had less power. Raina would more likely to trip her in the path of a bullet and say it was an accident than protect her.

Quill squeezed her hand. "You're safe with us," he said, and she wondered how much of her emotion he could pick up. Did he know her suspicion was aimed at Raina alone? It pained her to think that he might feel it as suspicion towards him or the coven.

"What if that guy somehow found out where I live," Sagely said, shivering. True, he hadn't looked through her glove box for her identity. But he could have looked up her license plate or something. She imagined her meek roommate trying to fend off her attacker. If Sagely was helpless against him, Annie had no chance. Finding her chopped up in their apartment as a warning suddenly became a possibility.

"We won't let anyone hurt you," Quill promised.

"Just lay low, don't draw attention, and take care of whatever business you have. We'll keep a lookout. And under no circumstances show your magic."

"What if someone is about to murder you, like last time?"

"I don't think you could get away with blowing up a guy in the middle of a town," he said. "I mean it, Sagely. No magic. It's the one sure way to alert every witch in the state to your presence."

"Fine," she said, slumping back.

"He's right," Shaneesha said. "A strong pulse of magic like that is a beacon for other witches. You felt that one drive by. What if they'd been broadcasting a signal, doing magic right then? You'd have felt it even stronger. And it takes a lot more to alter the course of life—to save or end a life."

"Okay, okay, I won't use magic while I'm in town."

"Good," Quill said. "Then you'll be safe."

They reached Fayetteville late in the morning. Sagely ran up the pathway towards the door of her apartment, surprised at how much she missed it. She could hear yowling through the door. Rizzo could always tell when Sagely was coming home.

The moment she opened the door, Rizzo leapt into her arms. Sagely stroked the soft black fur on the top of her head.

"I'm sorry," she whispered. Rizzo rested her white paws on Sagely's shoulders and looked into her eyes as if searching for answers. But after a moment, she contented herself with rubbing her head under Sagely's chin.

Suddenly, Rizzo pulled back, her eyes wide and ears held high. Behind Sagely, the others had approached, including Raina with her seal.

"Oh, your familiar is a black cat," Raina said with a smirk. "How original."

"This coming from the girl who named her seal *Seeley*."

Rizzo hissed, and Sagely held back her laughter. *You go girl.*

Seeley opened his mouth, revealing long jagged teeth, and gave a quavering roar. Rizzo hissed again and swiped her claws, but they weren't close enough for her to reach.

"Control your familiar or take her outside," Sagely said. "He's upsetting Rizzo in her home."

"I'm just here to help," Raina said, smirking again. As Rizzo's claws raked Sagely's arm, she wished she could throw her in Raina's face and let her feel the wrath of her cat. But she didn't want that savage seal to eat up Rizzo like she was a penguin. She probably looked like one with her tuxedo markings.

Seeley struggled, snapping his jaws open and closed. Instead of taking him outside, Raina set him down on the floor, where he went waddling towards Sagely at a quicker pace than she would've imagined. She jumped back, ready to dropkick the seal if she had to. She dropped into ready stance, about to give him the vulture treatment when he suddenly flopped to the floor, lifeless.

For a second, Sagely thought she'd somehow willed him to die out of hatred alone, accidentally killed him like she had that dark warlock. She braced herself for Raina's attack.

But Raina spun on Quill, her eyes flashing. "You put a sleep spell on my familiar?"

"She told you to stand down," Quill said blandly.

"You had your chance. It's her home. We're guests."

Sagely shot Quill a grateful look and stroked Rizzo's head, calming her down. Raina snatched up her seal and stormed out, slamming the door behind her so hard that the wood cracked.

After that, they worked in awkward silence, no one mentioning Raina. Sagely packed up her clothes and a few items from the kitchen. She didn't have much. She left a note telling Annie that she was moving out but would pay rent for the rest of the summer. Annie would be able to find a roommate easily in the fall when school started, and she'd get the whole place to herself for the summer.

Sagely didn't offer much explanation why. She made sure to tell Annie it had nothing to do with her, but that she'd found some distant family. For once Sagely was glad they hadn't become close, that they weren't even good enough friends to miss each other.

At last, the three of them loaded the final bag of clothes into the bed of the truck and climbed in. Raina was sitting in the backseat with her seal draped across her legs.

"You're not allowed to interfere with another witch's familiar," she snapped at Quill. "You taught me that."

"I also taught you to train your familiar to behave himself."

"If it wasn't for her freaky void magic, he'd be comfortable here."

Quill's voice went quiet but forceful. "Stop this. Now."

"Wake him up, right now," Raina demanded, leaping from the truck and rushing towards Quill. Maude stood up on his shoulder and hissed.

"Maybe he could use a little nap for a few hours,"

Quill said. "Unless you make a cage to hold him, he'll be riding in the same truck with all of us and the cat the whole way back. That's a long way to endure an angry seal-cat fight."

"You had no right," Raina screamed. To Sagely's surprise, Raina's eyes filled with tears. Sagely had to remind herself that a familiar was more than a pet. That there was some magical bond she would never have with Rizzo, no matter how much she loved her.

"She's right, Quill," Shaneesha said. "It's like drugging someone without their knowledge. Not cool."

Before Quill could answer, Raina leapt at him, palm outstretched, like she'd do that palm-heel strike with the fireball. But nothing came from her hand. She pulled it back, grasping at her throat as if she couldn't breathe, tears pouring down her face. The seal slipped from her arm to the pavement, and she fell to her knees beside it. Still grasping her throat, she choked out a sob, touching the seal before raising her face to Quill once again.

"That's enough," Shaneesha said, her face darkening. "Let her go, Quill. You're in the wrong here. And you're still standing by it, sticking up for a stranger who's not even part of the coven. Betraying your own people for this pretty little piece."

Sagely blinked back the hurt. She had to remind herself that the other girls had known each other for years, and she'd only just met them. And Shaneesha knew the coven rules. Obviously Quill had done something inexcusable by messing with Raina's familiar.

When he didn't respond to Shaneesha, she leapt forward, muttering under her breath and making strange motions with her hands. Motions that looked suspiciously like she was tying invisible ropes. Quill's familiar shrieked in protest. Sagely remembered what she'd heard about binding magic. She was not about to let that happen to Quill. Just as Shaneesha raised her arm to cast her spell Quill's way, Sagely screamed inside her head. *STOP!*

EIGHTEEN

At the last second, she tried to take it back, remembering the pulse between her palms when she grabbed the dark warlock's head. Remembering the sudden release of that pressure, the splatter of warmth across her face, the strands of hair stuck between her fingers. The crunch of bone. She shuddered, unable to look at what she'd done to Shaneesha.

Finally, not knowing became worse than knowing. She could feel magic crackling inside her, around her, making a strange silence in the outside world. Again, she thought of the black hole. The void. She opened her eyes.

Shaneesha's head was very much intact. Intact with the rest of her body, which was locked inside a shimmering bubble.

"Let me go," she yelled, stamping one foot. Sparks exploded from the pavement, raining down around her, and the hedge burst into flame. If anyone looked out the window or drove by, there was no way witches were staying hidden from the regular world.

"Let her go," Quill commanded sharply. Sagely dropped her hand, and the bubble disappeared. Shaneesha scuffed out some remaining sparks from around her feet, and a shower of water doused the burning bush.

"We need to get out of here right now," Quill said.

Even Raina didn't argue. She scooped up her seal and climbed into the back seat of the truck, her fingers lingering at her throat. Whatever Quill had done to her, it didn't look very pleasant. Soberly, Shaneesha hopped in the truck, too. After slamming the door, her eyes wide and her breathing coming quick, she leaned forward to where Sagely had climbed into the front seat with Quill.

"How'd you do that?" she asked, looking at Sagely with a kind of terrified awe.

"I don't really know," Sagely said. "I just wanted to stop you."

"I've seen a shield before," Quill said. "It looked just like that. Except a shield is around the people you're trying to protect. It doesn't keep someone in."

Great. More strange magic. Just what she needed.

Quill whipped the truck around one corner and then another, his tire hopping the curb. His jaw was set, his hands gripping the wheel with white knuckles. He stared straight ahead, but Sagely caught him checking the rearview. Maude was racing over and under the seat, keening as if she'd lost something. And his magic was in chaos—Sagely could feel the swirl of emotions tumbling through him.

"What is it?" she asked, touching his arm, hoping to calm him.

"I told you not to use your magic until you were trained," he said in a quiet, solemn voice.

"You're mad at me? I just saved your ass from two witches ganging up on you. Two of your own supposed friends, I might add."

"Hey, I wasn't going to hurt Quill," Shaneesha protested from the back seat. "I would never hurt someone from my own coven." She gave Quill a meaningful look, but he missed it.

He'd already pulled out onto Highway 16 and taken off. But he must have sensed it somehow, the way he sensed Sagely's emotions, too, because he responded. "This is between me and Sagely."

"Fine," Shaneesha said, crossing her arms and sitting back. She stared out the window, her full lips pulled into a pretty pout.

Raina sat silent, letting tears drown her face. She didn't wipe them away. Sagely respected her for not hiding them, but it also felt like a passive aggressive move, forcing them to see her misery at the fact that Quill betrayed her for Sagely, a new and untested witch with no alliances to their coven until she went through the initiation ceremony.

She couldn't wait—if only so the others would stop looking at her like some kind of poisonous freak. Since her parents had died, she hadn't really felt like she belonged anywhere. Certainly not with the families who fostered her. A long time ago, without even noticing, she'd stopped wanting to feel like she belonged.

So this was a new experience for her, this yearning to be a part of something. In a way, she felt like she already was, and by saying otherwise, they were denying her her rightful place. She was not anxious that she wouldn't get in—she was pissed that they were acting like she wasn't already one of them.

She reached for Quill's arm again. He could be pissed at her, but she was not missing what she came for. "Hey," she said. "We need to go back to the Tae Kwon Do studio. I have to say goodbye."

"It's not safe now," he said. "We'll have to go another time."

"No," she said. "We'll have to go now. I need to say goodbye and tell the masters I won't be back for a few months at least. It's that, or I'm not going at all."

"What's the big deal?" Raina asked. "You get to quit your job and have everything you want. Just call them from a phone booth on the way."

Sagely twisted around in her seat. "It's not just a job. I love it. I love those kids. They're counting on me. I can't just disappear on them like…"

She broke off then, catching Quill's look of concern. "What is it?" he asked, his anger melting when he saw that she was hurting. He took her hand and squeezed.

"I just have to go," she said, swallowing past the tightness in her throat. "I know what it's like to have someone be there one day and gone the next, okay? Don't make me say it in front of the whole car."

He nodded and swung the truck onto a side road before turning back toward town.

"You're going to get us killed for her," Shaneesha said.

"It's important to her," Quill said. "You knew this trip could be dangerous, and you wanted to come. Let's do what we came for."

NINETEEN

When they arrived at the studio, a wave of nostalgia swelled in Sagely's chest. The studio had always been an oasis for her turbulent emotions. When she stepped through the doors, calm descended. There was no drama, just the centered, disciplined feeling of the studio. Everything was in order, the cubbies on the wall filled with shoes, bags with sparring gear and pads on the floor along one mirrored wall.

Sagely stepped onto the familiar tough rubber mat where the kids were going through their patterns. She hugged them all for a long time, and shed a few tears, promising she'd come back for a visit.

"Don't forget what you've learned," Master Zuchowski said, giving her a rough hug. "And we'll expect to see you back here for your fourth-degree test." She held both Sagely's hands in hers and gave her a long, searching look. "Is everything okay?"

Master Zuchowski had been a mentor to Sagely, though she wouldn't call her a mother-figure. She would never have the kind of close, loving bond with anyone that she'd had with her mother.

"I'm great," she said, avoiding her teacher's eyes. Master Zuchowski wasn't the warm and fuzzy type, but she could always see right through B.S. excuses.

"Are you sure you want to leave us?" she asked. "If you're in some kind of trouble, you'd let us know, right?"

Sagely nodded, this time lifting her eyes. She couldn't leave her instructor worrying. This was not the kind of trouble a Tae Kwon Do master could help with, not the kind that required an intervention or a police call. From outside, Sagely felt the thrum of tension in Quill, his worry and concern for her. It was killing him that she'd told him to wait outside, where he couldn't get to her in a second if something happened. But Sagely knew there were no witches in there and had insisted it would draw suspicion to show up with bodyguards.

As Sagely stepped out the glass doors, it felt like the last time, despite her promises. Quill rushed to her and took her hand. The magic between them instantly connected, as if she was a boombox that had been running on batteries and was now plugged into her power source. Everything felt right again when they touched.

"Everything okay?" he asked. "You seemed sad in there. Did something happen?"

"I don't like goodbyes," she said, remembering the last goodbye she had with her parents, how lame it was in retrospect, how little weight it carried. If only she had known she wouldn't see them again. Not alive, anyway.

"No one forced you to say goodbye," Raina said

bitterly as they climbed back into the truck.

Sagely had just about had enough. This day had been exhausting, and it wasn't over yet. She turned in the seat to face Raina. "Look, I don't know what your problem is, but I'm here, and I'm not leaving. So you better get used to it. I'm going to be a part of the coven whether you accept it or not."

Raina quirked an eyebrow and smirked. "I choose not."

"You're stronger than me, anyway, so what's your problem with me?"

"My problem? Oh, I don't know. How about this for a reason? You came in out of nowhere and have this bond with Quill, the most desirable guy in the coven, not to mention the strongest. At least he liked me for real reasons, not because of something he can't help."

"Raina," Quill said, his voice a dangerous rumble.

"You're acting like this because of a guy?" Sagely asked, choking back laughter. "That's just sad. I expected more from such a strong and powerful woman. It really is like we're still in high school. Don't we have better things to fight about than a man?"

"If he means so little to you, I guess you won't mind if I add him to my collective, then?"

Sagely's skin bristled with a charge of jealousy, as if she were a dog getting its hackles up. Quill was a bone worth fighting over.

"Not a chance," she said.

"Hey, let's just calm down," Quill said, setting a hand on her knee. "You know what happens when you get angry. It could be dangerous. No more magic today, okay?"

She turned to face forward, but she couldn't help but wonder what had passed between them before she entered the picture. How long ago did it happen? How much did they love each other? Why weren't they together now?

"We've got a follower," Shaneesha said. Quill cursed under his breath as the rest of them twisted around to see a black Jeep taking every turn they took.

"I'll lose him," Quill said. "Sagely, take the wheel."

Surprised, she grabbed the wheel and steered while he kept his foot on the gas and twisted around in the seat. He rolled down the window and hung his arm out like he was just getting some air on this hot day. But a second later, she heard two distinct pops. Quill grabbed the wheel and twisted, hopping another curb and gassing it. As they speed down a side street, she just had time to spot the Jeep tilted to one side at the edge of the last street, both right tires popped.

"Good thing Hollywood doesn't know about you," she said. "It would make the chase scenes so much less exciting if you could just bust everyone's tires."

"I'm not here for excitement," Quill said with a scowl. "I'm here to protect you and keep you safe. And you might want to help out with that by not showing off your magic in the middle of town."

"I said I was sorry," Sagely snapped. "And unless I'm mistaken, you were all doing magic back there, too."

On the drive home, the silence wasn't the comfortable silence of four people lost in their own thoughts and listening to Bon Jovi on the radio. This time, it was an uncomfortable, intense silence. Halfway back, Sagely turned to Quill.

"I'm sorry," she told him. "I was just trying to help."

"You don't trust me? You don't think I can handle Raina myself? I know how to solve a confrontation within my own coven."

"I didn't think," she said. "I saw they were ganging up on you, and I got defensive."

For a minute, he didn't answer. At last, he said, "That's all right. You didn't know." She could see him holding back a grin, but he refused to answer when she asked what was up.

They were almost home when she noticed Quill obsessively checking the rearview mirrors. She twisted around in her seat to see a black Jeep rolling along the winding two-lane road behind them.

"How long has that been there?" she asked.

"A while."

"Is it the same one from town?"

"Yep."

"How did they know where we went?" She tried to detect any strange magic around it, but she didn't feel anything. Maybe they were too far away. "Are they witches?"

"Nope."

Shaneesha had fallen asleep with her green snake coiled around her neck. Sagely shivered and turned her eyes to Raina, who was staring out the window with a blank, faraway look. Her seal lay curled into the crook of her elbow. On the sliver of seat between Quill and Sagely, Rizzo had curled up and fallen asleep. Maude had made herself at home on Rizzo, as if the cat were her own personal pillow. So much for Rizzo wanting to eat the mink.

Sagely turned back to Quill. "Anything we need to

worry about?"

"Not sure," he said, swinging off the highway onto a narrow dirt road that led to their coven's home.

"And this is why we don't use big, flashy magic in the middle of town," Raina muttered just loud enough so they all heard.

Sagely bit her tongue, because maybe it was true. Even Quill was mad at her. She seemed to have crossed some line that was worse than Quill tampering with Raina's familiar.

They bounced along faster than they should on a dirt road. The night of the attack flashed before Sagely's eyes, and she gripped the dash, breathing hard. Quill glanced over, his lips tight. When he saw her distress, though, he slowed the truck. He reached over and stroked the back of her head, smoothing her red hair.

"I'd die before I let them hurt you," he murmured, his green eyes intense. The warmth of their bond washed over her, soothing now that she was used to it. Magic coursed between them. Not just his magic protecting her, but their magic, protecting them.

She smiled at him, and for just a second, she thought everything would be fine. And then the Jeep rammed into the back of the pickup.

TWENTY

Shaneesha slammed into the back of the seat, her braids flying. Quill spun the wheel, maneuvering the truck to keep from sliding into the ditch as Shaneesha let out a stream of curses that would make anyone blush under other circumstances. But this was no time for polite language.

Already Sagely's blood was pounding in her head, and every muscle in her body was taut, ready to fight. This time, she'd have help. This time, she was not an unsuspecting girl just getting done with a relaxing evening at the park, with no idea that warlocks existed, let alone wanted to murder her.

This time, she was ready for the bastard.

"Stay in the car," Quill growled when she reached for the door handle. The Jeep roared up behind them, smashing into the truck's tailgate again. The truck's back end slid off the shoulder into the ditch, but Quill gassed it, and it lurched out again in a spray of gravel.

"Can I use my magic now?" Sagely asked.

"Get down," Quill said. "I don't even want them to know you're in the truck."

"Can't you make a bullet and shoot them or something?"

"Good idea," Shaneesha said. "Too bad Quill's the only one here who can do that with ease, and he's busy driving."

"Not too busy," Quill said, and Sagely was sure she caught a flicker of satisfaction in his determined eyes. So he wasn't completely good after all—he was itching for the fight, too. Sagely could feel adrenaline pulsing inside him like a high. With one hand on the wheel, he swerved the truck out of the way of the Jeep, dodging it this time. His other hand cranked the window down. He reached out, and a handful of gravel flew up from the road and into his hand as if magnetized.

Dropping it into his lap, he grabbed the wheel and twisted furiously as the Jeep once again bashed the truck, this time roaring up beside it and swerving to slam into the side panel. Metal screeched against metal, and Quill yelled for them to get down. Sagely ducked, wondering why the others couldn't make bullets, and why they were invited to come along if they couldn't be of any help when attacked.

Quill flung his hand out the window, and something flew from his palm and smashed the Jeep's windshield into a spider web of cracks. Instead of stopping, the Jeep plowed ahead, knocking the Datsun sideways into the ditch and barreling in front of it. The Jeep stopped in a spray of gravel and a swirl of dust.

Raina coughed and sputtered as the cloud of dust

billowed through Quill's window and into the cab of the truck. Quill leapt out, yelling for them to stay there.

Fat chance.

Sagely was out of the truck seconds after him, the others not far behind. She gathered the magic swelling inside her, converging it into a ball of energy as intense as the sun. There was nothing void about this—it was all here, all presence, all substance. Her instincts homed in on the figure emerging from the Jeep as if she were looking at him through a scope.

When he stepped from the cloud of Arkansas red dust, she froze. It was not the man in the black cloak and hat. For a moment, she couldn't swallow, couldn't breathe. She'd never seen someone so beautiful in her life.

Oddly, he was not someone she'd normally be attracted to. He was barely taller than her, only a bit over five feet, with black hair that fell in baby-soft waves to his chin, and features delicate to the point of femininity. His eyes were a rich brown that she couldn't tear her own eyes from once they met. His flawless skin glowed with an almost iridescent sheen.

"Fox," Quill growled.

"Quill," the stranger said, his voice surprisingly strong and commanding for such a pretty little guy. "I want the girl."

"Over my dead body," Raina said, stepping up beside Sagely.

Sagely glanced at her, surprised.

"If it can't be avoided, so be it," the man named Fox said.

"Wait," Quill said, turning to Sagely. Their eyes met, and she registered agony there. He swallowed hard.

"Sagely, I'll fight to the death for you if you want to be a part of our coven. But if you don't, now is your chance. You haven't been initiated. You're free to do as you please." His eyes were haunted, full of uncertainty, and she could feel what it cost him to release her and the part of him that she carried inside her.

She thought about it for a second. If she wanted to go, if she didn't want to live underground, she could leave. But she didn't even know who this guy was. He was definitely not full of darkness and evil like the man who had attacked her, even though Fox had attacked her, too. In fact, she couldn't feel any magic coming from him at all. Just a feeling of something unfamiliar, foreign. If she went with him, she could spare the coven more attacks from strangely alluring creatures like this one as well as dark witches. She could spare them the danger of her own magic, the accidents that could happen while she was learning to use it.

"I don't want you to leave," Quill said in a voice so quiet that she could barely hear him. "I...I'll protect you. You'll be as safe with us as anywhere else."

"Safer," Raina said, her voice venomous and her lips drawn back from her teeth in a sneer. She looked like she was ready to rip the guy's throat out, and the magic inside her was pulsing out an ugly rhythm.

"It's your call," Quill said quietly, his voice straining to hold back the emotion behind those words. "You're part faerie, so I'll understand if you want to explore that part of yourself."

Sagely spotted the pointed ears then, mostly concealed by Fox's gently flowing locks.

"Give us the girl, and everyone leaves happy," Fox

said. He slunk forward a few steps, and she couldn't help but admire his gait, as sexy and supple as… well, a fox.

Quill growled beside her, and she realized he was picking up on her strange attraction. It wasn't like she meant to find this guy hot!

"If going with you makes her happy, she may," Quill said. "Otherwise, no one is leaving with you. But it's her choice. Not yours."

"I'm not going anywhere," she assured Quill. "Not if I can help it."

"Not my first choice, but if I have to take you by force, I will," Fox said. The doors to his Jeep flew open, and three more little faeries stepped out. They were all impossibly beautiful and delicate.

One of them crouched like a panther, ready to spring, and bared her blindingly white, sharp teeth. When snarling, she was a little less delicate looking—but only a little.

They all leapt forward as one, seeming to hang in the air before dropping to the ground in front of the witches, a good ten feet from where they started. Quill threw up his hands and fired magic bursts at them in rapid succession, like tiny blue bullets.

"Get back," he yelled to his companions as he fended off the fae.

Shaneesha braced herself and began swirling her arms as if pulling invisible threads from the air. With a heave, she threw a blast of flame at the fae. It knocked the panther-like girl to the ground. With a screech, Maude leapt onto her and began to shred her skin with her claws. Another faery, this one as blonde and ethereal as an angel, staggered but stayed on her feet. The ground beneath her heaved, and she tumbled backwards, scrabbling at the dirt rising under her.

Sagely focused on the last faery, a guy with a long, fuchsia braid that reached his waist. He looked confused for a second, and then fixed his sky-blue eyes on her.

Oh, shit.

He was so beautiful that for a second, she lost concentration. He seemed to glow with unearthly light, an enchanting smile stretching across his face. He dove at her. She spun, delivering a roundhouse kick right on his pointy little faerie ear.

Quill sent a wave of earth over the blonde and turned just in time to knock the fuchsia-haired guy off his feet with white-hot ball of light.

Fox somersaulted toward them, sailed through the air, and body slammed Sagely. Her arm jerked up in a high block, almost involuntary, and cracked against his chin. He didn't even blink. He weighed at least a thousand pounds, or so it seemed. She was crushed into the hard-packed dirt, the breath knocked out of her. With a roar of fury, Quill sent a stream of blue light into him like a laser beam.

The blonde faery came whirling towards them like a cyclone and smashed into Quill. His beam of magic broke off, and she sank her teeth into his neck. Maude shrieked and raced to him, clamping onto the faery's delicate ankle.

"If you won't come, then give it back," Fox commanded, his eyes boring into Sagely's. Suddenly, she was frozen, suspended in time, his eyes trapping hers like they were the only two people in the world. His breath was gentle against her cheek, like a flower-scented breeze on a spring morning. His hypnotic gaze ensnared her, and she nodded mutely.

A smiled turned up the corners of his red mouth.

"Good girl," he said, his voice deepening, his eyes as hungry as a starving man's. A shiver of pleasure ran through her, and her pulse raced. Her body responded to the pressure of his in the most carnal way, and she quivered under him even as she felt something cold and hungry invading her, like tendrils of ice searching her fevered veins.

Beside her, Quill flung off the blonde faery. Shaneesha slammed her with a blast of flame that knocked her twenty feet down the road. She crashed into the trees, shrieking and beating at the flames consuming her.

The guy with the braid and the second female now converged on Quill, and while he was busy holding them off with flashes of blue fire, Fox reached for Sagely's throat.

Suddenly, he cried out and froze. Literally. His hand hovered inches from her neck, frozen into a claw. He drew back, holding it to his chest and gasping.

When his eyes snapped to Raina, the spell was broken, and revulsion dropped into Sagely's gut like a rock. Was she just lusting after this sweet little faery who was at that very moment trying to kill her?

She bucked her hips, knocking him off balance, and punched him square in the face. Her knuckles flared with pain like she'd just punched a brick wall. She rolled sideways and leapt to her feet, barely clearing his grasping claw. He arched backwards with another cry. Though she stood ten feet away, Raina's hands were extended towards him, locking him in some kind of twisted hold. Meanwhile, her seal waddled over to sink his teeth into Fox's calf just as Sagely delivered a solid front kick to his chest. He grasped for her one last time with a frozen, blue hand.

Sagely chopped his wrist with a knife-hand strike. To her horror, his thumb snapped off and tumbled to the dusty road between them. Fox fell to his knees, grappling for his dismembered thumb.

Sagely shot Raina a grateful smile, still flustered by the strange effect Fox had on her. Shaneesha had blasted the blonde to the ground again, and Quill grabbed the last guy's braid and wound his hand in it, twisting him around and around. With a heave, he hoisted the faery into the air and spun him around his head before letting go. The boy flew through the air, flailing, before landing over a branch and hanging there, as limp as an empty pair of clothes.

"Get in the truck," Quill barked, scooping Sagely up in his arms. He raced to the truck and set her in the seat hurriedly but gently, before leaping into his seat. Shaneesha dove into the backseat, her snake curled snugly around her neck. Rizzo, who had been lounging across the back seat, gave her a look that said exactly how put-out she was at having to wake up and move.

We'll have to work on her fierce familiar routine, Sagely thought.

Raina gave Fox one last savage kick, then scooped up Seeley and streaked to the car. The guy with the braid was just dropping from the tree, into a crouch, when Quill floored the gas pedal.

TWENTY-ONE

As the truck leapt forward, Maude came sailing through the window and landed in Sagely's lap. The truck roared over the mound of earth Quill had made, and Sagely winced, hoping she didn't hear the crunch of bones along with gravel. Was a faery buried in that mound?

"I thought witches didn't fight or kill," Sagely said, her heart pounding as the truck bore down on the faery.

"We don't," Quill said, not letting up on the gas as he veered around the Jeep. "If we can help it."

"Faeries aren't people," Raina said, wiping a smudge of blood off her cheek. Something hit the truck from behind, sending the back end reeling off the road again.

"Oh, hell no," Sagely said, turning in her seat. "Not this time, asshole."

She threw out her hand the way she'd seen the others do, trying to blast Fox off the back with her magic. Nothing happened. Great. When she didn't need magic, she could make a bubble to contain her own coven, but when she needed it most, her magic refused to show itself. Like Quill said, it was mischievous.

"I got this," Shaneesha said, turning and throwing open the window at the back of the cab. She flung her hand out, but before she could knock him off, Fox leapt forward and sank his teeth into her wrist. She shrieked in pain.

Sagely scrunched up her mouth in concentration and tried again. This time, a sheet of ice formed across Fox's face, and before he could recover, Maude jumped up and scratched him across the throat. Shaneesha wrenched her arm free, tearing off a chunk of her flesh as she did so. A stream of blood blew from Fox's mouth as she slammed him with another blast of fire that rocketed him backwards off the truck.

Sagely was still watching him when she was flung forward, and she felt the sickening thud of the truck hitting a small, fragile body.

"Don't look," Quill barked.

Sagely whipped around in her seat in time to see the fuchsia-haired faery rolling off the hood of the truck and flopping into the ditch.

"I said don't look," Quill said, his voice tight.

"Sorry, I'm not very good at following directions."

"I've noticed."

"Don't worry, it's not just you," she said. "Ask any of my professors."

"Are they gone?" Shaneesha asked through clenched teeth. She was cradling her wounded arm against her abdomen, where blood was seeping into her shirt.

"Let me see," Raina said, taking Shaneesha's hand

gently and turning her arm. A gaping hole bled freely on Shaneesha's forearm. "I'll close it up, but you'll have to get the venom out later."

As Raina covered the wound with one hand, Shaneesha gasped through clenched teeth and squeezed her eyes closed. Sagely kept watch out the back window as Quill drove, blood trickling from his neck wound.

"What the hell?" Sagely asked at last, turning to face forward when she didn't see anyone following.

"Faeries," Quill said darkly.

Sagely wanted to heal his neck, but she didn't want her magic to go wrong and turn him to stone or something. She looked at Raina, swallowing hard. "Can you...fix him?" she asked, though it just about killed her that she couldn't do it.

Raina gave her a haughty smile and reached up to cover Quill's neck with her palm. When she finished, she gave his neck a few caresses before retreating.

Sagely bit back her jealousy and smiled at Raina, locking eyes with her to show her she wasn't intimidated. "Thank you."

"Anything for Quill," Raina said, sliding her long blonde hair back over her shoulder.

"You can heal people?" Sagely asked.

"I'm a water witch," Raina said with pride. "We have healing abilities, since most of the human body is made of water."

"I thought you said your coven is all earth witches," Sagely said to Quill.

He smiled and arched an eyebrow at her. "I said most."

"That's why he chose us to come," Shaneesha said.

"The more elements we've mastered, the better we can fight as a team."

"So you manipulate fire," Sagely guessed. "No air witches?"

"Not enough room in the truck," Quill said. "We have a couple. It's pretty epic when the four of us work together."

"And now five, once you learn to master yours," Shaneesha said, her eyes lighting with excitement. "We've never had a fifth. This will be so rad."

"I wonder what it will be like," Raina mused, dropping her bitchy act for a second.

Sagely turned her. "Thanks. You know, for saving me from Fox."

"We take care of our sisters," Raina said with a shrug. "Whether we like them or not."

"At least you're honest," Sagely muttered, turning back around as the truck chugged into the driveway leading to the unremarkable cabin that hid the cave's entrance.

"You're a good fighter," Raina said grudgingly. "It's not your fault you're part faerie."

She said the last word like it was something dirty.

Quill cleared his throat and glanced at Sagely like he was about to speak, but he shut his mouth and shook his head instead. She could feel their bond, though. She wasn't the only one struggling with jealousy. He'd felt her strange attraction to Fox, and he wasn't happy about it.

"What?" she asked. "I can't help it. Don't tell me you're not attracted to those hot faerie girls."

"Faerie attractiveness is legendary," he said. "Among the fae."

"What does that mean? You don't believe it?"

"Oh, I totally believe it."

"Let me guess. You're immune because you have so much magic?"

"No," he said slowly. "I'm immune because I don't have fae blood."

TWENTY-TWO

After letting Rizzo wander and do her business, Sagely looked around for Quill, hoping he'd give her some indication of what came next, but he'd disappeared inside with the others. She found him in his room wearing only a towel wrapped around his waist, and it was all she could do to keep breathing. She seemed to have forgotten how.

His chest was so sculpted, his shoulders so muscular, his abs flat and strong as a washboard. When at last she tore her eyes away, he was grinning at her with one eyebrow cocked.

"Ready for the mud baths?" he asked.

"I think so," she said, biting back her own smile.

A few minutes later, they were standing at a tiny room off the cavern that smelled like eggs. Now she knew why. This room smelled like sulfur so strongly that she was surprised she couldn't see clouds of green gas in the air like a cartoon. The bubbling, green mud looked like something out of a cartoon, too—something like a swamp. Or maybe a cauldron of witch's brew.

"Come on in, the mud's great," Quill said, sliding into the side of the pool one leg at a time. When he was seated, it almost looked like he was sitting in a hot tub. Taking a deep breath, Sagely stepped in, sliding down across from Quill. The mud was divine. It felt like she was submerged in liquid velvet. The warm mud coated her skin, and she had to hold back the urge to just moan with pleasure.

"Why didn't you make me do this earlier?" she asked, leaning her head back against the edge of the bath.

"I tried," he said with a grin. "I guess this is one of our rain checks."

Suddenly she wasn't sure she wanted them to be called rain checks. All she could think about when he said that was *Raina*. She pushed the jealousy away and said, "I guess so."

"Why are you sitting so far away?" he asked. "I don't bite. You can come over here."

She realized then that maybe she had thought he was still mad at her. But when he gestured with his mud-coated hand for her to join him, she knew that everything was okay between them. She slid across the tub, relieved.

"How about those other rain checks?" he asked.

"What other rain checks?" she asked with a mischievous smile.

"This one," he said, sliding his hands behind her neck. He pulled her in, his gorgeous, gorgeous lips covering hers. She melted into him, the combination of the relaxing atmosphere and the magic vibrating through her body making her forget everything.

She was sunk in pleasure, wallowing in it. His lips

moved over hers, caressing them, nibbling them, needing them. At last his tongue slid into her mouth, hot and hungry. His warm hand slid against her neck, coating her skin with mud. She didn't care. She just wanted him to keep touching her.

But after a minute, it was all too overwhelming. Her attraction to him, the magic, the heat in the room and between them. She pulled back, breathing hard.

Quill's eyes swam with desire. "Sagely…" he said, but he didn't add anything else.

She drew back from him, back from the intimacy of the moment. "So how do we get this stuff off?" she asked, examining her green-coated hands.

"We wash very…" He trailed a finger down her skin under the surface of the mud. "Very… thoroughly."

She didn't answer. A tingle shimmied from the crown of her head to the soles of her feet, making her toes curl. But suddenly, her mind was invaded by the thought of things she'd rather not think about, things that had happened when she was a kid. Things that, for some insane reason, she was about to tell someone after keeping them hidden all these years.

"What's wrong?" Quill asked, a frown forming. His eyes searched hers, their green a deeper shade than usual.

She shook her head, not sure she could go through with this. What would it get her? There was no point. She kept repeating all the things she'd told herself all those years, but this time, it wasn't working.

"I can tell when something's wrong," Quill said quietly. "Tell me what it is. You're all dark now. And be careful if you use magic right now, because it will be dark."

"I don't think you want to know this," she said

slowly, but she didn't think he was going to give in.

"I do, though," he said, stroking the frown off her forehead with his thumb. "Tell me. I want to know you, Sagely. Everything about you. Every part of you. Even the dark parts."

She let out her breath in a rush. "I've never told anyone this, and if you tell anyone or use it against me in any way, or throw it in my face, I will kill you. I'm not saying that lightly. I will freaking explode your head."

"Okay okay," he said. "I'd think you would trust me after today." He looked at her hard.

"I can't believe you did that, by the way," she said. "I can't believe you stood up for me against your coven."

"You're important to me," he said. His face went serious, his eyes locked on hers. "You're important."

"Thank you." She wasn't sure what else to say. He was definitely not like commoner guys, and that was definitely a good thing. She didn't know if anyone had ever told her she was important, not directly. Her parents had made her feel important. But since then, no one had made her feel that way.

"That was a nice change of topic," Quill said with a small smile. "But I want to know what you were going to say."

Again, she hesitated. She wasn't sure what she hoped to gain from this revelation. She hadn't told anyone since right after it happened. For the first time in her life, she suddenly wanted to, and not just because she was afraid of what power it had to turn her magic into darkness. This was something even scarier. It meant she was thinking about a future with him.

A future where it might affect their relationship,

where he might need to know this. Maybe it was a defense tactic to drive him away, the way she'd driven away other men. She swallowed hard and opened her mouth to speak. "After my parents died, and I was sent to a foster home, I was abused."

Quill's hand pulsed around hers, and his face darkened like a deadly storm. His eyebrows drew close, the frown on his forehead murderous. "Who?"

"It doesn't matter," she said, her voice flat as she recited the rest like a robot. "A foster brother. I tried to tell my foster parents, but they just shut me down. I was there for two years. After I told them, they must have asked him, because it got worse. When I left, I got a great family. They just wanted a child. They were everything a foster kid dreams of. I was lucky to have that experience."

"But?"

"But the damage was done. I never really felt close to them. I don't trust people, even good people. They gave me everything I asked for, and what I asked for was Tae Kwon Do. I wanted to be able to defend myself, to take care of myself if anything like that ever happened again."

When she stopped speaking, Quill's hand was like steel around hers, squeezing it so hard she was losing feeling in her fingers. What was it with witches and the death grip?

For a minute, he didn't speak, and her heart began to pound. She'd never told anyone this before, so she had nothing to compare his reaction to. When at last he turned to her, his jaw was clenched, the muscle jumping as he swallowed. His green eyes glowed, almost ultraviolet in their intensity.

"It's not your fault."

Sagely pried her fingers loose. "I know it's not my fault," she snapped. "What the hell kind of thing is that to say? I was eight."

"What do you want me to say?" he asked, his voice tense with barely suppressed rage.

"Nothing," she said, standing. Thick, warm mud clung to her entire body. "I'm going to go shower. This is making me claustrophobic."

In truth, she wasn't claustrophobic. She just needed to get away for a minute, to breathe. To put away those memories where she'd stored them for years, where they belonged. Far, far from her mouth, from the ears of people who would never understand.

By the time she was scrubbed clean in the shower, she already felt stupid. What did she expect him to say?

When she stepped out of the bathroom, into the tunnel, she collided with a hot, mud-covered marble statue. That's how hard his body felt, anyway.

"I'm sorry," Quill said.

"No, I'm sorry. I don't think I was ready for that," she admitted. "I shouldn't have blown up at you."

Great. It was all awkward now that she'd acted like a complete psycho and showed him how totally screwed up she was.

"If that's what you call a blow-up, this will be smooth sailing," he said, smiling down at her.

"So you're not mad at me?" she asked, giving him a coy smile and trailing her fingers from his chest, down his stomach, sliding slowly in the mud. She wanted to erase what she'd told him, make him see her the way he'd seen her before. Playful and sexy instead of damaged.

His eyes stayed serious for a moment, as if he were

contemplating whether to play along. But when she traced a finger along the top of his shorts, he smiled. "You'd better let me go shower off before I lose all control, seeing you in that towel for so long."

"Make it a cold one," she teased.

"Oh, I will," he said. "Trust me."

"Well, you did get mud all over me again, too," she said. "Maybe I'll join you."

"Sagely…" His hand covered hers. "Are you sure about this? Now? After what you just told me?"

"Forget what I told you," she said, tugging at the band of his shorts.

"Is that what you want?"

"Yes," she said, slipping her hand under the band of his shorts. "Besides, we're just showering. Totally innocent."

His eyes widened and his Adam's apple bobbed as he swallowed. "You're not going to make this easy on me, are you?"

"Not even a little," she said, ducking back into the bathroom.

TWENTY-THREE

Thirty minutes later, as they stepped out of the bathroom into the corridor, Raina emerged from her room. She stopped short, her mouth falling open. It would've been funny if Sagely hadn't caught the wave of pure pain rolling off her.

Raina recovered quickly, though, the flicker of hurt covered by her usual poise. "I was just coming to apologize for the way I acted today," she said. "But I guess it's not necessary. It seems like you're feeling all better on your own." With that, she zipped her finger across another constellation and stepped through the wall. Sagely had the feeling if she tried to enter that room, she'd run smack into solid granite.

Quill called after Raina, but she was already gone. Sagely turned to him, a flare of jealousy rising inside her. But he avoided her eyes, looking uncomfortable.

"Ex-girlfriend?" she asked, though by now it was

obvious. She just wanted him to say it.

"Yeah," he said, glancing off down the corridor, distracted.

"Well, feel free to go comfort her," she said. "I'll be going."

She turned and made her way down to the Corona constellation on her door before turning back. "But you might want to get dressed before you go visit your ex in her bedroom."

To her annoyance, she caught a hint of a smile forming on his delicious lips before she slipped into her room.

*

After dressing, Sagely joined the students in the cavern for dinner. As usual, she found the normality of their food comforting. Tonight, they had spaghetti with freshly grated Parmesan cheese on top and salad on the side. It was a meal she could make at home and often had. But she felt no sense of nostalgia for home now that she had Rizzo with her. Her cat was the only thing in that world she had a real attachment to.

When she walked in wearing her own clothes, skin-tight jeans and a t-shirt knotted at one hip, along with her ever-present red boots, she noticed a couple of the girls glancing her way and then turning to whisper together. Great. She'd avoided being one of the freaks in high school, but apparently high school never ended.

Just then, the comforting warmth of Quill's magic washed over her as he entered the cavern. She almost melted with relief...until she remembered their shower earlier. Her face warmed. Now she was melting for other reasons. His hand grazed her lower back as he passed, and she shivered at the pleasure of it.

"Don't mind them," Quill said, leaning close to speak into her ear. A warm shiver curled down her spine at the closeness of those lips. "They've just never been around someone quite like you. I can't say I have, either."

When she was seated at a table, Quill insisted on going to get her plate. Sagely smiled as she watched him scooping food onto their plates. Maybe she could get used to having a man around who liked taking care of her, even if she was used to doing it all herself.

Just as she was feeling smug about him, a tiny girl floated up to the food table beside him. Sagely recognized her as Willow, the gorgeous witch from her magic test who'd left her so distracted she had to look away to win. She smiled up at Quill adoringly, then reached for his neck, her fingertips skimming over his skin. He bent in her direction, and she hooked her finger in the neck of his t-shirt and pulled it away from his neck.

Anger boiled inside Sagely. She clutched the edge of the table, wishing she could hurl the huge slab of stone at her. How many exes did Quill have? And why was this chick touching her man?

The thought gave her pause. She didn't know when she'd started thinking of Quill as her man. But she definitely did. And she definitely didn't want that hot girl's hands on him, even if Sagely hadn't claimed him officially.

Willow's fingers traced the faerie bite on his neck, and her perfect lips parted slightly as a look of concern creased her forehead.

While Sagely had been distracted, a girl with kinky dark hair broke away from the pack of girls at their table. She approached Sagely, smiling excitedly. Sagely remembered her from the magic test, too. She was right in the middle, power-wise. She'd chatted nervously during the test. Her name was Ingrid. Now, she sat opposite Sagely and tossed a heap of hair back over one shoulder.

Sagely knew that gesture. The bitch flip.

Ingrid was there to tell her off or lure her into some trap where she could make fun of her. Although she wasn't sure how witches made fun of each other.

"Is it true?" Ingrid asked, her eyes bugging.

"Is what true?"

"You know," Ingrid whispered, leaning forward. "Is it true that you made a reverse shield?"

"Considering that I don't know what that is, I have no idea," Sagely admitted. Instantly, she regretted exposing her naïveté. Of course she should've acted superior, like she knew all about it, and flicked her hair back, too. Like it was everyday stuff, and she did it on a daily basis.

"Oh wow," Ingrid said leaning back. She looked at Sagely with big eyes and placed a closed fist over her heart. "I'm Ingrid."

"I know," Sagely said, placing a fist over her heart, too, although she felt clumsy with the new gesture.

"I've seen someone do a shield before," Ingrid said. "But I've never seen someone do a reverse shield where someone was trapped in a bubble." She lowered her voice and leaned forward again, giving Sagely a conspiratorial smile as she glanced over at the other girls. "I wish it had been Raina, and I'd been there to see it."

Sagely couldn't help but smile back at the girl, who she had obviously read wrong when she approached. Just as they were grinning their heads off at each other, Quill plopped down beside Sagely and pushed a plate of spaghetti her way. She decided to suck up her jealousy and be an adult about it. If she had multiple husbands down the road, he'd have plenty of time to feel what she was feeling now.

Plus, he'd come to sit with her while the unearthly beautiful Willow sat by herself at the end of a table, her head bent over her plate.

"I guess you two are getting along famously," Quill said, arching an eyebrow at Ingrid.

While Quill was busy twirling noodles around his fork, Ingrid gave Sagely a grin that was so transparent it might as well have been spoken out loud. *Oh my God! He talked to me.*

Immediately, she looked guilty and cleared her throat, attempting to erase the giddy grin from her face.

Sagely shrugged and shook her head, gesturing that it was okay to crush on her boyfriend. But she wasn't so sure. Ingrid wasn't exceptional, but she was pretty, with crimped black hair past her shoulders, fair skin, and curves for days. Sagely had to respect the witches, though. They were so transparent—even the mean girls, the ones who didn't like her, didn't play games.

Ingrid had broken rank to come talk to Sagely, to make her feel welcome and forget about the other girls whispering about her. She owed Ingrid for that, even if Ingrid didn't know it.

After dinner, Sagely hurried back to her room to find Rizzo lounging on her bed. She scratched behind the cat's ears and collapsed onto the bed, exhausted from the long day. Soon she was asleep.

Suddenly, the man with no face was standing over her. She was terrified, more terrified than she'd been when he slit her throat. He loomed over her like a reaper—dark, hooded, and undeniable.

"I compel you." The voice came from around her, inside her, like the voice that came from the cave walls that day. Booming through her, it vibrated her bones. She looked down to find Quill's head between her hands. She pulsed her fingers, and it exploded.

She sat bolt upright, sweat slicking her body, her heart hammering, her ears still ringing with the cry she'd let out. She slipped from the bed, goosebumps running up and down her spine, sure that the noise must have come from the waking world. Sure that the others had heard it. They'd be crowding into the hall, racing for the cavern, ready for a fight.

When she stepped through the wall into the hallway, though, no one was there. She looked up and down the tunnel, lit now by a single wall sconce. No one.

Cradling Rizzo in her arms, she tiptoed down a few doors until she reached Quill's. Slipping through, she didn't stop to think what she would do if she found him with someone else. She pushed the thought away. He was not with someone else. He was in the bed by himself, sleeping. She could feel him, his magic and his warmth. Tiptoeing over to the bed, she lifted the blanket and slid in with him. Rizzo settled onto their feet and began to purr.

"Sagely?" Quill asked groggily, his hands finding her waist and pulling her close. She tried to melt into the warmth of his chest, but she was still shaken.

"What's wrong?" he asked.

"I had a bad dream," she admitted, feeling childish. What was she supposed to say, that a man with no face compelled her to explode his head in her dream? But that was exactly what she told him after a moment of consideration. She wouldn't feel better until he told her that it was nothing, just a dream from feeling guilty about murdering someone. Because that had to be it.

Good or bad, that man had been a human being. She'd killed a warlock who just happened to be using his powers for evil. But Quill had explained to her that they didn't kill because no matter how evil someone was, they had the ability to turn good. No one was beyond redemption.

Quill was silent for a long minute before he spoke. "You probably won't be surprised to learn that we believe in the power of dreams."

"So it's going to happen?" she asked, a shudder wracking her body. If she saw herself kill Quill and there was no way around it... She definitely should have gone with the faeries to protect the coven.

"It's more likely something that they are planning," he said. "There are too many variables to be sure, but a dream like that can often be an omen warning of ill intent."

"What if... What if that man I killed gave me some of his magic?" It was a question she hadn't wanted to ask, because she felt things sometimes, things influencing Quill's magic inside her, things that weren't exactly nice.

She expected Quill to deny it, but he only snuggled her closer into his arms and kissed her forehead. Her heart began to beat faster, but she had to say it now, while she had the courage. "I can feel it inside me," she whispered.

She waited for him to say they needed to have a cleansing ritual, to purify her and rid her of the evil magic that she was tainted with. Instead, he smoothed back her hair. His hand rested gently against her cheek and he tipped her chin up. "I know," he said, his thumb stroking her cheek.

She drew back a little. "You do?"

"Of course," he said. "I can feel it through our bond. I don't know if the others can feel it or not, but I've felt that since you killed that man. He didn't just let my magic go when he died. He let his go. And some of it has found its home inside you."

"Great. So I'm half good witch, half wicked witch?"

"You can't be a dark witch without choosing it," he said. "Everyone has a choice what kind of witch and person they want to be. You have dark magic inside you now because someone else made it dark. Not because you made it dark or because you are dark."

"So what do I do to get rid of it?"

"You don't. It's up to you to turn it into creative magic instead of destructive magic."

Quill slid his arms around her and kissed her cheek, snuggling into her neck. Sagely lay awake staring up at the ceiling thinking of how she could change dark magic to light. She didn't know how to do that. She wasn't a super shiny happy person. There was a part of her that wanted to go scratch Raina's eyes out just because Raina used to have Quill before she did. She didn't really blame Raina for hating her. If some other girl came in and took Quill away from her, she *would* scratch her eyes out.

But she was not giving him up. She may have thought he only loved her for their bond, but she liked his idea better. What could be better than magic to bring two people together?

And Quill trusted her. Even with the dark magic

inside her, he trusted her enough to fall sleep right next to her, even knowing that she'd had a dream in which she killed him. Even knowing that she was perfectly capable of killing a man.

This powerful warlock, with some of the most potent magic in the world, was sleeping as innocently as a baby beside her. And when she thought of it, she trusted him just as completely—otherwise she wouldn't be in his bed. He could have stopped her earlier, stopped her from doing any magic. He could have bound her magic because she'd killed someone. But he hadn't.

She'd found a man any girl would want. A man who could make stones into diamonds but was happy just to goof around, swing through the trees like Tarzan, and kiss her until she couldn't think straight. No wonder Raina hated her. When she thought about how lucky she was, she almost hated herself.

TWENTY-FOUR

Sagely woke up slowly on the morning of her initiation and stretched across the bed. It was empty. She sat up and looked around. Rizzo and Maude were curled up on the foot of Quill's bed. Sagely lay back on the pillow, snuggling in and smiling at the delicious memory of his warm arms cocooning her as she fell asleep, making her feel safe. She turned her head to inhale his woodsy scent on the sheets.

Damn, I've got it bad.

As she lay there reveling in the softness of Quill's sheets, she realized she hadn't really looked around his room before. With all the drama, there was always something else on her mind. That, or it was dark and Quill was the only thing on her mind. She'd been sleeping in his room for the last week.

Now she had a chance to study his room. Like hers, the walls were made of dirt and stone. But otherwise, the normalcy of it comforted her. He had a shelf of records with a small record player on top. Led Zeppelin and Bob Seger record covers were taped up on the wall. She liked that he was a normal guy as well as a powerful warlock. It made her feel safe that he was both, not too foreign but also able to protect her in ways a commoner never could.

She sat up when he slipped through the wall, carrying a tray in both hands. He was wearing drawstring grey sweatpants and nothing else, and she couldn't keep the smile off her face. God, he was gorgeous.

He returned her smile, licking his lips before setting the tray across her lap. Two plates heaping with bacon, scrambled eggs, and biscuits with gravy sat on the tray.

"Oh, wow, this looks amazing," she said, grabbing a fork. She dug in, stuffing her mouth with the salty, rich food before noticing he hadn't taken a bite yet.

"Glad you're enjoying it," he said, grinning as he picked up a fork. His hair was all mussed and curly in the morning, before he brushed it. She was touched that he'd gotten up to make her breakfast in bed before he even went to comb his hair.

They ate in silence, enjoying the simple pleasure of good food after such hard days lately.

"That was totally ace," she said when she was done. She set her fork on the tray and leaned back on the pillows. "How come you eat such normal food? Not complaining. It's just that looking at this place, I'd expect to be eating roots and herbs or something."

"There is a special brew you'll have at your initiation ceremony tonight," he said with a grin.

She groaned and closed her eyes. He'd outlined the ceremony for her so she wouldn't be nervous. The whole coven would come to welcome her, drink together and vow to treat each other as family as long as they shared one coven.

"Seriously, though," she said.

Quill gave her a teasing smile. "I can't reveal all my secrets," he said. He leaned over and gave her a quick kiss, then lifted the tray. Before he could stand, she knelt up on the bed and wrapped her arms around his neck, pulling him in for a deep, passionate kiss.

"Does this mean what I think it means?" he asked, glancing meaningfully at the bed.

"Not even," she said, swatting his muscular backside. "I have to get ready for my big day, and I don't need any distractions. Now, what should I wear?"

"You're such a girl," he teased, leaning in to nuzzle her ear. Delicious shivers ran through her, and she pushed him away with reluctance.

"Says the guy who thinks one kiss means I'm ready to hop in bed with him," she teased back.

"You are in bed with me," he pointed out, leaning in to brush kisses across her collarbone.

"Okay, I can spare a few minutes," she said, melting into him. "But just for kissing."

"Just for kissing," he promised, his voice rough with desire as he murmured into her neck.

*

That evening, she was a bundle of nerves as she made her way to the big cavern. She must have changed twenty times, trying on every outfit she owned. At last, she settled on a yellow sundress that made her red hair stand out and suited her warm skin tone. The damp breeze in the tunnel swished her skirt around her legs as she made her way into the cavern.

Her heart sped up when she heard the clamor of voices, and for a second, she was sure those dark witches were back to ruin her ceremony. She'd only been there two weeks, but it felt like she'd been waiting for this day forever.

But the sounds from the cavern weren't the angry ones of a fight. They were excited, and when she stepped into the room, she spotted Eli talking to the drop-dead gorgeous girl who had been a little too handsy with Quill after his faerie encounter. A few others were standing around chatting, holding copper mugs, above which swirls of silvery mist hovered.

"If it isn't the woman of the hour," Quill said. His freshly washed hair was slicked back into the little knot he wore at the nape of his neck, and he gave her a closed-mouth smile, pride shining in his eyes. "Ready?" he asked, his fingers brushing the small of her back.

She nodded, swallowing hard. He gestured to the stairs, and together they climbed them and emerged into the cabin above. That was when she heard more voices, and saw that outside the screen door, the yard was teaming with people.

Half a dozen grills lined the edge of the yard, and the smell of meat and vegetables filled the air. She turned to Quill, and he slid his arm around her and gave her a squeeze.

"You look beautiful," he murmured in her ear.

"Good, because I feel sick," she muttered back.

"Aww, don't be nervous," he said. "They've all been waiting to meet you."

When they stepped out onto the porch, she looked around, confused. She didn't know any of these people!

"It's the whole coven, remember?" Quill said.

Damn. He had said the coven would be there, but she'd imagined all the people she'd met the first day. The students. Not a bunch of families. There were kids of all ages, from babies to teenagers, and adults, too.

"Can I introduce you around?" Quill asked, pulling away to study her face.

"Yes, please," she said. She wasn't scared of the witches, she just wasn't expecting to have to make small talk with the whole First Valley. Holding her head high, she descended the steps. This was her day. They were here to meet the girl with the weird magic. She was not going to show weakness by letting them see how rattled she was.

Deep breaths, she told herself.

"They're gonna love you," Quill said, taking her hand. "How can they help it?"

She pulled her hand away discretely and walked beside him like an equal, not a pretty arm piece. He introduced her to each person, telling her something meaningful about each one and then standing by while she made polite conversation. When the food was ready, they sat at the picnic tables and ate.

Eli and Ingrid squeezed in on either side of Sagely, and she realized that at some point, she'd forgotten about her nervousness and wandered away from Quill, too interested in all the other witches to remember that she was making a first impression.

They had all been warm and welcoming, from oldest to youngest. No one had been jealous or snooty like some of the student witches. Now she glanced around as she ate, noticing that some students were eating with adults. And then she saw Quill, and her heart stopped.

He was sitting at one of the wooden picnic tables, and Willow had planted herself beside him. Her hand was on his shoulder, and she was stretching her mouth up to his neck, kissing him. Right there for the entire coven to see.

Oh, hell no!

For about two seconds, Sagely considered going on eating like nothing was happening, like she didn't see a thing. It was the classy thing to do. But some situations called for class, and some called for kicking ass.

She stood and drew herself up to her full height, which, when she faced facts, was not very intimidating. Luckily she'd chosen to wear her trusty red boots, which made her feel a little more like she could stomp someone than if she'd worn cute sandals. She'd be damned if she'd sit there and let some other girl move in on her man without at least calling him out on it. She marched over to his table with all the dignity she could muster.

"Hi," she said, dropping onto the wooden bench opposite the necking couple. An older witch and a young warlock who looked like mother and son were eating together at the table, too. Sagely would have preferred to do this where no one could overhear, but it needed to be said right then, so it couldn't be helped.

"I guess all that 'magic brought us together' crap was just a ploy to get in my pants?" she said, her voice shaking with barely contained fury. "Well, good thing I caught you before it went that far, huh?"

"Sagely," Quill said, an arch smile on his face.

The girl pulled away and dropped her head, hiding

her face behind a wall of silky hair. At least she had the decency to be ashamed. Quill just smiled indulgently at Sagely, bringing his hand up to his neck.

"You think I'm the kind of girl who will just sit here and pretend this isn't happening right in front of my face? After you went on about how I was a part of you forever? Let me guess. She's a part of you forever, too? How many other girls are a part of you, Quill? Inquiring minds want to know."

"What?" the girl asked, raising her head. Her perfect lips parted, and Sagely saw a shiny smear of blood on her lower lip. What the hell?

"Sagely, this is my sister, Willow," Quill said, standing and stepping over the bench.

"Hi," Willow said in a soft, breathy voice, giving Sagely an apologetic wave.

"Why is your sister kissing your neck?" she asked.

"She's half fae," he said, dropping his hand from his neck. That's when she saw that the bite from last week was ripped open, bleeding again.

"And faeries drink human blood, so you're feeding her in the middle of a cookout?"

He laughed. "No, but she's the only one here with enough faerie blood to heal a faery's bite. They're venomous. She's immune to it."

"And you thought it was appropriate to do that at the dinner table?" Sagely asked, grasping at straws.

"She's right," the woman at the end of the picnic table said, standing. She held out a slender hand. "I'm Bea Golden, their mother. I'm afraid we don't always teach our children human etiquette. But this is your party, and we should be respectful of your customs."

His mother. Oh God.

Sagely shot him a murderous look, but he just couldn't stop grinning.

"Mom, meet Sagely, the girl I saved. And who probably saved me. I hope to one day be a member of her collective," he said with a wink.

"Don't count on it," Sagely growled.

The boy at the table was watching them with a big grin on his face, obviously finding the whole situation as hilarious as Quill did. Sagely could see the family resemblance then, how he looked just like a ten-year-old version of Quill. Willow, however, had the unearthly glow of the fae, an unnatural and alluring beauty that had the unfortunate effect of hypnotizing Sagely into a brainless lump of lust, thanks to her own trace of fae.

"Half faerie, huh?" she asked, sitting down across from Willow. "How'd that happen?"

"Our mother has eclectic taste," she said, avoiding eye contact.

Bea just laughed and sat back down to eat. She looked like a cool hippie with her brown hair in two braids that hung to her waist, each one woven with little feathers and beads and ribbons. She had Quill's green eyes and square jaw and tall figure, though she was wearing outdated bell bottom jeans and a cream-colored peasant blouse.

Quill told his brother to get Sagely her plate, and he scampered off to do his brother's bidding over her protests.

"It's okay," Quill said, joining her on the bench opposite his sister. "He loves to help. It makes him feel useful."

She shot him a questioning look, and he leaned in. "He's a commoner."

"A commoner who's anything but common," Bea said with a smile. "Just like his father."

"So you don't have to marry warlocks to preserve your magic?"

Bea laughed, a musical, tinkling sound. "Of course not. You can marry whomever you choose. For a century or so, that wasn't the case, but now we have plenty of strong witches." She smiled fondly at Quill. "Like my son."

"I think I need to know more about this collective thing," Sagely said.

"Just don't expect the rest of the coven to be happy if you marry a fae," Bea said with a sly smile. She really did have eclectic taste in men. Sagely wondered what her collective looked like, and how they all interacted. Though the idea of having a collective of guys intrigued her, she couldn't picture it actually working.

"Hey," she said, turning to Quill. "Is your dad here?"

He took a huge bite of his burger and pushed it into his cheek before answering. "Nope."

He went on chewing, and his brother brought her plate from the other table just as she was about to ask more. She decided to leave the questions for another time. He obviously didn't want to elaborate.

TWENTY-FIVE

As people finished eating, they made their way towards a fire in the center of the yard, where, no joke, a huge cast iron cauldron bubbled. People stood around it in the warm, lingering evening, fanning themselves with paper plates. At least the smoke was keeping the mosquitoes away.

When Sagely finished, Quill's brother took away their plates, and Quill leaned in to her. "Are you ready?" he asked in a low voice, his eyes searching hers.

The concern radiating from him calmed her like a healing balm. She smiled. "How bad can it be?"

"I'm ready for it to be official," he said. "For you to be one of us." He stroked her hair, cupping the back of her head and drawing her in for a fierce but tender kiss. When he pulled away, he locked eyes with hers again. "I won't let anything threaten your safety," he said.

She shivered at the apprehension in his words.

Something was going to happen, and he knew what it was, but she didn't. It put her on edge, but before she could pry it out of him, Majori Yordine stepped away from the cauldron and held up a copper mug, steam rising off it.

"Welcome, sisters and brothers," she said, her commanding voice rising over the gathering, which fell silent as every face turned to her. "Our coven is our family, and today, it is my privilege to welcome a new member to the family. Sagely was gifted magic and would like to train to become a witch."

She gave Sagely an encouraging smile. Sagely stood and squared her shoulders, hoping she looked fierce even in a yellow sundress. Yordine's strong features and voice made her wish she'd worn something that conveyed the kind of power the older witch had.

"Sagely, please come up for the laying-on of hands."

Sagely walked up to her, keeping her steps even, not hurrying. Quill had told her about this part. He'd told her that she could talk to the Majoris and explain that because of her past, she didn't feel comfortable being touched by strangers. But she was determined not to let one asshole from her childhood hold her back any longer. She was ready to move on, and this seemed symbolic of letting go of that pain. This time, she was choosing to be touched.

"Magic is often spiritual, mental, and invisible," Yordine said. "As energy, it isn't always apparent. But it's also a very physical energy. It is most strongly conveyed through mind and body at once. When we welcome a sister, we share with her a trace of our magic. Therefore, we are all bound in one coven and can sense when someone needs help. I'm sure you have sensed magic in us, and you have a bond with our strongest member.

Today, you will get a small fraction of that bond with each and every member of our coven. Together, we form one magical family. And you become a member of that family."

A family. It had been over a decade since she'd had one of those. She'd never let herself want one after that, knowing it was impossible. She'd never allowed herself to imagine a foster family becoming permanent. Though she'd had a good one for six years, she'd petitioned for emancipation the moment she reached sixteen. She knew she would never have a family again.

But now she did.

Unexpectedly, her eyes throbbed with unshed tears. Could it be real? After years of being on her own, counting on only herself, could she really have such a huge group of people who cared about her, what happened to her, and if she was safe? She'd be sharing something with them that she hadn't allowed herself to share with anyone since she was eight years old.

She would no longer rely solely on herself. She'd feel their pain, their need, their loss. She'd be called to save them and protect them if they were in danger. And they would protect her, share her pain. It was a huge responsibility, and suddenly, all she could think about was that warlock she'd accidentally killed. It was *too much* responsibility.

"Now, as we accept you into our coven, we share our magic with you as you share yours with us."

Majori Yordine handed her a copper mug. A layer of blue flame danced on top of the liquid, which released a silvery mist when she blew on it. She took a small sip, and was surprised by the slightly spicy, clean flavor of it. Basil, mint, lemon, and something sweet. She took another sip, and her body started to relax. She could feel her magic pulsing stronger, but also steadier.

The Majoris motioned for her to lie on the platform beside the cauldron, which looked like a narrow picnic table without benches. This was it. A hundred strangers were about to put their hands all over her body. Her throat tightened, and her breath started to come quicker. But she forced herself to think of this differently. To welcome and relish their nearness, the hands she had given permission to touch her body. Quill stood beside her shoulder, as if ready to spring into action the moment she'd had enough.

She could do this. She was in absolute control. The moment she told them to stop, they'd stop. No one would touch her if she didn't want them to.

Quill smiled down at her, smoothing her hair back. "Try to absorb their magic," he said. "Feel each witch's signature. It's like a fingerprint—similar, but no one's magic is exactly the same."

Eli stepped up beside her first. "I accept you as a member of my coven and my family."

A feeling of power surged through her as he waited for her answer. Not one person would touch her until she said yes.

"I accept."

Eli pressed a hand briefly on her forearm, smiled at her, and stepped away. One by one, the witches came up to welcome her, each one pressing a palm onto her body somewhere—her arms, legs, torso, and head. As she accepted each one as part of her family, she began to relax and absorb their magic like the gift that it was. Quill was right. She could recognize some signatures before they even touched her—Ingrid's, Raina's and Shaneesha's, and a few of the other students.

When at last she'd been gifted magic from everyone, she sat up and scooted to the edge of the table. Quill looked relieved as he helped her up.

"Were you afraid someone would try to steal my magic?" she whispered.

"No, of course not," he said. "I trust our coven. But I'm still a man as well as a warlock. I don't like seeing all those people touching you."

She shoved him playfully. "You're such a guy."

"And now, we partake of you, our new sister," Yordine said as she slid a silver knife from her belt. Its ornate handle fit into her hand, and the curved blade had some kind of symbols along the dull edge. The sharp edge glinted in the firelight.

Before she could move, Quill was between them, looming over Majori Yordine. She didn't flinch when he stepped up to her, dominating her space.

"Sagely will not share her blood."

Share her blood? What the hell?

"It's only one drop," Yordine said calmly. "The welcoming ceremony requires it. We drink of the elements. Plants from the earth, water from the rain, air from the sky, and fire from the spark of life." She tossed something new into the cauldron with each word—a handful of basil leaves, a pitcher of crystal clear water from the platform next to the cauldron, and something that looked like steam pouring out of a bottle when she removed the stopper and dropped it in. Lastly, she thrust her palms at the bubbling mixture, and fire danced across the top like a *flambé*.

"And a bit of the new member's essence for our coven when she becomes one of us."

Quill loomed over her. "No."

"What's going on?" Sagely asked, stepping up to his elbow. She dropped her voice to a whisper. "Is it because I have faerie blood?"

His jaw tight, Quill shook his head, his eyes locked on Yordine's. They seemed to be having another silent conversation, leaving Sagely to wonder again about their close relationship as student and master. After a minute, Quill turned to the rest of the coven. When he spoke, his voice was every bit as commanding and powerful as his Majori's. The coven listened with as much respect as they did when she spoke, too.

"Sagely was gifted magic from me," he said. "But she already had an ancient magic locked within her. The intense burst of magic I gave her inadvertently unbound the parcel of magic already within her—one that had passed from generation to generation in her family."

Quill faced the coven, filling them in on what the students already knew.

"But Sagely's magic is different," Quill said, his brow furrowed with concern. "We have spoken with the Wise One, and even she has no firsthand experience with it. Up until now, it was believed to be gone, if it ever existed. Some believed it was only a legend. Until now."

"Void magic," Majori Yordine said.

Several people inhaled audibly and glanced around nervously. Sagely was getting a little tired of the gasp-and-stare-at-Sagely routine.

"Since we don't know exactly what it does, or how to use it, we will be learning along with Sagely. If you've heard of it, you know it can be used for the dark arts. What we don't know is whether a trace of it will enter us with her blood. So before we perform this part of the ceremony, she'd like to give you a choice. If you don't want to risk a trace of this unknown and unpredictable magic, with whatever it entails, we will not drink together tonight."

Several people nodded and look relieved.

"You should also know that if you are bound to Sagely, it might be dangerous to you and your family," he said. "We already know that the faeries want the magic back. And we also believe that the dark witch attack that happened recently here in the school may be connected."

"It may be Viziri's doing," Majori Yordine added. "He had almost certainly come into possession of void magic at some point as well."

"If you choose to share in this unknown magic, you take on the responsibility of protecting Sagely at all cost, with your life if necessary," Quill said. "And judging by recent events, it may be necessary. You might have to do things you wouldn't normally do. If you don't want to compromise the lightness of your magic, or you fear it might be tainted from joining with Sagely's void magic, abstain from the drink."

"Great," she muttered. "You make me sound like an STD."

"On the contrary," Majori Yordine said. "Your magic is sacred. You're the only person in the witch community who carries it, as far as we know. It must be safeguarded at all cost, until we have mastered it and know its uses."

"*You* must be safeguarded," Quill said, frowning at Sagely. "No more spontaneous trips into town. It's too dangerous. We can't risk anything happening to you."

"And should you not wish to participate in this part

of the ceremony, we do ask that you keep this quiet," Majori Ory said, stepping forward. "If Viziri has not gotten word of it, we want to keep it that way. It's bad enough that the fae know."

Sagely shuddered, remembering the black cloaked figure slicing her throat open. *Give me what's mine.* That's what he said. Was that what the Jeep full of faeries had said, too?

Quill took both her hands in his. "This is serious, Sagely. When these people take a part of you, they might absorb a trace of your magic. Whether they do, or you keep it inside you, you are bringing back a lost art to our people. They will treat you with the respect you deserve. And they will fight for you if it comes to that. Only you can give this to us. But we won't take it if you are unwilling."

"Give me the knife," she said, taking it from Yordine.

"One drop," Quill cautioned. She could feel the magic coursing through her. She made a small cut in her finger and held it out. Yordine chanted steadily as she took Sagely's outstretched hand and held it over the cauldron. At last, she tipped it and let a single drop of blood fall into the bubbling mixture.

Sagely looked down in time to see a swirling blackness spiral down from the drop to the bottom of the huge pot, as if a whirlpool had opened in it. A black hole. A few people gasped, and others craned their necks to see in.

Next, the Wise One took Sagely's hand in hers. "On behalf of the Winslow Witch coven, I invoke the spirit of our mother earth and her four elements. Let all here bear witness to your union with our coven. We invite you now to become one with us and one of us, our sister."

From the folds of her skirts, she drew a dull metal ring. This one had a single marking, a circle within a circle. The other witches strained forward to see the strange new marking—no one else had the mark of void magic on their ring. She'd learned about the rings in class, how each witch started with a single marking, that of their original magic. They gained more through mastery of other elements.

"I accept," Sagely said, sliding the ring onto her finger.

Instantly, the inner of the two circles turned a featureless, infinite black. Several witches gasped and stepped back, while others squeezed in closer to see. Sagely held up her hand for a minute, so they could all stare.

Then she dropped her hand and turned towards the house. "I'm going to go lie down," she said. Quill followed her onto the porch, but she stopped and pressed her hand to his chest. "No, stay with your family."

"We're your family now, too."

She swallowed hard, a lump in her throat at the thought. A new family. Not one she'd been born with, but one that had taken her in nonetheless. "Don't get me wrong, I'm happy to be a part of this," she whispered. "But I still want to be me, too."

He caught her wrist. "What's wrong, Sagely?"

"I just want to be alone," she said. "Being the freak gets old fast. And…I'm a little overwhelmed by all this. I was a regular human just a couple weeks ago."

"You're not a freak," he said, cupping her cheek in his palm. "You're a treasure."

"Well, that gets old, too," she said, her lip trembling. "I just need to be alone for a minute. That's all it is. Please trust me."

She smiled up at him, and he nodded and leaned forward to place a gentle kiss on her forehead. "I trust you."

"And you'll make an excuse for me while I be an introvert for a minute?"

He laughed. "Anything for you."

She stood on tiptoes to plant a small kiss on his lips before she turned and went into the cabin, down into the hidden school, and into her room, where she changed into sweats and curled up with Rizzo. Ready to get lost in someone else's problems for a while, she picked up a book and read until she fell asleep.

TWENTY-SIX

Sagely woke to the sound of footsteps outside her room. Sitting up, she glanced around. Rizzo was curled against her hip, and her wall sconce was sputtering. Her heart pounded, and she held her breath. It was probably Quill.

But what if it wasn't?

After a minute, someone tapped on the wall outside.

"Quill?" she asked. Maybe he thought she was mad at him. Usually he didn't knock.

"Can I come in?" asked a shy, girlish voice.

Sagely nodded, as if she could see her through the wall. But it worked, somehow, because…magic, she supposed. Willow stepped through and perched on the edge of the bed.

"Is your hand okay?"

"Yeah, it's fine," Sagely said, holding up her hand, where only a red dot remained where she'd pricked her finger.

"Do you want me to go?"

"Not really," she said honestly. "What's up?"

"It's just…I don't know any other witches who are part faerie," Willow said, giving her a shy smile.

"Before yesterday, I didn't know you were, either," Sagely said.

"Witches don't usually like faeries," Willow explained. "If you couldn't tell from the biting and stuff the other day, when they attacked you."

"I thought that was because they wanted the magic back."

"Yeah, it was," Willow said, twisting her hands in her lap. "Anyway, I just wanted to see if you were okay. Maybe, since we're both part fae, I could heal you. But I don't know. I only really know I can heal a faerie bite."

"What else can faeries do? I know they don't have the same kind of magic, but they have some other powers, right?"

Willow's face pinkened. "Do you think I'm pretty? Like, you might like me?"

Crap.

"Sorry," Sagely said. "I'm not into girls. I can't seem to stop staring."

"It's the faerie," Willow said, nodding. "It's how they keep the blood pure. Most faeries are only attracted to other faeries. So you feel a pull towards us that normal witches don't."

"Well that explains some things," Sagely said slowly, remembering her mad lust for Fox, even when he was about to kidnap her. Quill had said he was immune, but she hadn't realized exactly why she wasn't.

"I think you're pretty, too," Willow said, still looking

at her hands. "Like, faeries are as attracted to you as you are to us. If you wanted me in your collective, I'd say yes."

"Wait—what?"

"I mean, no one is going to say yes to me," she said. "Warlocks think I'm a vicious, sly faery."

"But you're so pretty. And they don't get to make a collective, anyway."

"Yeah, but they can accept or not," she said, raising her head at last. "Just like with humans. When a man asks, you get to say yes or no, right? Well, with us, the woman asks, and the man can accept or not."

"Oh, right." Sagely hadn't really gotten down to the logistics of how this polyamorous thing worked. But if it was all based on love and respect, everyone would have to be okay with it. She wasn't sure if she liked the idea of proposing to a guy or not. She put away the thought for later.

"It would be weird, with you and Quill," she said slowly.

Willow brightened. "So you're going to ask him?"

"We've talked about it," Sagely admitted, biting back a smile.

Willow grabbed her arm, her green eyes shining. "That's so exciting. I can't wait. We'll really be like sisters." Her face fell then. "If you want, I mean. Most of the others don't want to be friends with me. Faery and all. I just thought maybe, since you're part faerie, too…"

"Of course we'll be like sisters," Sagely assured her. It was strange, to have someone want to be part of her family so badly.

"My element is air," Willow said, ducking her head again. "And I'm not that strong. You should know that, in case…you know. If that changes your mind."

"What's wrong with air?"

"It's just pretty lame," Willow said. "Earth is what our earth mother is made of. Fire is powerful and fierce, and it powers the spark of magic inside all witches. Water is healing and gentle. Air? It's useless. That's why Quill didn't ask me to go on your trip to town."

"I'm sure it's not that," Sagely said. "He wouldn't want to put you in danger. And honestly? I don't really care how strong you are or what magic you have. My magic is the magic of nothingness. Annihilation. We probably make a good pair."

"I drank the brew," Willow said after a minute. "I just wanted you to know, because you left before we did. I'm sworn to protect you now. And if you ever want to experiment…try something out…maybe I could help. You could teach me. Or I could be your guinea pig."

"I better learn to control it first," Sagely told her. God, her skin was so creamy, she just wanted to touch it. How did faeries keep from mating like bunnies all day long if they were this attracted to each other?

"I'm glad we're friends," Willow said, standing. "I'll leave you alone now."

"Me, too." Sagely watched her float to the door, her filmy white dress dancing around her like feathers. When she reached the wall, Sagely spoke. "Wait. Who else drank?"

"I'll make you a list," Willow said. "Almost everyone did, though."

"Did Raina?"

Willow hesitated a long moment, her fingers disappearing through the rock face. It still unnerved Sagely to see someone sinking into stone. "No."

Sagely swallowed hard. She should have expected that. "Did your brother?"

Willow studied the wall in front of her feet for a long moment before answering. "No."

TWENTY-SEVEN

Over the next month, Sagely dove fully into her new life. She attended the coven's weekly gatherings, prepared and ate meals with the students, and practiced Tae Kwon Do forms in her room at night. During the day, she learned magic, at first with Majori Ory, who was as kind and encouraging as she expected. After a few weeks, she moved up a level with lots of praise from Ory about how quickly she mastered the basics. Really, she thought he just felt bad for her, training with a group of witches ten years younger than she was.

At the next level, she studied under Majori Romero. He was hard on her, as she expected, sometimes pushing her to tears. But he was also fair, and under him, she learned to control the initial wave of magic that pulsed through her when she had a flash of terror or fury.

There were more advanced witches and warlocks in this class, though most were still younger than Sagely.

Willow and Ingrid were both in the class, and Sagely took to spending time with them, trying to test if Willow had gotten enough void magic to use when she'd drunk the brew. Despite her love of teaching, she made zero progress.

One day, as she sat alone on the porch, attempting to move a plant's leaves with water magic, Quill stepped out of the cabin.

"Hey," he said, sitting down on the step. "Want to get out of here a while? Maybe go swimming?" He wiggled his eyebrows at her, and she laughed. They'd spent at least half their nights together, but true to his word, he had let her set the pace for getting physical. It wasn't that she'd never had a boyfriend. But she'd never really trusted people since her parents died, so she'd always put up a barrier, both emotionally and physically. She wanted to do it right this time, to tell him when she needed to pull back instead of putting up a wall between them.

"Okay," she said. "I could use a break. Moving stuff with your mind takes a lot more energy than just picking it up with your hands and doing it the easy way."

"Blasphemy," he said, standing and holding out a hand to her. Laughing, she took his hand and let him pull her up. They ran into the woods and sprang up, grabbing the vines. Now she could feel their magic, the magic of the entire forest coursing through the trees around her, the air, and her own blood. When they arrived at the pool, it was much smaller than in early summer. Mosquitoes buzzed around it, but they jumped in anyway. The water was still cold, though the waterfall was barely more than a trickle now.

"How's your training?" Quill asked when he surfaced,

his blond hair slicked down over his skull. "I can't wait until you move up a level and I get to start telling you what to do."

"As if."

He reached for her, but she slid away in the water. Though it was hard for her, too, a part of her liked making him wait. She wanted to make him prove he would always respect her boundaries, but she also liked having the power to command the most powerful warlock in Arkansas.

"Can I ask you something?" she said, treading water in the shallow pool. She swallowed hard before asking. She didn't know why it was hard. She could have asked any time. But it had been on her mind, the one concern she hadn't shared with him. "How come you didn't drink the brew that had my blood in it the night of my initiation?"

"We share enough magic," he said easily. "I didn't think it would make a difference."

"Are you sure you're not scared of my dark, unpredictable magic?"

"I'm not scared of you," he assured her, swimming over to her. He caught her hand and pulled her closer. She could feel the heat of his body in the cold water as it drew near. "I wanted you to keep something for yourself, something that's not mine. I wouldn't have let anyone have it if I could've avoided it, but it was the only way to connect you with the coven and keep you safe. But it's your gift, Sagely. I don't want to take any of it away from you."

She slid closer, until the water between them vibrated with an electrical current. Their eyes met, and he arched one eyebrow, asking permission. She slipped her arms around his neck. Their warm bodies entangled under the cold water, and a bolt of lightning electrified her. There was nothing between them. Maybe this would be the day she couldn't hold back. A part of her was tired of holding back, and that part was growing more impatient every day. She pressed her lips to his, and he cradled the back of her head in his hand.

"You are too damn sexy," he said, pulling away at last.

An eerie chill that had nothing to do with the water zipped up her arms. Quill's body stiffened, and he broke away, swimming towards the shore and pulling her with him.

"What's wrong?" she asked.

"Danger in the coven," he said, running up the bank. He grabbed his clothes and tugged on his shorts. "We need to get back there. Now."

She pulled her cotton dress over her head, glad that she'd worn something simple today in the heat. Shoving her feet into her red cowboy boots, she took off after him.

"When we get back, go straight to your room and wait for someone to come tell you it's safe," Quill said over his shoulder.

"Not gonna happen," she told him, running to catch up. This time, they raced through the woods, swinging on the vines at a breakneck, terrifying speed. As they drew closer, a crawling, panicky feeling overtook her. She could feel the wrongness in the coven's magic inside her, but she didn't know what it was. Not until they raced into the clearing in front of the cabin.

She skidded to a stop behind Quill, who threw out an arm to hold her back. A handful of students were on the porch, and a few more in the yard. Majori Yordine was standing at the bottom of the steps, her hands held out in a supplicating gesture to the tiny woman with shimmering emerald hair standing at the edge of the clearing. The woman held Willow in a headlock.

Damn. Sagely knew she should have been teaching the witches Tae Kwon Do. Then Willow would know how to break out of the faery's hold, even with the ornate silver blade pressed to her throat. The faerie woman held it in her free hand as if she might puncture Willow's jugular at any moment.

Pulses of blind, red fury ricocheted off Quill. He tensed to spring, but Sagely put a calming hand on his arm.

"Getting mad is not going to help," she whispered, repeating something Romero often told his students.

The faery turned towards them, a smile turning up the corners of her mouth. She looked like a hummingbird, tiny and fragile, with that shimmering dark green hair. "I knew you'd come," she crowed. "And here you are."

After their last faerie encounter, Willow had told Sagely to avoid their eyes so she wouldn't fall prey to their seductive influence again. And now she was hanging in the faery's grip, clutching on with both hands to keep the faery's arm from tightening and choking her.

"Release my sister," Quill said, his voice low and deadly.

Sagely had never heard him use that tone before, but when she shot him a look, his eyes were locked on the faery. When Sagely saw the terrified expression on her lovely face, rage boiled inside her, too.

"I was hoping you'd say that," the faerie said lightly.

Quill's brows drew together in a murderous frown.

"Aren't you going to ask why?" the faery taunted.

Quill's arm flexed under Sagely's hand, and she held him back again.

"What do you want?" Majori Yordine asked calmly.

"Stay out of this," Quill growled without taking his eyes off the green-haired lady. "This is between me and the *faery.*"

Hearing the disdain in his voice, Sagely dropped her hand, stung. She was part faerie.

"I'm glad you asked," the faery said, as if she didn't notice the tension. "I want the girl you have, you want the girl I have. It should be an easy exchange. No one has to get hurt."

"That's not going to happen," Quill said, curling a protective arm around Sagely's waist. His arm muscles felt like granite against her, and she held onto him in return, glad he was on her side.

"Then you'll have to fight me for her," the faery said. She took one step back, and suddenly, a dozen faeries materialized from the trees behind her, stepping silently onto the grass to flank her. Sagely shivered when she caught Fox's hungry eyes on her, but she tore her gaze from his before his beautiful eyes could hypnotize her.

"You know witches don't like to use our magic for fighting," Majori Yordine said, her accented voice clipped. "But if you insist, then you'll have to fight me and leave the children out of it."

"No," Quill said, releasing Sagely to step forward. "They're here for what's mine. This is my fight."

"You're not ready," Yordine insisted.

"He looks ready to me," the faery said, eyeing Quill's broad shoulders, down his sculpted torso to his narrow hips. She grinned and ran a slightly pointed tongue along her sharp teeth.

"No," Yordine said. "I forbid it. He's still training."

"He's bigger than me," the faery pointed out. "Are you afraid he'll be hurt? I'm the most powerful faery in the Three Valleys. The Queen. And I want to fight your most powerful witch. Is that you?"

"No," Quill growled. "It's me. And I'm a warlock, not a witch."

Before the faery could answer, Quill leapt at her. Lightning fast, he slammed a ball of magic into her face and grabbed his sister.

"Get inside," he yelled at all of them. But no one moved except Willow. She scurried across the lawn to where Sagely stood, her breath coming short as she gripped her arm. Raina stepped up on her other side, and Yordine fell back to join them, her jaw tense.

The faery recovered from Quill's initial attack and leapt to her feet. He aimed a punch at her face, but she leapt five feet into the air, slamming her heel into his cheek. Sagely heard bones snapping as he roared in pain. But before the fae queen got in another kick, he grabbed her foot and slammed her to the ground. A heavy thud sounded, and the ground tremored beneath their feet.

Sagely squeezed her eyes closed for a second, not wanting to see her boyfriend beating up a woman, even if she was an evil faery. She opened them again when Raina nudged her, hard. "Watch," she said. "If Quill needs your magic, you need to be ready to give it."

For the first time, Sagely realized how serious this was. The strongest faery in the valley was fighting him. What if he didn't win? What if he lost...and died? If the faerie queen killed Quill, what would happen to Sagely and the rest of the students? The entire coven? If their strongest warlock was out of the picture, they'd be open to all kinds of attacks. They should have been protecting Quill, not Sagely. He had all the magic.

Sagely would probably end up as a sex slave to these faeries, maybe by her own choice. But it wouldn't be her choice, really, because she'd be under their spell.

"Send him positive energy," Willow whispered, her nails digging into Sagely's arm.

A month ago, Sagely might have scoffed at that idea as silly. But now she knew a little about how magic worked. She squared her shoulders and watched as the faery spun in the air like the Frisbee she'd been throwing around the first time she saw Quill.

The faerie queen moved so fast she was nothing but a blur. Quill chopped through the blur with a solid hit, though. The faery toppled to the ground but sprang back up and threw herself at Quill. Her arms and legs wrapped around him, and her teeth sank into his shoulder.

Raina sucked in a breath.

He's got this, he's going to win, Sagely chanted inside her head.

"Don't worry, we practice how to fend off attackers in my classes," Majori Yordine muttered. "Quill is a skilled fighter."

"I thought witches were all about that 'I'm a lover, not a fighter' mantra."

"Quill has an abundance of magic," Yordine said as he ripped the faery loose from his shoulder. She came away with a chunk of his flesh, and blood spurted from his wound.

Sagely swallowed hard so she wouldn't puke. But she didn't close her eyes. "Enough magic to heal that?"

Sagely's eyes were riveted to the scene in front of her, to the delicate, beautiful faery with her sharp teeth streaked with gore, her chin dripping blood. Quill's blood.

"He has the means to protect his magic," Yordine said. "His strength as a warlock is not matched by a faery."

Sagely wanted to ask if she was sure about that. But she knew better than to put those thoughts out into the world. Voicing them made them stronger, so they might come true more easily.

Quill pinned the faery to the ground and knelt above her, his hands flat on her shoulders as he chanted under his breath. Sagely felt his magic swelling as he worked his spell on the faerie queen. She started to relax.

But just when she thought he had won, the faery's hands flew up and gripped his neck. Her nails punctured his skin, sinking into his flesh. Blood began to seep from the holes her fingers made. Sagely tried not to gag as she saw the faery's delicate fingers burrowing into his flesh, up to the first joint. Blood trickled down her clenched, claw-like hand.

Quill's magic wavered inside Sagely, growing cloudy and then ebbing.

"What's happening?" she whispered, grabbing Majori Yordine.

"The faerie bite," Willow said, her hands flying to her mouth. "It's poisoning him. I need to get out the venom."

"Should I go get his familiar?" Sagely asked, turning to run.

But before she took a step, Raina grabbed her arm. "You can't leave him," she hissed. "He'll see you go and think you gave up on him, and he'll give up. Besides, there's no time."

"How's it happening so fast?" Sagely asked, remembering that the last time, Willow had healed his bite long after the attack.

"They can bite without injecting venom," Willow said. "Like a snake. This time, she injected venom."

TWENTY-EIGHT

Quill's magic flickered inside Sagely like a candle about to sputter out. His eyes caught hers, and his panicked, bewildered expression ripped her heart in two.

"Return his magic," Yordine said. For the first time since they'd met, Yordine sounded flustered.

"What? How?"

"You have his magic," the Majori said. "Don't give him yours. You can't do that without endangering him. But his own magic is familiar to him and can flow back easily."

"Tell me how," Sagely yelled, grabbing her shoulders with both hands.

"Open yourself and release it, just as he did when he gave it to you," Yordine said, clutching her forearms and staring hard into her eyes. "Breathe deeply in, and when you breathe out, feel it leaving your body. It knows where it belongs. It will return to him."

Sagely tried to breathe, but she was hyperventilating. Eli slipped up beside her and put his arm around her waist, and she saw his eyes signal to Willow. She got into position at Sagely's other side.

"Close your eyes now, and open the channel between you," Raina said, coming up behind her and putting her hands on Sagely's shoulders.

Sagely tensed under Raina's touch, not liking her enemy behind her, where Sagely couldn't see her. "You're my sister," Raina said softly. "I'd never hurt you. And I won't take the magic you release. No one will. It's only for Quill. Let it go."

Sagely's body began to relax as she stared into Yordine's wise brown eyes. She took a deep breath, closed her eyes, and felt the magic humming inside her at a fever pitch, as if it already knew it was needed elsewhere. It was trying to get out, to go to Quill's rescue. She pursed her lips and let it out in a long stream. When she opened her eyes, she saw a silvery vapor curling in a long spiral from her lips across the grass to Quill. He inhaled deeply, his shoulders rising and his chest expanding.

With a jerk, he clamped a hand down on the faery's face. She shrieked as his fingers tightened, his other hand circling the back of her head. With one swift wrenching motion, he twisted. Her shriek was cut short, and silence fell over the yard. Quill slumped sideways into the dirt beside the faery. The magic Sagely had returned had been enough to give him the strength he needed to kill the queen, but it wouldn't save him. The venom was still poisoning him.

Fox stepped forward. His eyes met Sagely's across the yard, and a traitorous thrill passed through her, shimmering in her blood. She realized then that Quill wasn't ready to pounce, his nostrils flared with jealousy. He couldn't feel her anymore. She couldn't feel him. His magic was gone.

She wanted to howl with the loss of it, the emptiness it left inside her.

Fox smiled and glided forward. "She's no longer the strongest faery in the Three Valleys," he said to Quill's slumped form. "I am. I want the human with the faerie blood. I challenge you, strongest of our kind to strongest of yours. Winner gets the girl."

"No," Sagely gasped. "He won't win."

The stricken looks on the faces of the witches told her she was right.

"I will fight in his stead," she said, stepping forward and clearing her throat. "Right now, he's not the strongest in the coven. It's my magic you want, anyway. So challenge me."

Quill's head snapped up. "No," he roared, his green eyes sparking.

"I challenge you," Fox said to Sagely, a greedy smile on his red lips.

"Challenge accepted."

Fox sprang at her, flying through the air over Quill's head. He landed in front of Sagely in a crouch, and their eyes locked. Crap. He was sexy as hell. Before she could go completely under his spell, she leapt into the air and planted a front kick directly on Fox's gorgeous face. He leapt to his feet, stumbling backwards with blood gushing from his nose. Magic coursed through her, pulsing dark and light, dark and light.

Before Fox could recover, she delivered a quick series

of blows. One to his face, then a high block when he tried to hit back, and while his arm was up, she sank her fist into his gut. He doubled over, and she grabbed the back of his neck and hurled him to the ground using his own momentum. She crouched in ready stance, waiting for him to stand.

He pushed up on his hands and spun like a top, knocking her to the ground. They tangled together, and while she was still disconcerted, he pounced on her, pinning her down. His face sank to her shoulder, and she felt a strange pull as her body melded with his.

Suddenly, she was jerked up towards him, electrified. Waves of ecstasy rolled through her, and she curled her hands into his soft curls, scratching her nails against his scalp. She wanted more of him, to absorb him and devour him. The thought startled her, and she realized he'd bitten her just where her neck and shoulder joined. It was going to be over in seconds, when the venom hit, and she'd barely landed a blow.

She caught a glimpse of the coven, holding Quill back by both arms as he sagged against them, struggling forward even as his strength failed. He was dying, and now she was going to die, too.

"Add Quill to your collective." The voice came from inside her head, booming and commanding. It wasn't Quill's voice, but something bigger, like the voice of the coven itself.

Her head snapped up, but Fox gripped her hair and pulled it back down. She gasped and writhed beneath him, tortured into helpless submission by this faery gnawing at the hollow of her throat. She couldn't seem to move. She thought she might be about to die of pleasure, if that was possible, though she could clearly feel the pain of his tiny teeth ripping apart her flesh. It didn't compare to the waves of pleasure racing across her skin, through her veins, in her flesh and bones and blood.

His fingers were tight in her hair, and his breath was coming fast. With his free hand, he shifted her leg so he was between her thighs, his hard body tight against her soft one. As his tongue caressed her torn flesh, he pressed himself harder against her. She shuddered against him, losing herself completely for a moment. The pleasure of being devoured by a faery overcame her. Blackness swallowed her vision, stars exploding across the midnight canvas.

"When you add a warlock to your collective, you can share magic," the voice inside her head urged, jerking her back into a dazed awareness. "Add him and open the channel to get your magic back."

"But how? I'm not old enough to have a collective."

"That's a coven rule, not a law of magic. *DO IT.*"

"How?"

"Invite him. Joining a collective forms a bond that lets you hear each other's thoughts. Hurry, before it's too late."

She felt silly even thinking it inside her head, but she didn't know if she could do it out loud. "I'm inviting you to join my collective, Quill," she said inside her head.

This time, Quill's voice growled, "Accepted."

A burst of his beautiful magic exploded inside her like a firework, and the symbols on her ring lit up with blue light. She threw off the artificial pleasure charging through her veins and hurled Fox into the air, leaping to her feet. Every second counted, and she had to do whatever damage she could while she was able. She leapt at Fox, now on his feet, too. Suddenly, she felt like a ninja, jumping five feet into the air and delivering a spinning side kick to Fox's head, then flipping over, still in the air, to swipe his legs out from under him.

What the...? She'd never been able to do *that* before.

She landed on Fox, her thighs tightening, her knees crushing his hips.

"Don't meet his eyes," Willow screamed.

Sagely grabbed his head in both hands, covering his eyes. Now would be a great time for some exploding heads. The magic vibrated inside her, threatening to blast him straight to hell. His lips were shiny with blood, her blood, like he was wearing lipstick on his perfect, round little mouth.

"I'm not your girl," she said. "I'm not anyone's girl except my own. I can make my own choices, and if I choose to kill you right now, I will."

"I surrender," he said quickly, his hands gripping her forearms. But he didn't pull them away, maybe feeling the magic building there and knowing if he tried, she'd squash him like a bug. His fingers stroked her arms, and shivers raced through her, making her arch her back like a cat being petted. She couldn't seem to shake the faerie allure. She wanted to kill him and kiss him at the same time.

"Don't touch me," she barked, lifting his head and slamming it onto the dirt.

"You might be a witch now, but you can't deny the faerie inside you," he said. "That's why my venom strengthened instead of weakened you. We're of one blood—fae blood. Killing one of our own is like cannibalism. Let me go, Sagely."

"Why should I? You wouldn't have let me go."

"Did you not hear me? I'd never kill a faery. I was giving you strength, not trying to kill you."

That gave her pause. Because in all that time he'd been pinning her down, he certainly could have ripped out her jugular, or broken her neck, or any manner of things to kill her. And when he let her up, she'd been freakishly strong, like a superhero in a comic book. No normal human could jump that high and fight like that no matter how much Tae Kwon Do training they had.

"You have a funny way of showing affection," she said at last.

"You even have a faerie name," he said. "We all have the names of plants. Don't you want to know how your mother knew that?"

"Shut up," she growled. "Don't you dare mention my parents. You know nothing about them."

"But I do," he said softly, raising his hands to her arms again.

This time, the shiver that went through her was more like a chill. "Did you kill them?" she asked, her throat dry.

"I'd never hurt a faery," he said. "It's impossible for a full-blooded fae to kill one of our own kind. I wanted to take you home to our troupe, not kill you."

"Oh, and that's so much better? Kidnap me and hypnotize me into being your sex slave? How merciful you are." Her fingers tightened, and a pulse of magic traveled down her arms. She stopped it at the last second, before it left her hands. But he must have felt it, because he winced, then rushed to speak, his breath coming short.

"There are things I can tell you," he said. "Don't kill me. I'll agree to let you stay in the coven if that's your will.

No more attacks."

"No violence, and stop hypnotizing me with your eyes, and I'll let you live long enough to make a deal with the coven."

"Agreed," he gasped, his face contorting with pain.

She released his head slowly, and he blinked up at her with bewildered eyes. Eyes that pulled her in like a whirlpool of desire.

"Stop it," she warned, clamping her hands over his eyes again.

"I can't," he said, throwing up his hands. "I can't stop it any more than you can."

She lifted her hands again, pressing them into his shoulders to hold him down. "What the hell does that mean?"

"You don't think I feel the same thing you do when our eyes meet?" he whispered, his silky brown eyes full of vulnerability.

Crap. A faeries had that attraction to each other. Willow and Quill had both told her that. But was she really like that to Fox? How did faeries survive the relentless lust without it killing them?

Someone cleared her throat behind Sagely, and she tore her eyes away, confused. For a minute, she'd forgotten anyone else was there. It had been just the two of them.

"Why don't you dismount the faery now, and we can work on that truce," Majori Yordine said dryly.

Sagely's cheeks burned as she leapt clear of Fox. He staggered to his feet and brushed off his tan pants and green shirt.

"Wait," she said, narrowing her eyes at him. "If all

faeries are named after plants, how are you named after an animal?"

He bowed slightly and held out a hand. "Fox Glove," he said, taking her hand and kissing it, every inch the chivalric gentleman. "Pleasure to make your official acquaintance. You've proven yourself a formidable foe. Let's talk politics."

Sagely had no interest in talking politics.

She turned to see Quill lying on the ground, Raina with her hands on his chest, her attention laser-focused as she chanted under her breath. Willow was bending over his bite, her mouth suctioning out the venom. Sagely pulled her eyes away, still a little squeamish about that part. She ran to Quill's side and dropped to her knees, lifting his head into her lap.

"Is he going to be okay?"

"He'll live," Shaneesha said, standing behind Raina with her hands on her shoulders. "But his magic is all jacked up."

Sagely brushed back a strand of blond hair that had come loose from his little knot. She felt what Shaneesha meant. His magic was roiling and dark. Had she done that?

"The venom is gone," Willow said, sitting back on her heels and wiping her mouth.

"I've healed his physical wounds," Raina said, standing.

"He needs to rest now," Majori Ory said. "Get him inside."

Eli, Ingrid, and some of the other young witches lifted him and carried his unconscious body inside. Sagely started to follow, wanting to be with him, needing to. It was a physical need now, some kind of bond beyond their magic. Panic crept through her when Majori Romero stepped into her path and held up a hand. "You need to stay here," he said, his voice a quiet rumble.

"But he needs me," she said, her own voice bordering on hysteria.

For once, she saw kindness in his eyes. "Being apart from someone in your collective when they are hurting is one of the hardest things you'll ever have to do," he said. "But what he needs most right now is for us to establish peace with the faeries and end these attacks. If we don't, this could happen again next week, next month. Tomorrow."

She felt Quill's body receding, as if her heart was a spool of thread and he was unwinding it as he went. Squaring her shoulders, she swallowed the anguish. Romero was right. She needed to be strong for Quill when he couldn't be. Showing the faeries that she was undaunted, that she was not ruled by emotion, was what Quill needed right now.

So that was what she'd do, even if it crushed her to do it, even if it meant letting Raina go inside to nurse Quill back to health in Sagely's stead. This was no time for jealousy.

TWENTY-NINE

Sagely turned back to the clearing. The Majoris carried out a few picnic tables from their spot beside the house while the faeries lingered near the forest's edge, watching with distrust. Most of the witches didn't look any more eager to make this truce than the fae.

Sagely spotted Willow and Eli emerging from the house. She ran up onto the steps and grabbed Willow's arm. "How is he? Is he awake?"

Willow shook her head. "He almost didn't make it. But he'll be okay once he recovers. I got all the venom in time."

Without thinking, Sagely threw her arms around her future sister-in-law and squeezed her hard. "Thank you," she whispered.

When she pulled away, Willow's eyes were shiny with unshed tears. "Thank you," she said back. "You saved him."

"No, that was all you," Sagely said. "But could I? Since I'm part faerie? And apparently immune to the venom, I might add."

"I'll teach you how I do it," Willow said. "I bet you can."

"Thank you." Sagely squeezed her hand.

Willow dropped her eyes, her cheeks pinkening. "Thank you for not treating me like a freak, like everyone else does."

"Was that you, who spoke into my mind?" Sagely asked. "Once I got the venom, I heard someone talking to me. Was that through some faerie bond we have now that I got venom in me?"

"No," said a scratchy voice behind them. "That was me." Sagely jumped, not having realized anyone was listening. When she turned, the Wise One was sitting on the porch swing, making it swing forward and back slightly with a gnarled, polished cane she held gripped in one hand.

She winked at Sagely and smiled, her cloudy eyes sinking into her wrinkles. "As the coven's oldest member, I have access into anyone bonded to the coven. Including you, my dear. I seldom invade your thoughts to read them or speak to you, but I can, when needs be. You did well, little sister."

"Thank you," Sagely said, her own face flaming when she realized she could also feel how much Sagely had enjoyed getting sucked on by the enemy.

"Go now, child, and make the coven proud." The Wise One nodded to the yard, where fae and witches had taken seats along opposite sides of the picnic tables. The tables were arranged end to end, like a long conference table, but with a lot more mosquitoes.

"Come on," Sagely said, taking Willow's hand.

Willow hesitated and shuffled her feet. "I'm still in level two," she said. "I don't have anything to add. I'm not even a real witch."

"Stop that," Sagely said. "You're as important as any other member of the coven, and besides, you're half faerie, which makes you the link between the two peoples."

Willow's eyes stayed glued to her feet. "Then how come they came for you and not me?"

"I don't know," Sagely admitted. "But we're going to find out. And you're going to be with me." She linked her arm through Willow's and marched over to the tables where the witches made room for them on a bench.

"Now that we're all here, let's get started," Fox said, smiling at her.

"We're not all here," Majori Yordine said. "This is a training facility. Only students and young witches are here, as I'm sure you know, which is why you chose to attack now instead of when the entire coven was in attendance at a Gathering."

Since living there, Sagely had attended each weekly Gathering of the Coven, which was a sacred time for bonding and trading...and some gossiping.

"Your warlock has killed our queen, so we're not all here, either," Fox snapped back.

"Let's not fight," Majori Ory said. "We are intrigued by your offer of a truce. We have to share this valley, and as you know, we prefer to do it peacefully. Your kind is more prone to violence and conflict, so in the past, we have remained separate, like the werewolves in the Second Valley."

"Werewolves?" Sagely whispered.

Willow nodded. "The Three Valleys are safe for magical beings like us. We're in the First Valley with a lot of other supernatural beings. Werewolves live in the Second, because they are territorial and don't like to share. Shapeshifters of all persuasions live in the Third Valley."

Sagely thought of the playful trees conveying them through the valley. Too bad it was not just them instead of vicious, seductive faeries.

"Once, our people were united," Fox said. "We had understanding of our differences and respected each other's cultures. That's why your people gave us their void magic to protect. Fae are loyal and honorable, and they trusted us above all other beings."

"That's true," Majori Yordine said, narrowing her eyes. "But why are you offering a truce now, after centuries of conflict?"

"Because it benefits us as well as you," Fox said. "We would be united against a common enemy."

"A common enemy?" Sagely blurted out. "The only reason you're offering a truce is because I was going to kill you, and you needed to offer something we'd want."

"True," Fox said, flashing a disarming smile. "Since you're new here, I'll explain. Faeries don't have such a democratic society as witches. I've long wanted a truce and thought it best for our people, but Amaranth didn't agree, so I could say nothing. As the new fae king, I'm now in a position to offer such things."

"You're the king? Just like that?"

"Yes," he said. "I was second in line. When she died, I instantly became king."

"And what's in it for us?" Sagely asked.

"Protection," he said without missing a beat. "We'll

be twice as strong with our two races joined together against Viziri. When he's ready, he'll come for your magic and strip your entire coven."

A collective intake of breath met this statement.

"The world's most powerful warlock is coming here?"

"The warlock who attacked you," Fox corrected.

Sagely shivered, her fingers clutching the edge of the table involuntarily. Glancing around the table at the fae and the witches, she saw sober, knowing faces. No one looks shocked. "You knew?" she whispered. "I thought you said it was a faerie."

"We weren't sure, but we suspected," Yordine said quietly.

"We are sure," Fox said. "He has attacked and killed a dozen of our people in the last quarter century. Only those with void magic."

"But why?"

"When a witch dies, her magic is released into the universal energy field of magic," Yordine said. "But if she's murdered, her murderer has a chance, the moment the magic is released, to steal it."

"Our people don't do that," Shaneesha said.

"No, but a power-hungry warlock who has practiced the dark arts will," Yordine said. "We've known Viziri is the strongest in the world for some time. We just weren't sure how he was gaining such power."

"And now you know," Fox said. "All you had to do was ask. We have the void magic, and he has found those of our people with it, murdered them, and stolen the bound magic."

"Can't you fight him with it?" Sagely asked.

"Faeries don't use the kind of magic witches do," he said. "Though we do have our own powers, as you witnessed." He gave her a smile that made her pulse race and her skin crawl simultaneously.

"So it was Viziri who attacked me," she said.

"Yes," Fox said. "And it's likely the reason he killed your parents."

Sagely choked, gasping for breath as if he'd punched her in the gut. "What?"

"I told you I knew about your parents." The heartless bastard was gloating.

"How do you know?" she demanded, strengthened by her anger.

"We've been keeping tabs on him for the last twenty years," he said. "He probably came across your parents by chance, sensed their void magic, and thought they were a childless couple. He didn't know that the magic would be transferred to you upon your mother's death, as bound magic always is."

Sagely tried to steady herself. Fox's gloating smile had turned to one of sympathy, and he reached across the table. In his outstretched palm was an iridescent stone that looked almost like a pearlized piece of sea glass.

"It's a seeing stone," he said softly.

The fae let out gasps of shock. The fuchsia faery they'd fought during their first confrontation covered his lips with his fingers, his eyes bugging.

"Thank you," Sagely said, bowing her head, aware that he was giving her something precious, though she didn't know exactly what it was.

"Take it," Fox murmured. "It holds their last moments. I could have transferred the memory to you

201

now by touch, but I thought you'd rather watch it in privacy. Put it behind a mirror, and it will show you what you wish to see."

Touched by his thoughtfulness, she reached out and took the stone. It was smooth and almost greasy between her fingers, artificially cool in the summer heat.

"Thank you." She swallowed and tucked it away for later, forcing her mind back to the present, back to the man who had killed her parents and tried to kill her. Now she had answers. She knew who had attacked her and why. And she knew her parents fall had been no accident.

"How did he know about my magic?" she asked. "Even I didn't know I had it. It was bound up until Quill released it."

"Like magic calls to like magic," Yordine said. "If he's been taking it from the murdered fae all these years, he has quite a bit. And the more void magic he hoards, the easier he'll be able to find others who possess it."

"We can help protect you," Fox said. "And our own kind, as well. We would rather return your magic than have a faery murdered for it."

"Return it?" Sagely asked. "How?"

"That's what we don't know," Fox said, turning to Yordine. "None of our people have been around long enough to remember the transfer."

"Nor ours," Yordine said. "There was a book that told of its uses, but it disappeared twenty years ago."

"Right around the time Viziri showed up," Sagely mused.

THIRTY

They all sat there staring dumbly at each other. The obvious answer was that they could get the magic back the way Viziri did—by killing the faeries who possessed it. But that wasn't going to fly with the peace-loving witches *or* the fearsome fae.

"Do you know which faeries in your troupe possess the parcels of bound void magic?" Sagely asked at last, surveying the row of faeries.

"No," Fox said. "That's why we wanted you. Your magic may call to theirs, and we can identify who is in mortal danger from Viziri."

Sagely threw up her hands in frustration. "And you couldn't just come ask? You had to try to kidnap and murder me and Quill, and get your queen killed?"

"It was her idea," he said, rising halfway from the table, his fists clenched.

"Down, boy," she said.

"Faeries are quick-tempered," Ory murmured. "Don't provoke him."

"Sorry," she muttered to Fox, shooting him a dark look. He looked like he might leap across the table and rip into her throat with those sharp little teeth of his.

A shiver of delight passed through her traitorous body at the thought. What was wrong with her? No wonder witches looked down on faeries. She had nothing but scorn for this weakness, and it was part of her!

"The ambush on the road was not my best idea," Fox admitted, returning her glower. "I realize now that probably scared you. I was alerted by your use of strange magic in town. The same magic I am cursed with. And I knew you must be part fae to possess it. So you may understand why I was overly eager to find out what you knew."

"By attacking us? Because *that's* obviously the best way to get someone to talk."

"It may have been impulsive," Fox said. "But I never tried to kill you or your leader. Amaranth injected venom into him. The day I led the attack, I instructed them not to give venom, and no one did. No one died, either."

"No, they were just mangled when you chewed on them like an animal." Sagely touched her neck where Fox had bitten her, but there was no pain and no wound, just an indentation in the shape of his teeth.

Fox smiled. "We use the weapons we're given. No one asks you to fight without using your fists."

"Okay, truce," Sagely said, holding up her hands. "I'm sorry. You're not like an animal."

Fox wiggled his dark brows at her. "I'm only an animal in one place."

Yordine cleared her throat. "Working together, with all the magic of the coven and the strength of the fae…"

"Our magic cannot defeat void magic," the Wise One's quavering voice said from her perch on the swing. They all turned to her as one. "Fire and water both defeat and balance each other," she said. "As do earth and air. That's why we have a few of each element in our coven, though it is an earth coven."

Sagely glanced around, counting the elementals. The Majoris were all earth mages, as well as most of the coven. Besides Raina and Willow and Shaneesha, she thought everyone was a dirt-worshipper.

"The only way to fight the void is with the void," the Wise One said. "Void magic can destroy, but it can also create something out of the void, out of nothing. Right now, only one member of our coven possesses the ability to fight Viziri."

Sagely froze as all eyes landed on her. Her blood ran cold as she remembered that man-shaped nothingness looming over her, filling her with dread and terror beyond measure. The flash of his knife, the bewildered helplessness as he flipped her over so she could see him while he slit her throat. She was jolted by the thought of what she'd gone through as a child, after she lost her parents. Because of him. Had he killed her parents in the same sadistic way he'd almost killed her?

Rage electrified her like a lightning bolt.

She was yanked out of the grip of fury by a thrumming of magic inside her, pulling her towards the house with irresistible force.

"Then I'll have to find out which faeries have the void magic," she said, standing. "Because I'm going to need help taking down the bastard. But right now, there's someone who needs me. So I'll leave you to do your blood sacrifices or whatever ceremonies unite us with the faeries. I have to go."

"You agree to an alliance?" Fox asked, his eyes appreciating her body a little too much as she turned back to answer.

"Yes," she said. "If it gives us the best chance of defeating that sick freak, I'm all in."

"Good," he said. "We'll fill you in after you answer the call of your loins."

She turned and stomped up the steps, her face raging with heat. How dare he make fun of what she and Quill had? It was much more than sexual—unlike whatever magical pull he had on her.

As she descended the stairs into the cavern, the magic and coolness of the place calmed her, bringing her down to an even, peaceful state. That was the power of earth magic. By the time she reached Quill's room, she was almost running. But when she stepped into the tunnel with the bedrooms off it, Raina was waiting for her.

"He's asking for you," she said, avoiding Sagely's eyes.

Sagely forced herself past the resentment. "Thank you for taking care of him."

"Of course," Raina said, finally meeting her gaze. "He's a great guy, Sagely. Not just powerful, but good. I don't mean his magic. I mean him. He's good through and through. Take care of him."

"I will."

"You're lucky to have him in your collective," Raina said. "I knew it was inevitable, but I can't say it doesn't hurt. Be good to him, okay? He's vulnerable right now."

"I wouldn't hurt him."

Sagely watched the other girl working to swallow. "He's lucky to have you, too," Raina said. "What you did today... I respect your claim to him, not just because it's the way of our people, but because you're a good match. I can see that."

"Thank you," Sagely said, glancing past her at the constellation on his door. This conversation could wait.

Raina sensed her impatience and stepped back, a sad smile on her face. "Go on," she said. "He doesn't need me anymore. He's all yours."

Sagely stepped into the room to find Quill propped up on his pillows next to his familiar, looking sheepish and groggy. "Come here, Little Red," he said, motioning lazily with one hand. She sat carefully on the edge of the bed.

"Are you okay?" she asked. "Your magic, it's all...wrong."

"Dark," he said. "I had to kill someone, Sagely. That's the darkest act there is. The laws of magic don't differentiate between a person with good deeds and one with evil. All life is equally sacred to the universe."

"Your magic turned dark because you killed a faery while protecting your coven? That doesn't seem fair."

"Protecting someone I love," he said, catching her hand.

Sagely swallowed hard. "How can we fix it, change it back to good?"

"There is one way," he said, giving her that charming smile. His green eyes crinkled at the corners, and the dimple sank into his stubbly cheek.

"Nice try," she said.

"A burst of creative energy," he said. "What could be more fitting to balance taking life than making life?"

"Whoa there, buddy," she said, pulling her hand away. "That is waaaay too fast. I'm not having kids for years."

"I'm joking," he said, snagging her hand and pulling her closer. His rock-hard pectorals flexed under her palms when she leaned over him, and suddenly, her heart was hammering. "Unless you're ready…"

"I'm not. I'm barely an adult myself."

"Not for kids," he said. "Though I think you'll be a great mom one day. But we could mimic the process…you know. Practice."

"You're shameless, you know that?"

He wrapped an arm around her back and pulled her even closer. She stretched out on top of him and kissed his gorgeous lips.

"We're connected by more than magic now," he said, suddenly serious. "Did you mean that? About your collective? Because you did it under duress. You can release me, if you want."

"You said you can break it off whenever you're not happy, anyway, right?"

"Yes, but that doesn't mean we don't take it seriously," he said. "It's a sacred covenant between two people. There's a bond of magic, too, not just words. It can flow freely between us now. It will flow into whichever one needs it."

"I feel it," she whispered. "Flowing between us."

"We don't take commitment lightly, Sagely. If you release someone from your collective, you sever not just the ability to exchange magic freely but the ties of your love together."

"Do we?" she asked, suddenly nervous as she searched his serious eyes. "Love each other, I mean? Maybe I did it too soon, and it'll mess up what we have."

"You didn't," he said, linking his fingers through hers. He kissed the back of her hand, his eyes still on hers. "I love you, Sagely. I want to be your husband. If you meant it when you took me into your collective, I'm honored. I meant it when I accepted."

"I meant it."

He kissed her gently but passionately, and she could feel his magic pulsing into her, against her. Their bond was different now, stronger and filled with need as well as want. She reached back and pulled the tie from his hair, burying her fingers in his thick blonde mane.

"Good," he said, rolling them over so they were lying on their sides, faces inches apart. He circled her waist with his hands and pulled her tight against him, his mouth finding hers and hungrily claiming it.

"Wait," she said, pulling away before she completely lost her head. "So this is like our wedding night?"

"Don't look so panicked," he said, the corner of his mouth pulling up in a smile. "I'll be a gentleman."

"But I want a wedding," she said, sitting up and swinging her legs off the bed. "I mean, I know I don't have parents to walk me down the aisle, or family to come, but...I just always thought I'd have at least a small wedding."

"It's not really our wedding night," he said, sitting up and rubbing her back. "Think of it as our engagement night. If you want a wedding, we'll have a wedding. Whatever size you want. I want you to be happy, Sagely."

209

"So I proposed? This must be the least romantic proposal of all time. Propose or your fiancé dies?"

"I told you, we can call it off," he said. "I'm not going to make you marry me. Whatever you want, whatever makes you happy, that's what I want. For the rest of my life, all I want to do is make you happy, and protect you, and be the man you want me to be." He took her hand and gazed into her eyes. "I love you, Sagely. Be my wife."

"That sounded like a proposal," she whispered.

"That didn't sound like a yes."

"Yes." Somehow, she was laughing and crying at the same time. He leaned in and kissed her, an intense, lingering kiss. "But this," she said, putting a hand on his chest and pushing him back gently. "This will have to wait until the wedding night. Not the engagement night."

"Of course," he said. "If that's what you want. But you have to give me something I want tonight."

"What's that?" she asked, leaning away from him and searching his face.

"You have to stay here and let me kiss you all night long." His blond hair fell in loose curls around his chin, almost to his shoulders, but it was his smoldering bedroom eyes that did her in.

She swallowed hard and nodded. "All night's a long time," she said with a nervous laugh. "I might fall asleep."

"I think I can find ways to keep you awake," he said. "But if you get too tired, spooning is an acceptable compromise."

"Okay," she said, laughing as she kicked off her boots. She slid her bare legs between his sheets, pleased at the way his eyes followed her every move.

THIRTY-ONE

The next morning, Sagely took some time alone to shower and sit in front of her mirror, combing her wet hair straight. She had to talk herself into slipping the stone behind the mirror. She wasn't sure she actually wanted to see her parents being murdered by a dark warlock.

At the same time, it felt like cheating not to watch. After all the years of wondering, of thinking it was impossible that they'd both slip off the same ledge and fall to their deaths together. After all the years of thinking it couldn't be true. Now she knew. It wasn't true. It wasn't an accident. They'd been murdered.

Maybe, when she watched it, she'd get some clue as to how it happened.

But when she scooted back and looked into the mirror, nothing happened. She spoke to the mirror, feeling silly, calling upon it to show her what was stored in the stone, what she wanted to see.

Maybe it was all a trick, Fox's way of getting her to sympathize with him and think he was giving her a gift. It could be nothing but an odd pebble. When she retrieved it from where she'd set it beside the mirror, she knew that wasn't true, though. She could feel the magic in it, not like hers, but something supernatural.

With a sigh, she left her room. She didn't know how Quill would react to the news that Fox had given her something special on the night she was engaged to *him*. But she didn't want to keep secrets, and she needed to unlock the memories in the stone. She slipped into his room, only to find him sitting on the edge of the bed with Raina.

A growl built inside her, and her magic pulsed red with anger and jealousy. Quill's eyes flashed up and meet hers. His magic was still all wrong—not as dark as the previous night, but not the usual warm energy radiating from him. He smiled and dropped his hand from Raina's back, which he'd been rubbing in a comforting way. Her eyes were red, but she wouldn't look at Sagely.

Sagely pushed away her jealousies for now. She could ask him about it later, or he could tell her himself. There were more important questions than whether her fiancé could innocently rub his ex-girlfriend's back.

"Fox gave me a seeing stone," she said, holding out her palm for them to see. "But I can't get it to work. Do you know how to activate it?"

"He did what?" Quill leapt to his feet, sending out a shock-wave of anger and pain that made her step back. He grabbed his head in both hands and turned away, breathing hard.

"Let me see," Raina said, slinking from the bed and

approaching. She bent Sagely's fingers back and peered at the stone lying on her palm.

Sagely cut her eyes at Quill, silently asking if he was okay, but Raina still wouldn't look her in the face. She pinched the stone between the tips of all her fingers and picked it up.

"Are you okay?" Sagely asked Quill. "He said it can show me what happened to my parents. That's the only reason I took it."

"I'm fine," he said, dropping his hands and slumping onto the bed. "It's fine. I wasn't there to protect you, and he was."

"Um, if by protect me, you mean try to gnaw a hole in my throat, then yeah. Otherwise, no."

"Right." He raised his eyes to hers, and she could feel the wounded edge still under his words, although he sounded normal enough. She had already filled him in on everything else that had happened, on the meeting between the witches and fae. Though she didn't stick around for the treaty-signing, she'd told him everything else. Except for the stone.

She didn't know why she'd kept it secret. Maybe because she knew it carried some weight even when Fox gave it to her. She shouldn't have taken it, she could see now. Not if it hurt Quill.

"I can give it back," she said. "But I want to see what happened first."

"No," he said, holding up a hand. "This is part of being a warlock. Being one of several or many husbands to the woman we love. Supposedly, it makes us stronger. But that's a strength I haven't yet mastered."

She went to him and wrapped her arms around his

neck, pressing her lips to his. "You're the only one I want," she told him. "You're the man I love, and I want to make you happy as much as you want to make me happy. So stop worrying about a stone I took without knowing its meaning from a man I don't give a lick about."

"Then stop worrying about someone I was with before I met you," he countered. "Yes, I had a relationship with Raina, but we're *only* friends now. There is absolutely nothing between us. Absolutely nothing I would ever do to jeopardize what I have with you, Sagely."

"He's right," Raina said from behind her. "I meant what I said last night, when I told you he's *all* yours. I can see this is what you both want. I won't stand in the way of that. Besides, I was just talking about leaving."

"Leaving the coven?" Sagely asked. From the redness of Raina's eyes, she could tell the other witch was conflicted.

Raina shrugged and crossed her arms, hugging herself. "I never meant to make this my permanent home. But I had a reason to stay...until recently."

"Because of Quill," Sagely said, bristling again.

"You have nothing to worry about," Quill said, smiling and pulling Sagely in again. "I knew from the moment I laid eyes on you that I had to save you, even if I was killed trying. I knew you were someone who mattered. Someone who was going to change my life. I just didn't know how much." His hands slid around her back, and he pressed her body to his, his lips finding hers.

The magic between them was different now, darker and more animal, but also stronger. She couldn't tell which was their promise to join in a collective, and which was the fact that they'd both killed someone now. They were both "impure" witches.

Raina cleared her throat, and Sagely dropped from her tiptoes and pulled away quickly, her face flaming. She'd forgotten Raina was there. Even if she still didn't completely trust Raina, she respected her. And she didn't want to rub this in her face when Raina was obviously hurt that Quill had chosen Sagely over her. But she just had.

Raina frowned down at the cloudy white stone, still pinched between her fingertips. "You have to put it into your mirror somehow. Like into the frame, or bind it on somehow. Then you look into the mirror and open yourself. Give your faerie powers permission to show you."

She dropped the stone into Sagely's hand. Though she'd been holding it for a few minutes, it was still cool to the touch, the iridescent shine churning slowly inside it. The muscle in Quill's jaw clenched, and he looked away.

"Thanks," Sagely said.

"You know that's very powerful," Raina said as she turned away. "You can basically spy on anyone, anytime, unless they're blocking you somehow."

"Which means Fox gave up his ability to spy on you," Quill said bitterly.

"I guess that explains how he found us at just the right moment both times." Sagely was relieved to know he couldn't see her now, although he *could* have another one. From the reaction when he'd given it to her, though, she doubted that was the case.

Though Quill offered to watch with her in case the scene upset her too much, she turned him down. She needed to do this alone. He looked a little hurt but stayed back, assuring her he'd be right there if she needed him.

All she had to do was call to him through their bond.

The mirror atop her old dresser was an attached oval one with ornately carved vines around it, painted pale yellow like the dresser. She slipped behind it and pushed the stone into a carved loop, but it slipped through and fell to the surface of her dresser. After retrieving it, she wedged it into a tight curl at the top of the mirror.

When she sat in front of it again, she closed her eyes and set her hands on top of her dresser, palms up, as if meditating. She opened herself, letting in the flow of magic in the caverns and all around her. Then she strained to feel a different magic, the one that had grown stronger when Fox bit her and made her feel like a ninja. It was a frantic energy, though faint within her.

She made herself receptive to whatever the stone would show her, no matter how scary or upsetting it might be. When she opened her eyes, she was startled to find herself somewhere else. It was as if she was transported from the cavern to a mountainside. This was definitely not where her parents were killed. Snow was thick on the ground, and a biting wind whistled nearby. Her heart was hammering painfully, and something was coming. She recoiled in fear, only to drop back into her body. Her heart was racing.

Taking a deep breath, she tried again. Again, she was on the mountain. This time, she knew she was in someone else's memory, that it wasn't real, and she made herself stay. Someone was crouched beside her—someone safe, whom she loved. They were waiting together, sharing their fear like a last slice of bread. When a sleigh came into view, her heart pulsed so hard black spots appeared before her eyes.

"Wow," the boy beside her breathed. "Isn't she beautiful?"

She was. The woman looked like a queen riding in her sleigh pulled by two snow-white horses. As if she could sense them, her head swiveled their way. A crown of lilac braids circled her head, dusted with snow like powdered sugar. Though the day was dark and wind howled across the snow, when the woman smiled, the air around her seemed to brighten, as if a sunbeam was emanating from her.

But Sagely felt only sickening dread when the woman smiled, her teeth like needles.

"A faery," she breathed.

"She's calling me," the boy said, standing unsteadily.

"NO!" Sagely whisper-screamed, grabbing his coat sleeve. But it was too late. The faery had seen them, and her eyes fixed on his with the intensity of a laser. As if in a trance, her brother—because she knew that was what he was—stepped forward.

"I'm coming," he said.

"What are a pair of water witches doing on a mountain in the snow?" the woman asked, her voice teasing and chiding at the same time.

"We live here," her brother said.

"You must live near water or your magic will freeze as solid as this horrid stuff. I should know. I'm a sea faery myself. Only by special enchantment am I able to come here. But as luck would have it, I'm on my way back to the sea now. Come along, I'll take you with me."

Sagely felt the truth in the woman's words, even as terror immobilized her. Her magic had not been unlocked, so she did not yet know her element. But she despised the cold, hated the snow and the frozen ground under her feet. In all her life, she'd never seen the sea, but in some deep part of her bones, she knew that was where she belonged.

"She's right," her brother whispered, crouching next to her. "If I don't go, I'll die, Raina. I know I will. And you will, too. We don't belong here. I'll go with her and find ways to stall her. You go home and tell mother where I went. Then follow the tracks of the sleigh and join us."

Raina crouched behind the boulder, her fingers aching hatefully with cold. She wanted to leap out and drag her brother to safety. Their mother had warned of the Goblin King and the Snow Queen, who would take them away and steal their power. But although she knew better, she also wanted to dive into the sleigh with him, whip the horses into a frenzy, and fly down the mountain and away from this god-forsaken cold. She would never look back.

And so she watched, envy sinking into her very bones as her brother climbed into the sleigh. As soon as they disappeared into the snowy mountain pass, she leapt to her feet and ran after them, calling for them to wait. She'd come so close. She had to get out of there, too. They could send word back to their mother when they arrived at the sea. But already, the sleigh's tracks were nearly gone, as if the horse had been dragging nothing more than feathers. When they disappeared altogether, Raina fell to her knees, sobbing.

She knew in her bones they were never coming back for her.

Sagely jerked back into her body, hiccupping. Her cheeks were wet. It was so real that it took her a moment to remember why her face was warm when she wiped away the tears. She was not in the snowy mountains, a childhood version of Raina. But now she knew why Raina hated faeries so much. She had as much reason to be bitter over old losses as Sagely did.

Shaking off the memory, Sagely took a deep breath and put her hands on the surface of the dresser again, in front of the mirror. Later, she could dissect the reasons Raina had shared that memory with her. All she knew was that when Raina had taken the stone, she'd imparted that memory. A peace offering, perhaps, something she couldn't say out loud, but that she wanted Sagely to know. It was the closest to apology she could offer.

Pushing the memory aside, Sagely settled herself, wiped her hand on her shorts, and looked into the mirror again. This time, she didn't just open a channel to it. She didn't know who had put memories in this stone, but she was only interested in one of them. Raina said she could see anyone, at any time. So she concentrated as hard as she could on her parents' last moments.

The memory swam up at her, and her heart clutched so hard she almost lost it. But she relaxed, and it came back into focus.

Her parents were hiking on a trail that she recognized too well. The lookout trail at Devil's Den. She shivered, and the memory began to slip. Grasping it firmly, she sank into it fully, so fully she was no longer herself. Like the last time, she became someone else, someone who had witnessed her parents' death.

Fox, she assumed.

They walked up the trail towards him, over the stony trail and onto the ledge that jutted out over the valley below. It was fall out, and the valley was awash with reds, oranges, yellows, and rusts. Her dad had his arm around her mother.

Somewhere far away, tears wet the lashes of a girl in a cavern bedroom.

"I have to tell you something," her mother said as they settled onto the flat stone, a good five feet from the precipice. They didn't use picnic blankets, but her father untied a flannel shirt from around his waist and lay it down so her mother could sit. Her hair spilled in auburn waves over one shoulder, shining in the sun.

Sagely watched from the eyes of someone transfixed, in awe of her mother's beauty. Even though Fox knew he should get up and leave, that he was witnessing a private moment and he'd had his share of time alone on the point, he couldn't leave.

"Is everything all right?" her father asked, slipping an arm around her mother's back.

"I don't know," she said, laughing and sniffling at once. "I know we said one was enough, but…I'm pregnant."

Disappointment colored Fox's admiration, though he could clearly see her mother was already taken. Being married and having a child were two separate things. One bond could be broken, the other could not. He started to turn away, deciding he'd had enough. It would only hurt to see this beautiful stranger sharing her life with someone else.

Somewhere, Sagely's body was screaming no, clinging to the memory. Was this all she'd get to see?

But then she slipped back into it completely, because the person driving this memory wasn't leaving. Footsteps approached at a quick clip, almost like the steps of a shod horse, sending shivers of dread spiraling along Fox's spine.

The terror was suffocating. He jumped to his feet, on high alert. Something evil was approaching.

Sagely wanted to close her eyes, to scream, to tear herself out of this body that was not her own, but she was trapped, helpless to stop it, helpless to unsee what she was seeing.

A man came bursting up the trail, out of breath, a long black coat swirling behind him. He had the same cloak and hat, but he wasn't a black hole. He was very much a man, with an angular face that would have been handsome if not for the frenzy in his eyes. Ice turned her veins blue as he charged forward, gripped the woman who was her mother, and dragged her backwards on the stone.

Stunned, Fox let out a single cry before Viziri punched her mother in the face. Her head crunched against the rock with a solid, sickening thud. Fox leapt forward, but her father had already grabbed Viziri by the shoulder, spun him around, and punched him in the jaw. Viziri reeled backwards, then grabbed her father by the arm and slung him around. Off balance, her father's arms pinwheeled. He wrenched free, but he was too close to the edge.

NO!

Sagely couldn't do this. She couldn't watch, but she couldn't stop watching as he stumbled backwards, terror ripping across his face as his feet scrabbled against the rocky edge of the precipice. But gravity was a force he couldn't overcome, and he went down all at once. He was there one moment, and then gone.

Sagely ripped herself out of the scene, tears streaming down her face. She was breathing so hard she had to grab the edge of the dresser to keep from keeling over. Her stomach churned, and she had to fight not to vomit.

At last, she sat back, but the second she did, she saw the mirror, where the scene was playing on without her. The man in black was now hurling her mother over the point of the lookout, her head already bashed in and hanging at an impossible angle for a living person. Viziri was screaming and raging, running back and forth on the point, oblivious to the peril of the drop.

With an anguished, enraged roar, he fell to his knees, clutched his head in his hands, and sobbed.

She would find that devil and murder him with her bare hands if she had to. Just like he had murdered her beautiful, pregnant mother.

She felt a tug. Startled, she looked up and saw Fox in the mirror. "I'm sorry I didn't save them," he said, his face sober. Through the glass, she could study him without the unnatural attraction, which apparently did not convey secondhand. Even without the magical pull between them, he was still gorgeous, with round chocolate brown eyes, red lips, and wavy black hair.

"I knew what he wanted," he said. "He wanted the void magic. Unlike your parents, I knew I had it within me. It is a burden to our people, not a gift, since we cannot use it. I was burdened with possessing this magic and taught all my life to cloak myself with invisibility should someone come looking for it. So that's what I did, although I wanted very much to help your mother. If you hate me, I'm sorry, though I doubt I could have saved her. I did what I had to do to save myself. I was a coward once, but I will make it up to you, if you'll let me. I will protect you in a way I didn't protect your parents."

She wanted to blame him, but she couldn't. She knew

exactly how it felt to be a helpless against a stronger attacker. When she'd been put in the bad foster situation, she'd done everything she could to protect herself. Everything an eight-year-old could. But it wasn't always enough. And when Viziri had come for her, she hadn't been able to save herself despite all her martial arts training. So she knew all about being powerless against an insurmountable enemy.

"If you have questions," Fox said. "My troupe is gathering in three days. You may come then and speak with us about it, the truce, and which of my people have void magic. They will be anxious to return it to your kind." He gave a small smile and added, "I'll be looking forward to seeing you especially."

With a swirl of mist, he vanished, leaving Sagely staring at her own pale, stricken face.

THIRTY-TWO

The morning of the faerie visit dawned cool and smotheringly damp. Sagely could feel the air in the underground caverns clogging her lungs, the moisture sweating off the walls.

"Hey," Quill said sleepily from beside her, toying with her tangled red hair. "You look sexy in the morning."

"Hey, back," she said, smiling up at him. "You look sexy all the time."

He growled and buried his face in her neck, inhaling her scent. "You better stop that."

"Stop what?" she teased.

"Stop being so irresistible, damn it."

"Sorry," she said lightly. "I can't. I was born this way."

"Then we better get up," he said. "We've got a big day ahead, and if we stay here another minute, we're going to have to do something that takes all…day…long."

She laughed and sat up, pulling at the hem of her t-shirt. "You're right. We better go. I need to talk to your sister, anyway."

"Well played, Little Red," he said. "Mentioning my sister. Clever fox, you."

She laughed, but her mind strayed to Fox. Was he thinking about her visit, too?

She had already told Quill what happened with the mirror. He'd been pissed that she hadn't let him be there for moral support. But he got over it when she gave him the play-by-play, and let him comfort her for the rest of that day, and the night, of course. She had to admit, she'd been a mess, and it was a testament to his feelings for her that he could still love her after seeing her ugly cry for three hours straight.

But now she was ready for action. Ready to avenge her parents.

They met in the main cavern an hour later. Before she went off and opened herself to a bunch of faeries who, up until last week, had been intent on murdering her, she needed to test out the process with the one faery she trusted.

Willow was sitting outside at one of the picnic tables set up along the tree line, alone as usual. Quill hovered near the house, pretending to fix some of the other tables, though she knew he was there to make sure they were both okay. No one really knew how void magic worked.

"You'll be fine," she assured Willow, taking both her hands. "We're just doing a test run, okay?"

Willow nodded. "Thank you. For trusting me."

"Why do witches hate faeries so much, anyway? Besides being kind of vicious, they don't seem so bad."

Willow gave her a sad half-smile. "You mean aside from the fact that they tried to rip your head off?"

"Exactly."

"They're just natural enemies," Willow said. "Like werewolves and vampires. Some beings are just not meant to be friends."

"Well, your mother must have disagreed," Sagely said, squeezing her hands. "And she seems like a pretty smart lady."

Willow smiled gratefully. "Thanks."

"Are you ready?"

"Ready."

"Open the channel to your magic," Sagely said, remembering the Wise One's words. She opened herself, allowing her energy to sync with Willow's, opening the channel between them until she felt a slight tug. They were linked. She opened her eyes and smiled at Willow, who was grinning ear to ear. Sagely had never seen the girl so happy, and she knew she felt the connection, too. She was not just a half-faerie hybrid. She was a real witch.

Her magic swirled into Sagely's, and Sagely's back into her. Willow's magic was different than hers, so she could still feel what was hers and what was Willow's. She was surprised by how softly Willow's energy vibrated. But Willow was so quiet, it was exactly the pastel, gentle energy she should have expected. There was not a trace of darkness in her sweet heart, either.

Opening the channel between them was a beautiful, strange, vulnerable feeling. It was like touching someone in the dark, knowing who they truly were. She caught the surprise in Willow's eyes, even wariness, when the girl felt the twisted dark and light magic inside Sagely.

She reached, searching for the parcel of void magic that she'd be looking for in the fae. But as hard as she strained, she couldn't find it. Finally, she slumped back, completely drained of mental energy. It felt good to connect with someone, but the strain of searching her depths exhausted Sagely. The link between them blinked out like a TV being switched off.

"What happened?" Willow asked, looking both bewildered and slightly accusatory.

Sagely shook her head. "You don't have it."

"But I'm half fae."

"It's not in all faeries," Quill said, slipping onto the bench beside his sister. "Your father must not have had it."

"But you had it," she said, her eyes fixed on Sagely. "And you only have a trace of faerie blood."

"It's not about how much Sagely has," Quill said. "And it's not a competition."

"Easy for you to say." She tore her eyes from Sagely at last and glared at Quill. "You have the highest capacity for magic in the entire coven. Sagely comes in, she's brand new here, and she's already moved up a level. And she's got special magic. When do I get to be special?"

"You can heal people," Sagely pointed out. "I couldn't have saved Quill. But you did."

"Yeah, right," Willow said bitterly. "I can only heal witches when one of my own people bites them. Because my people are just that savage. I feel really freaking special." She jumped up and ran into the woods.

Sagely started to get up, but Quill caught her arm. "Let her cool off," he said. "She doesn't mean it."

"I'll go talk to her. Maybe she could use some

228

woman-to-woman straight talk."

"She's flighty, like her magic," he said. "She'll cool down and come back. She may be impetuous, but she can take care of herself."

"I wasn't saying she couldn't."

He smiled, his dimple sinking into his stubbly cheek. "I love how you want to take care of her. But trust me. I know my sister."

"You're right," she said, sinking onto the bench beside him. She leaned her head on his shoulder. "You're pretty good at taking care of her yourself."

"I don't know about that," he said. "She might look sweet, but she's a pain in the ass."

"I'm sure all siblings are." As soon as she said it, her throat tightened with the memory she'd seen in that mirror. She would have had a sibling if not for the warlock who murdered her parents. She wondered whether she'd have had a little brother or sister to look after.

"One day, you'll be taking care of our kids," he murmured, kissing the top of her head. She knew he was trying to be sweet, telling her she'd have her chance. But all she could think was...

What the hell! Kids!?

"You're going to have to wait a good long time for that, buddy," she said. "Like ten years."

"As long as we can practice for...nine?" He leaned back to give her a hopeful smile.

"So you're going to wait for a whole year?" she asked, giving him her most seductive smile in return.

"I'd wait ten," he said, his green eyes serious. "I'd wait forever. That's not why I love you."

"Why do you love me again?" she teased.

"You're not afraid of anything," he said, kissing her nose. "You're brave, and crazy, and all-around kick-ass."

"Eh, not your best," she said, giving him a quick kiss. "But it'll do for now."

Quill laughed and squeezed her shoulders. "You okay? I could see that wore you out. You sure you're ready to do that with the entire faerie troupe?"

"I'm sure." She straightened, her jaw set in determination. "Let's go."

THIRTY-THREE

"I don't know about this. You didn't get to try it on Willow," he said when they were in his truck. "You don't have any practice. What if they do something to you when you're vulnerable?"

"Wouldn't you do it, if you were in my place?"

He stared straight ahead as they drove towards the faerie community, along a dirt road through the woods. But he didn't lie about it.

"Does Willow have any fae siblings?" she asked after a stretch of silence. She picked up a book of magic the Wise One had given them and flipped idly through it.

"I don't know," he said. "Faeries raise their children more...communally. Our people are very attached to our children. Raising them is important to a couple, no matter how many husbands a witch might have, or if they are no longer together romantically. We still treat each other with dignity and respect once that bond is broken. Being able to leave a relationship that is no longer working makes that easier than for humans, who have all that guilt and shame and obligation tied up into their vows."

"You make it sound so nice to have your marriages like flings."

"It is nice," he said. "Every day, you choose to stay. If you love someone forever, you stay together forever. You don't worry it's out of some misplaced sense of duty. It's because you are truly loved every day of your life."

"I admit, it was hard to wrap my head around your marriage customs at first, but when you say it like that…"

He cocked an eyebrow at her. God, he was gorgeous.

"It sounds less like dating, and…well, damn romantic," she admitted.

"It is."

"So faeries don't take care of their kids?"

"No, they do," he said quickly. "I'm not saying that. For us, taking care of our children is a priority even once a marriage dissolves. But for faeries, the children are the responsibility of the troupe. They aren't neglected. But the stronger bond is between the husband and wife. I'm sure you can guess the reason." He glowered at the road ahead.

"What about your dad?" she asked. "I know you didn't want to talk about it at the picnic. If you're still not ready, I understand."

"No," he said, gripping the wheel with both hands. "If we're going to be together, I don't want to have any secrets."

A strange feeling crept over her. "Secrets? What does that mean?"

"My father was a very jealous warlock," he said, then swallowed hard. "Like me." He was quiet for a long moment as the truck slid on the gravel. Maude scampered along the dash and hopped into his lap as Quill righted the truck.

With another glance at Sagely, he continued. "He was my mother's first husband. And then she took another, Willow's father, and he just...couldn't handle it."

"He left?" she asked, praying that was all it was.

His knuckles were white on the wheel, and she could tell how hard this was for him. She scooted across the bench seat and put an arm around his stiff shoulders. He relaxed a little when she began to knead at his tense muscles. "No," he said quietly. "He didn't just leave."

"You can tell me," she said. "I won't think badly of you. You are not your father."

"I better not be," he grumbled, turning up a bumpy dirt track and gunning the engine. The tires spun, trying to gain purchase on the steep, nearly vertical slope. The truck rocked over the exposed stones in the road, slipping and sliding but slowly gaining the hill.

When they reached the top, he pulled up along the side of the road where several jeeps and four-wheel drives were parked. Quill turned to her.

"If this changes the way you feel about me, I understand," he said. "I'll step back and give you time to think it over, or...sever our bond." He swallowed and dropped his gaze.

Sagely wrapped her arms around his neck and forced him to look at her. "Nothing is going to change the way I feel about you," she said. "I love you, Quill Golden. So shut up and tell me."

He smiled sadly and untangled her hands, holding them both in his own. "Like most witches, my father distrusted faeries. He hated that he had to share a wife with one. One night in a jealous rage, he killed him."

"Oh."

"Oh?" He searched her eyes, and she could feel him exploring her emotions through their bond.

"That's definitely not cool," she admitted. "But it's not like you're a murderer just because your father is."

Quill swallowed hard and looked down. "But I am a murderer."

Crap. How could she forget?

She could see it was eating him up inside, what he'd done to the faerie queen. It was self-defense, though, and she didn't blame him one bit. If he hadn't killed her, she would have killed him, and probably kidnapped Sagely, too.

But Sagely had told him all this before, and he was still torn up about it. After the first week, the murder she committed hardly entered her mind at all. Maybe it was the trace of faerie in her.

"Look, I killed that dark warlock," she reminded him. "We do what we have to do to survive. That's not the same as what your dad did. Even so, it can't be the first time someone's gotten jealous. You have a polyamorous society. The way I figure, you've got to expect that kind of thing from time to time. And it's not just that your mother married another warlock. She married someone your dad hated."

"Maybe," Quill said, turning to stare out the windshield. "I know I need to get that part of myself under control. To be a better man for you. I swear to you right now, I'll never kill a member of your collective unless he's putting you or our kids in danger." He turned back and offered her a tentative smile.

"Okay," she said, laughing a little. "But right now, I can't imagine wanting to be with anyone but you. No offense, but you're quite enough."

"And you, my love, are more than enough." He slid his hand up the back of her neck and over her head, flipping her hair into her face.

"Hey," she protested, laughing and shaking it back as she stepped out of the truck.

They followed a footpath into the cool of the forest. The canopy of old-growth forest was thick, but sunlight dappled the ground at their feet. When they'd walked about five minutes along the twisting path, they came to a clearing where soft, lush grass grew, and sunlight streamed down through the break in the trees. Wildflowers dotted the tiny meadow, and butterflies flitted from one to another.

Suddenly, the serenity was broken when four fully-armed fae dropped from the sky. They seemed to hang suspended on the shafts of sunlight for a moment before landing, as softly as the butterflies on the butterfly weed. Except for the silver-tipped arrows strung and pointed at the witches' hearts.

"We come in peace," Quill said, throwing up his hands.

"Look out," Sagely screamed. "It's an ambush."

With a twang, an arrow left Fox's bow and flew straight at them.

THIRTY-FOUR

A shimmering bubble instantly materialized around the witches. The arrow lodged itself in the iridescent membrane, where it hung suspended, still vibrating. Fox grinned and lowered his bow. "I just wanted to see if an arrow would burst your pretty little bubble. Welcome. Let's go up, shall we?"

"What the hell!" Sagely screamed. "You could have killed us."

"I wasn't aiming at you," he said, his eyes raking over her body.

Quill dropped the shield and stepped forward ominously, towering over Fox's trim form. "Have your men disarm, or we won't be going anywhere with you."

"Fair enough." Fox's companions, two of whom were familiar from her first faerie encounter, lowered their weapons. Fox leapt nimbly back into a tree, and a second later, a rope ladder tumbled down. "For our cumbersome-bodied guests," he said with a grin, crouching on a tree branch as easily as a monkey.

When Sagely and Quill reached the top of the ladder, the faeries were all jumping ahead on the branches. She glanced nervously at Quill, who rested a reassuring hand on her lower back. "It's just like on the way to the swimming hole," he assured her in a low voice, leaning down to speak close to her ear. "The forest will take care of you. Don't be afraid."

She gave him a grateful smile, glad he knew her so well. He knew she wouldn't want to show any weakness. He gave her a little push, and she stepped forward onto the branch. She was part faerie. She needed to know their ways, too. So she embraced her faerie side, the part that was strengthened by Fox's bite. His venom was not poisonous to her. Feeling a bit invincible, she took three steps forward and jumped.

Instead of leaping for another branch, she jumped like she was sky-diving. For a split second, fear reamed her gut. She'd done it wrong. She was going to die.

Suddenly a branch slid under her, springing her back up like a trampoline. She was not as sure-footed as the fae, who leapt and scurried from one branch to the next, racing along their length and leaping impossibly far ahead, but she could move like a witch. She felt like a trapeze artist as she swung and leapt and fell, buoyed up by the leafy branches time and again. Quill swung along beside her, staying close. At last, still pumped from the adrenaline, they arrived at a wooden platform built into a huge, ancient oak.

The faeries were dancing across a bridge that hung suspended over a canyon about a hundred feet wide.

Below, a gentle stream glittered and gleamed in the sunlight as it twisted and turned along its path between lichen-covered boulders. Unfortunately, the bridge was made of what looked like tiny braids of dried grass, and the boulders may have looked nice, but that wouldn't stop anyone from falling to their deaths on them.

"Don't be scared," Fox called from ahead, turning to walk backwards on the swaying ropes. "It's perfectly safe." He gave them a toothy grin, and her damn, traitorous body quivered all the way through.

"Safe for a faery," Quill growled, taking a tentative step onto the bridge, Maude clinging to his shoulder.

"No," Sagely said, reaching out to grab his elbow. She pulled him back to the platform. "He's trying to test us. But we're guests here. They want to find out who has void magic? Let them come to us."

After a moment, Quill's full lips twisted into a smile. "I like the way you think." He pulled her in and gave her a slow, lingering kiss. Her toes curled in her boots. Wait a year? She didn't know if she could hold out another week.

"Are you coming?" Fox called from ahead.

She stood on tiptoes and kissed Quill another moment, harder and deeper. In case Fox had any doubts about whose side she was on here. Like she'd told Quill, blood didn't decide who they were. They decided. She may have a trace of faerie blood, but she was a witch.

Breaking the kiss, she turned to see the faeries on the other end of the bridge. "Either give us safe crossing or bring your magic to us," she said, her voice clear and strong. "If you want to get rid of it, that is."

When the faeries converged to talk, Quill leaned over and squeezed her hand. "Can I just say, you've never been hotter than right now?"

"You're looking pretty fine yourself," she said, giving him a once-over.

Fox hopped onto the platform, startling them out of the moment. "Come along, then," he said. "We'll carry you across."

"Never," Quill growled.

"You asked for safe passage, and we're providing it," Fox said as the blonde who attacked them on the road dropped down onto the platform and gave Sagely an excited smile.

"You're asking me to trust a faery with my life," Quill said.

"And you're asking us to carry you on our backs, and be vulnerable to your voodoo juju. Our word is good."

After searching Fox's face, Sagely nodded. With a bow, he turned and dropped to one knee. "Climb on and get ready for the ride of your life."

"I don't think so," Quill said, grabbing the back of Fox's neck. "You can carry me."

The blonde girl looked wholly delighted to be Sagely's steed. They climbed on the faeries' backs, who then turned and leapt. Sagely could feel every muscle in her steed's body tensing, like ropes of steel. For a second, two, three, they were airborne. Then the faery dropped onto the delicate braids of the bridge without so much as a wobble, and leapt again. In a few bounds, she made it to the other side.

Pushing aside a branch, Fox revealed a tiny house, camouflaged by wood and bark and leaves. The entire thing was shaped from a still-living tree, its branches bent at angles to make the house.

"We live in harmony with our surroundings," he said. "Come in. You can test my companions first."

Sagely sat down at a table made from a branch. She liked how light and airy the house was, the opposite of the coven's heavy earthen burrow. The blonde volunteered to go first, leering at Sagely as she sat opposite her. Fox took a seat against the wall while Quill hovered behind Sagely.

"If anything happens to her…" He cast an ominous glower in Fox's direction.

Sagely concentrated and opened the channel to her magic, reminding herself that faeries couldn't even use it, so there was no reason for them to steal it. Unlike Willow, the faery had no witch magic of her own to search through, so the connection was more one-sided. Sagely sifted around and felt a sharp tug, something dark and empty. Her eyes snapped open. "You have it."

"How do I give it to you?"

Quill was searching through the book the Wise One had given them. In it, she'd found a single page on void magic. Sagely listened as Quill read it aloud.

"Void magic can be fought with all other elements, and no other elements. Creation is the opposing force of destruction, and yet, void magic is neither creation nor destruction. It is nothingness."

"But how do I retrieve it?"

"Like all magic, void magic attracts its like. Therefore, it can only be transferred to a witch already in possession of it."

"Then how did the faeries get it?"

"Some kind of powerful sorcery," he said, frowning at the book. "And since they are not witches, maybe it didn't need like magic."

"Great. So I'm the only one who has it, which means I'm the only one who can accept it?"

"It seems like it," he muttered. "But that can't be true. We'll have to find out more. This book doesn't tell us anything." In frustration, he slammed it closed. "We need the *Book of Void Magic*."

"What's that?"

"It was a book on void magic, but it was locked up in a museum of sorts, in Paris, so no witch could access it and unlock it."

"It's a little late for that."

"A lot, actually," Quill said. "It disappeared from its magic-proof secure holding about twenty years ago. Coincidentally, about the same time Viziri appeared on the scene and started attacking faeries and stealing witch children."

More determined than ever, Sagely turned back to the faery and took her hands. She could feel the magic in her, that it wanted to be released. Opening the channel between them again, she started to pull at it. Quill murmured an incantation for transferring magic, and she repeated it.

Suddenly, she was thrown back in her chair. Though their hands slipped apart, the lines of energy between them stayed alive, pulsing for a moment. And then blackness knocked a hole in her middle.

THIRTY-FIVE

Gasping, Sagely struggled to sit upright, clutching her chest.

"Are you all right?" Quill asked, rushing to her and cradling her in his arms. "Did she hurt you?"

"No." When her breathing had slowed, she grinned. "I got it!"

"Oh, thank the spirits," the blonde said, hopping to her feet. "I swear my allegiance to the Winslow Witch Coven for the duration of your war with the dark warlock Viziri," she said, locking her hands behind her back and bowing deeply to Quill.

"I'm not declaring war for our coven," he said. "I'm no leader."

"You're the strongest in the coven, and therefore, in our eyes, you fill that role. Thank you for removing me from personal danger, Sagely." She bowed again, this time to Sagely.

Quill frowned as she ducked out into the trees, and another faery entered the tiny house. "I don't know if I like this," Quill muttered. "Viziri is going to find out that you're gathering power to fight him. If you take on all the magic from this troupe, and we can't figure out how to get the magic to the other witches in the coven, you'll be the only one who can fight him."

"At least someone will be able to," she pointed out. "And it said all magic can be used against void magic."

He didn't look happy, but she'd already taken the hands of the faery with the long fuchsia braid. She smiled and opened herself to him. Within seconds, she could tell he didn't have any void magic.

One at a time, the rest of the troupe came to be tested. Searching drained more and more of her energy. Most didn't have anything, but it was exhausting even when they didn't. When they did, it was both exhilarating and almost painful. As she did the incantation, and the magic dropped into place inside her, joining her own void magic, she felt a surge of energy. But her breath was knocked out of her, and she wanted to curl up and take a nap.

After a half-dozen fae had transferred their bound magic to her, Quill held up a hand. "That's enough," he said firmly. "Sagely, you're about to pass out. You can't keep doing this. They'll have to wait. You can come back."

"No," she said. "We don't know when Viziri might attack again, and we have to be as ready as we're able. It's not that bad."

"You're lying," he accused. "I can feel your exhaustion. You're going to break down. You need some time to rest and recover. If you don't have strength to fight, what good is all this magic?"

"He's right," Fox said, standing for the first time since they arrived. "Sagely, we don't want to put you in danger. You are a savior to my people. I would never wish any ill to come to you when doing a favor for us."

"I'm fine," she said, glancing at Quill.

Obviously taking this as a sign that she didn't want to admit weakness in front of Quill, Fox turned to the warlock. "Why don't you go home and take care of your coven, Quill. Sagely can stay here and rest, and when she's feeling better, she can complete the transfer of magic and come back to you. If she wants."

"Not a chance," Quill growled, holding out an arm to knock Fox back when he tried to touch Sagely's shoulder.

"I'm okay," she said, lying her palms flat on the table to hold herself upright. "I need to keep going."

"No," Quill said, crouching beside her and taking her hand. "You don't need to do this all today. It's okay to rest. It doesn't mean you're weak."

"I need to finish," she insisted. "He killed my father, Quill. My mother and her unborn baby. And he will kill me the moment he gets wind of what I'm doing here. If I don't get it now, I may never have another chance."

"I can't watch you do this to yourself."

"Then don't look. Quill, please. I've come too far to stop now."

Sagely could see the hurt cross his face as her words hit. "If that's what you want," he said, standing and stalking out.

Fox gave her a wicked grin but she held up a hand. "Don't."

He hesitated, and the smile dropped from his face.

"As you wish," he said, bowing to her before returning to his seat.

After a few more transfers, she was about to burst with all the magic that had been forced into her. She was gasping, trying to breathe and not spew it all up again. She remembered measuring her capacity when she arrived that first day, and she knew she couldn't take it from the last few faeries.

Looking over at Fox, she shook her head miserably. Tears were streaming down her cheeks, but she didn't know when she'd started crying. Fox sprang to her side. "Are you hurt?"

"I can't do it," she whispered. His small hand slipped into hers, and she was surprised by its strength. Though she was bursting with magic, she'd never felt so weak.

Quill burst in through the door. "What happened?" he demanded, rushing to her, their spat forgotten. "Sagely, I'm here. Tell me what you need."

She shook her head again. "I can't do it. I can't take any more of it. And it's not enough. It's not going to be enough."

"What if I take some of what you already have," Fox asked quietly. "And then you can get it out of the others. I'll take whatever you can't hold, and I'll keep it for you."

"What?" Quill asked, turning to him with a murderous frown. Maude hissed at Fox from her perch on Quill's shoulder.

"She can't transfer it to a witch," Fox said coolly. "But she can give it to a faery. I already have some, so it should be willing to slide over to me."

"What do you mean, you have some?"

"I'm one of the faeries with void magic," Fox said.

"Then why didn't you already give it to her?"

"Because a leader looks out for his people first," Fox said. "I'm the fae king now. I have to see every single faery out of danger before I'll get rid of my own curse."

Quill looked like he was ready to punch someone, but he raised his eyebrows to Sagely in a question.

She shrugged. What else could they do?

"Fine," Quill grumbled. "But I'm staying right here with her. Don't even try to do anything funny."

He sat behind her on the bench, so she was held between his thighs, and held her up as she reached across the table. Fox sat opposite and took her hands into his. Like those of all the fae, his hands were small but strong as steel. She tried to ignore his fine features and alluring eyes, and focused instead on opening that channel of energy. Forcing herself to go on, she pressed into his inner space.

He had the magic, like he said, but her body, her energy field, refused to release its overabundance. "I don't know how to give it back," she whispered. Quill said it took powerful sorcery. She didn't have that.

"Damn it," Quill cursed, pounding a fist on the table. "I told you to stop. You've taken on too much."

"What do I do?" she whispered, feeling sick and dizzy, as if she might pass out at any moment.

"I don't know," he growled in frustration. "You and Viziri are the only witches who have enough to use it."

"So I have to be like this until he finds me and kills me?" Her voice rose as she tried to stagger to her feet. She was drained physically, mentally, and spiritually. And yet, her body was buzzing with some sick energy that refused to let her relax, as if she'd just swallowed packages of cocaine instead of magic.

"We'll find some way to help you," Quill said. "Maybe, since we're intended, we can share it through our bond, like we did our magic."

She grabbed his hands and pressed them to her middle. "Try. I have to get some of this out. It's getting stronger. It's all joining together in there, and it's too big for me."

"Can't you just use it?" Fox asked.

"She can't, because it was bound," Quill said urgently.

Sagely rested her head back against his shoulder and let their magic join. But the parcels of void sat heavy inside her, weighing her down like a thousand tons of ebony.

"Try it with me," Fox said softly, reaching across the table. She checked him for trickery, but his eyes were sympathetic and earnest. "Make me your intended."

"No way in hell," Quill said, jumping to his feet.

Sagely looked up at him miserably. "I won't do it if you don't want me to."

His nostrils flared, and the muscle in his jaw twitched and twitched. Finally he sat down behind her again. His voice was deadly calm. "Try it."

"I'm sorry. It won't mean anything." Tears streamed from her eyes again as she took Fox's hands. Quickly, she recited the incantation. Why were her engagements always born of dire emergency instead of romance?

Oh, right, because she'd been a dumbass and not listened, and she'd stretched herself too far. If Quill was a lesser man, he would have pointed that out. He would have told her it was her fault she had to add a faery to her collective.

Instead, he held her steadily, his even breaths calming

247

her as she wondered if taking Fox into her collective was an even bigger mistake than taking the void magic.

"Though I understand his animosity, I want the same for you as your warlock," Fox said. "I would die to protect you just as he would. You are an irreplaceable treasure to the fae. I may be a king, but it would be an honor to spend my life serving you."

Sagely swallowed, and the world swam before her eyes. "I invite you to be the second in my collective," she whispered, her fingers clinging to his for dear life. If this didn't work, she might die. All she could do now was trust him.

"I accept," Fox said, his face serene and without malice.

Sagely pressed the bond again, though it was enough to almost knock her out. Fox's fingers tightened, and she felt him pulling at her magic. An instinct inside her clutched at it for a moment, not wanting to relinquish the power that weakened her as it grew stronger.

Suddenly, something lifted inside her, ripping from within her chest. She screamed, and the world went black.

THIRTY-SIX

Sagely woke in a strange bed, with the wind sighing through the trees and across her face. She sat up with a start, sucking in a huge breath.

"Whoa, you okay?"

She turned to find her man and his familiar beside her, and everything in her settled just a bit. Quill was propped on the pillows, holding a battered copy of *Mrs. Dalloway* in one hand. When she stirred, he set it on the bedside table and wrapped his arms around her, pulling her to him.

"What happened?" she asked.

"You mean after you asked a faery to marry you?"

She pulled back and studied his face, but she couldn't tell if he was angry. "Yes, after that."

"Nothing. I guess he took some of the magic back and relieved the pressure. And then you blacked out."

She glanced around at the warm evening sunlight

filtering through the leaves around their little room in the trees. "When?"

"Yesterday afternoon."

"I slept all that time? Why didn't you wake me?"

He gave her a look. "You needed it."

"Fine, you're right," she said, sighing and leaning back against his strong, warm chest. She ran her fingers across his defined pecs.

"I just want you to know," he said, his hand closing over hers. "I'm not my father. Your connection with Fox, it's not something I'm going to be super stoked about, but I'm not going to snap and murder the bastard, either. It's your private business with him."

"I didn't mean to get engaged to him," she protested, sitting up.

"But you are."

"I can break it off," she said. "You said I could with you."

"Don't do it for me," he said, shaking his head. The sadness in his green eyes almost destroyed her. "You might need to channel that magic, if it comes to a battle with Viziri. You can get it back from Fox faster this way, and if there's even a chance that could save your life, then you have to take it. And he's the fae king. He might break a pact with our Majori, but he'll honor a marriage vow. Fae may be a lot of things, but like he said, they honor their word. A marriage is an extremely strong alliance."

She looked at him doubtfully. "Really?"

"Really."

"So how does this work?" she asked, lying back against him. She couldn't imagine loving Fox the way she loved Quill. But she couldn't deny she was attracted to the faery, either. Kings had been marrying to form alliances longer than they'd been marrying for love. And Fox didn't seem to have any qualms about it.

"However you want it to work," Quill said. "You call the shots."

"Do we all live together? Do I tell you both everything?"

"Hell, no," Quill said, halfway laughing. "Unless you want to kill me."

"Okay, that's good," she said. "I'd rather live with you."

"When I'm done with my training, I'll move out of the school like all the adults in the coven, and we'll have our own place. And you can come over here, or whatever your arrangement is with Fox. I don't want to know any of the particulars unless it affects our relationship."

"That's fair." She stroked his chest for a while, lost in thought, in the warmth and safety of his arms. She couldn't believe she had all this. She felt like the luckiest girl in the world.

But after a while, she had to get up and face Fox. She found him checking in on some of the faeries whose magic she'd taken. They all seemed fine, as did he. But when he saw Sagely, he immediately stepped out of the faerie dwelling and joined her.

"We should talk about what happened with us," he said, his eyes shifting around the forest. "I've never been promised to a witch before, but I know it worked for plenty in the past."

"What, witches and fae?"

"Yes," he said. "Witches and faeries were allies. You gave us your magic to keep, and I'm assuming many did it the same way you did yesterday. Through the bond of intention or marriage. I can feel it on me, this spell you cast."

She didn't think of it that way, when she was saying the words, but she guessed that's what it was. A spell to tie them together.

"Look," she said. "I was overloaded with magic, I thought I was going to die...I wasn't in my right mind. If you want out..."

"I don't." His heart-shaped face with its pointy chin was serious for once. "But I don't know how it works any better than you do."

"Um. Well. I've already asked Quill into my collective. I don't know how you feel about monogamy."

Fox laughed. "We don't stand on all that ceremony. Whatever works for you will work for me."

"Really? You don't care that I'm intended to someone else?"

"No."

"You're okay if Quill and I go ahead and have our wiccan ceremony, and get married, and live together? Maybe even have kids."

He grinned. "How lovely. But you'll come visit me, yes? Or I can visit you two, if that's your thing."

A flame of desire pulled somewhere inside her, but she pushed it back, not wanting to be greedy. "For now, let's just concentrate on drawing that warlock bastard here and getting rid of him. Maybe a few years down the road, we can revisit this thing we agreed to. Once I'm settled into things with Quill. I don't want to take on too much at once. I'm not really a relationship person."

"A witch who doesn't do relationships. And you're

expected to have plenty of them." Fox laughed, his whole face getting in on the joy of it. His sharp teeth sent a chill along her spine, but it was not all fear.

She shrugged it off. "I've got a lot to learn."

"You teach me all your witchy tricks, I'll teach you the way of the fae," he said with a smirk.

Her face warmed, and she wasn't even looking at his seductive eyes. "I'd better go."

"Wouldn't want to make your *intended* jealous."

"You're right. I wouldn't." She turned to go, but hesitated at the door to the tiny house that they'd first entered. "And Fox?"

"Yes, my queen?"

That almost did it. Her temper threatened to make her forget her manners. But her parents had raised her better than that. So instead she smiled and said, "Thank you."

"Oh, no," he said, his eyes alight with pleasure. "Thank *you.*"

THIRTY-SEVEN

On the way home, Sagely lay across the seat with her head on Quill's thigh. He stroked her hair, letting her rest. When they turned into the yard in front of the cabin, Quill ground the truck to a halt, cursing under his breath.

Sagely sat up just as Raina skidded up beside the truck. Quill had his window down, his arm along the sill, and Raina breathlessly started explaining before Quill could even turn off the ignition.

"Willow never came back," she said, her words a rush. "She's not with you? Where have you been? You were supposed to be back last night. We're all freaking out. Did the faeries attack? Were they holding you hostage?"

"Damn it," Quill yelled, pounding the steering wheel. The horn went off in one sharp blast.

"It's okay," Sagely said, putting a hand on his arm. "We'll find her."

"It's my fault," he said to the steering wheel. "I told

you not to go after her."

"She's not with you?" Raina asked again, though she could see that no one else was in the truck.

"I told you, she went off into the woods," Quill said.

"The Forest is our friend," Sagely reminded him. "It wouldn't let anything happen to her."

"You're right, you're right," he said, turning the key in the ignition. The truck sputtered off, the fan still whirring. A second later, he turned it back on. "Something's wrong. I can feel it."

"The mirror," Sagely cried, leaping from the truck. "The stone. You said it could show any time and place. Let's go." Without waiting for an answer, she sprang for the cabin. Up the steps and into the house, down the stairs, through the cavern and down the corridor. It was second nature now, even running through the solid stone walls. A minute later, she arrived at her room, Raina and Quill close behind. She sat in front of her mirror and asked to see Willow.

A second later, white mist swirled over the screen. When it cleared, they saw Willow sleeping on a bed covered by a synthetic blanket.

"Where the hell is she?" Quill growled.

"The faeries probably kidnapped her," Raina said bitterly.

"That's not a faerie house," Sagely pointed out. "But I can go back and see where she went from yesterday." She asked to see Willow arriving at the house, and the mist covered the mirror again. When it swirled away, Willow was walking through an abandoned trailer, touching everything. They moved ahead and saw her at a stream in the woods. Three boys walked up behind her, and Sagely felt Quill's body tense.

The boys looked like bad news. They were around Willow's age, but one of them was football-player big. Another was short and chubby, and the last was skinny and pimply and smoking a cigarette. All three had their hair slicked back, and they strutted like they thought they were hot shit. When Willow turned from the stream, startled, the big guy smiled like a snake.

Okay, Sagely couldn't handle watching this. She asked the mirror to move ahead to when she went to sleep. Like fast-forwarding through a tape, it skipped ahead to another scene. When it stopped, Willow was lying on a bed, and three animals were attacking her. A bear, a mountain lion, and a bobcat were tearing away chunks of her flesh. She was so covered in blood they couldn't even tell it was Willow anymore. With a final, sickening scream, she flailed wildly and then went still.

Quill grabbed the mirror and tore it from the vanity, slamming it to the floor. Sagely covered her mouth, trying not to vomit. Raina was still and pale as paste.

"Is she alive?" she whispered at last.

"I'm going to get her," Quill said, heading for the door.

"Wait," Raina said. "Let me get Shaneesha. If the shifters have her, it might not be safe."

"I'm not waiting around," Quill said, turning and storming out. He called back over his shoulder, "I'll be at the truck."

When Sagely started to follow, Raina put a hand on her arm. "Wait. Can I…can I use the stone? I want to see if my brother is still alive."

"Take it." Sagely plucked it from the wreckage of her

mirror and handed it to her. "I've seen all I want to see."

Raina pocketed it, and they sprinted from the room.

"Shifters," Sagely said as they jogged down the corridor. "I thought you said they minded their own business."

"I said the werewolves almost never leave the Second Valley," Raina said. "The Third Valley…who knows what goes on there. Shifters live by their own rules. We stay away from both the other valleys."

"Obviously with good reason," Sagely muttered. They reached the cavern where Shaneesha was training with a handful of advanced witches. Raina quickly explained to Majori Yordine what had happened, and that Quill could not be stopped. Yordine said she'd alert the coven, and if they needed more help, she'd send reinforcements. But she didn't seem concerned, which Sagely tried to take as a reassuring sign.

As they passed the cavern where the younger students trained, Eli ducked out. "What's going on?"

"Willow's in trouble," Sagely said. "I think we've got it covered."

"Let us come, too," Ingrid said, joining Eli. "We're her friends. Maybe we can help."

Sagely didn't have time to argue, so they all raced up the stairs and out into the yard. Quill already had the truck turned around and running. They all piled in, the two younger witches in the bed. The doors were barely closed when Quill gunned the engine, sending gravel flying as the truck spun out onto the dirt road.

THIRTY-EIGHT

Though Sagely wanted to ask what was going on, what they could do, she bit her tongue. Quill wouldn't know much more than she did. How could Willow be sleeping peacefully now, with no sign of what had happened last night? Had the mirror instead shown the future, an attack that hadn't happened yet? Or, when she asked to see her right now, did it show a scene from before the attack? All she knew was that it must not be too dangerous, because Yordine hadn't come with them or brought the whole coven. She seemed confident they could handle the shifters themselves.

Quill was an adult with powerful magic who had almost mastered all the elements. That was enough to reassure Sagely, too.

They pulled up outside a cream-colored trailer house with a rusty car sinking into weeds on either end, slowly succumbing to the elements. The yard was patchy with grass, wild asters, Queen Anne's lace, and other weeds interspersed with bald spots of rocky Arkansas dirt. A huge grasshopper landed on the windshield when they parked.

Quill jumped out of the truck, leaving the keys dangling in the ignition. Maude launched herself after him with a whine of protest. Sagely turned off the truck and pocketed the keys before climbing out. Eli and Ingrid hopped from the bed just as Quill began pounding on the metal door of the trailer. The others hurried to join him. If they didn't calm him down, Quill might have another murder on his hands.

For a second, Quill stopped pounding and stood at the top of the cinderblock steps. Crickets droned in the midday heat. And then, inside, they heard footsteps. Quill started pounding furiously again. A second later, the door swung inwards. Willow stood squinting out into the bright sun at them.

"What the hell?" Quill thundered.

"I'm fine," she said, stepping back. Quill charged in, and the rest of the group trailed in one by one, a little awkwardly.

Seconds later, Quill was back from searching the rooms. "Where are they?" he demanded. "Who hurt you?"

"I'm fine," Willow said again. "I was hurt, but I'm healed now."

Quill stilled and took a breath, his nostrils flaring. His eyes narrowed. "What happened?"

"I'm a shifter now," she said, raising her chin defiantly. "I was changed last night. I'm exhausted, but otherwise, I'm healed."

"What the hell?" Quill asked again, dialing down the

volume this time.

Willow gestured at the worn corduroy sofa. "Sit down. I'll get you tea. We can talk."

"Let me help," Sagely said, following her to the little kitchen.

Willow opened the fridge and took out a plastic pitcher of tea.

"We were really worried about you."

"I'm sure you were," Willow said, a note of bitterness in her voice.

"Did you do this by choice?" Sagely opened the cabinets to find a bunch of plastic cups with logos from various gas stations, radio stations, and local events. She couldn't find any glasses, so she used those.

Willow didn't answer until they were all seated. It was a tight fit, and half of them had to sit at the table while the rest took the couch.

"We saw you in the mirror," Sagely explained. "With the seeing stone Fox gave me. It looked…really horrific."

"So you spied?" Willow asked.

"You're a shifter," Quill growled.

"Would you rather I was dead?" she shot back. "I'm a shifter. I made an alliance with them, too. They're going to help us fight Viziri. So you're welcome." She raised her chin in that defiant way again, and Sagely was reminded how very young she was.

"You. You made an alliance. When?" Shaneesha asked.

"Yesterday," Willow said. "They wanted me to be a shifter. They want me. They think I'm special."

"You are special," Sagely said gently.

Willow turned to her, eyes flashing. "I thought you'd

be different," she said. "When you showed up, you were an outsider, too. But when you had weird magic, did anyone treat you like an untrustworthy mutant? Nooooo. Everyone wanted to protect you."

"Well," Sagely said, glancing at Raina. "I'm not sure I'd say no one treated me like a freak."

"I have always protected you," Quill said to Willow, his voice brimming with emotion. "Ever since our mother let you go to school with us. It was my job to protect you."

"And you did," she said. "As well as you could. But you can't change the way witches see faeries, the way *you* see faeries. I've made my decision. You don't have to like it, but I expect you to respect it."

"We do," Sagely said quickly, taking Quill's hand and squeezing it, hard, when she saw him about to protest. "But are you sure about this? It seems like you're just trying to get back at us for…something."

"I'm not," Willow said. "I'm a shifter now. You can't undo it, even if I wanted you to. And I don't. I want to learn about this part of me now. I'm probably the only shifter-witch-fae in the world. I'll still work with the elements. But I also want to know about this lifestyle. Maybe I'll like it better. If I don't, I'll come back to the academy."

"You're only sixteen," Quill said. "You can't live on your own."

"I'm not," she said. "There's a guy…he lives here. He's a bear."

Quill's fingers flexed, and his ring glowed with magic. "You're my sister."

"And I always will be," she said. "If you need me, I'm here. I'm a healer. That's what I want to be. If someone gets bitten, I'll be there to help. But I want to go to school here."

There was a long beat of silence.

"School?" Ingrid asked, like she'd never heard of it. "What school?"

"You know, regular-people school," Willow said. "I've barely ever met a commoner. I want to know about them, too."

"I guess it's time she spreads her wings," Sagely muttered to Quill. "She wants to see the world outside your burrow. Can you blame her?"

"Yes," he roared.

Before he could go on, something strange happened.

A chill raced up Sagely's spine, and she was instantly cold, as if a dark cloud had blotted out the sun on a hot day, and a chilly breeze appeared out of nowhere. Except there was no breeze through the trailer. It was just a feeling, a coldness and darkness that wouldn't go away, gnawing at her.

For a second, she thought it was her void magic doing something weird. But then she saw the others looking around with wide eyes. Willow hugged herself, and Raina sniffed the air like a dog. Quill's mink hissed, and Ingrid's crow squawked.

"What was that?" Sagely whispered.

Quill jumped to his feet. "Something is wrong. Something's happening to the coven."

An uneasiness tugged insistently inside her, as if she were being pulled by a magnet from far away. It was an unbearable feeling, an itch to go to them, to be with them, to save them. "Then let's go help them," she said, standing, too.

Quill held out a hand to stop her, his head tilted to one side as if listening. A look of intense concentration crossed his face, followed by one of dread. He looked at her, his face stricken. "We can't," he said, shaking his head. "It's too late. All their magic has gone dark."

THIRTY-NINE

"Rally the shifters," Quill said, turning to Willow. "Sagely, can you communicate with Fox through your—bond?"

"I don't know how," Willow cried. "I've been a shifter for one day!"

"Figure it out," he said. "You made the decision to be one of them, and you said they'll help us. We need all the help we can get."

"Who are we fighting against?" Ingrid asked. "Our own coven?"

"Something turned their magic," Quill said.

"Viziri," Sagely whispered. She could feel that pull in her gut, but now that she was paying attention, she knew it was not a call to help the coven. It was the pull of his magic. And it was massive.

"Quill." She grabbed his arm. "He's way more powerful than me. More than we imagined. There's no way I can fight him."

Quill took her face between his hands and kissed her hard. "You won't be alone. I will be right beside you every step of the way."

"I don't even know how to unlock the magic that's bound," she reminded him.

"We'll figure that out, too," he said, his brow knitting into a frown. He didn't say what would happen if they didn't, but she already knew. Viziri would kill her to get the magic, just like he'd tried to do that day on the side of the road.

Once it was unbound, she could use it. So she was going to have to figure out how to do that, because he obviously had.

But even with that, it was a long shot. As she looked around the room at the frightened, determined faces, she knew that these were her sisters and brothers. They'd fight to the death together, for each other. She was glad for the strong ones, Raina and Shaneesha and Quill, and scared for the others. She vowed that she'd protect them to her last breath.

If Viziri would be satisfied to leave them alone and kill her to get the magic, then she'd make that sacrifice. But she wasn't going to go down without giving him the fight of his life.

*

Sagely reached through her bond with Fox, trying to psychically communicate by sending him as much urgency and need as she could convey. She'd have to hope it was enough, because she could feel the pull of Viziri drawing closer. He must have attacked the coven when they'd gathered to discuss Willow, and finding Sagely absent, he'd taken them over. Now he was coming for her.

Meanwhile, Willow was on the phone, anxiously winding the curly cord around her finger as she dialed, barely slamming the receiver down before picking it up again. With trembling fingers, she dialed the numbers that Eli read off, one after another, and hurriedly asked each shifter who answered for help. Each time she hung up, she nodded or shook her head to let the witches know if help was coming before dialing the next number.

It struck Sagely how odd it felt to be in a house again, but the thought was pushed away by the sound of a truck bouncing into the drive. Quill sprang to the door, grumbling about teaching those shifters a lesson.

Sagely started to get up, but Raina motioned for her to continue summoning the faeries while she dealt with Quill and the stream of shifters arriving. For once, Sagely felt no qualms about letting Raina tend to Quill. He was hers now, all the way. She closed her eyes again, and let her fae blood and her witch promise summon her second intended.

Twenty minutes later, Sagely's eyes snapped open. A strange smell had entered the trailer, damp and scorched at once, but it was not in the air around them. It was inside her, bubbling up. The smell of Viziri. The bound parcels of magic strained inside her, yanking her to her feet. She was being sucked in, as if he really was a black hole. A black hole intent on consuming her magic and leaving her for dead.

"Sagely," Ingrid cried, leaping to her feet. But she was already opening the door, stumbling out into the hot, dry yard. She managed to overcome the pull and stop, grinding her heels into the red dirt. It was not just Viziri. The whole coven was in the yard, not just the students but whole families. She couldn't sense a single one of them. He'd done something to them.

"Mom," Quill said, starting down the steps behind Sagely. She held up a hand, warning him and the others. As soon as she saw Mrs. Golden's eyes, she knew that Quill's mother was no longer on their side. Her eyes met Sagely's, but there was nothing behind them, just a blank, black stare with no recognition.

"He's controlling them," she yelled. One of the shifters leapt from the bed of his truck, whipped his shirt over his head, ripped off his shorts, and turned into a stag. As his huge antlers pierced into the nearest witch, Sagely tried not to cry out. That was someone from her coven. Someone who was no longer a friend but an empty-eyed zombie who had come to kill her.

The witches started throwing magic at the shifters, who began shifting into animal form and charging. None of the witches had their familiars, so it was animal against human. Screams and snarls echoed through the yard. Yordine bared her teeth and leapt for Sagely. Sagely spun away, delivering a side-kick to the Majori's head before she was thrown to the ground. Quill leapt in front of her to protect her while she clambered to her feet. She couldn't see what had knocked her down, and a second later, she was slammed down again.

"He's controlling you," Raina screamed behind them. "Resist his magic."

"Help her," Quill shouted, throwing Majori Romero across the yard with a volley of fire. "I'll hold them off as long as I can."

"How?" Shaneesha asked, leaping from the door to crouch over Sagely.

Suddenly the Wise One's voice slipped into their minds. "Void magic can be combatted with all magic and no magic."

"How?" Sagely cried as she was jerked to her feet. She slammed into Quill's back, and he stumbled forward, just enough to be hit with a blast of gravel that pierced into his flesh like shrapnel. He sucked in a breath and steadied her with one hand.

"She's telling us to fight with all magic and no magic," Shaneesha said. "What the hell does that mean?"

"Use all our magic?" Raina asked, looking frantic as she grabbed hold of Sagely to stop her from pitching forward.

Something dark descended over Sagely's mind like a funeral shroud. His magic surrounded her, sank into her.

No, no, no!

She didn't want his magic, but her void magic sucked it up like a hungry sponge.

Suddenly, her fist flew out and punched Quill in the gut. He doubled over as she fought against her own body. Viziri was a puppet master, and she was now one of his puppets.

Oh, hell no! She would not be controlled, would not be helpless.

"All the magic," she cried. "All the elements. Let's see what happens."

A look shot around their little circle as the puppet witches advanced on them.

Seven of us, a small army of them.

But she could tell she was on to something.

"We've never done it with a void in the circle," Shaneesha said. "But that bastard isn't getting one more witch tonight. Let's do this."

She grabbed hold of Raina's hand, and they began to chant an incantation.

Sagely swung around, a knife-hand strike ready for Quill's throat. He ducked under her and gripped her in a bear hug, pinning her arms.

"Willow," he yelled. "You said you'd always help. We need you."

Two trucks bounced into the drive, slamming to a halt in a spray of gravel, and a dozen more witches jumped out. To Sagely's relief, they had clear, normal eyes, and their familiars in tow. They homed in on the circle around Sagely, and she felt a surge of power as they joined their familiar magic with hers.

Suddenly, clouds appeared out of nowhere, roiling across the sky. Ingrid and Eli huddled close, holding hands. Ingrid took Raina's free hand, joining the chant. Quill leapt in front, blocking a ball of magic from one creepy-eyed warlock after another.

As the storm swirled overhead, they became faster, angrier, agitated by the chant. A charge built in the air, and the trees whipped in a sudden wind. Like the feeling they'd had earlier, the day had gone dark and cold.

"Let 'em have it, Shaneesha," Quill yelled over his shoulder, ducking a witch's fireball. "Hurry, I can't hold them off much longer on my own."

Out of the tossing trees, a dozen tiny people floated down, as light as dandelion fluff. "The enemy of my enemy is my friend," Fox said, leaping into the air and crashing his heel into a warlock's blank, black eyes.

"The void is in them," the Wise One said in Sagely's head. "Unlock it within yourself, and you can share their magic once again."

Anyone with void magic could share with her. Almost all the witches had drunk the brew. If only she could unlock the parcels the fae had given her.

Shit. This was her fault. They'd drank the brew at her initiation, taking a tiny bit of her magic. That was why Viziri could control them, and he wasn't controlling the group around her.

Except Willow.

When she looked back, Willow's eyes were rolled back in her head, flickering from white to black. Her pure, untouched goodness was now polluted with the void.

Sagely fought against her puppet-body. "You're part of this," she yelled to Willow as her hair whipped across her face in the swirling wind. "Without you, the circle won't be complete. We need you. You're the fourth element."

Willow blinked dumbly at her, sight coming back to her eyes after a moment. "And you're the fifth."

"Complete the circle," said the tall shifter from the vision in the mirror. One of the boys who'd attacked Willow. He sets a hand on her back and pushed her forward. "Show us what you can do, Goldie."

Willow hesitated, then stepped forward. Eli, who had been working on the wind with what mastery of the element he had, fell back to let Willow take his place. She clasped hands with Shaneesha on one side and Ingrid on the other.

But as soon as Eli dropped the hands of the others, his eyes darkened.

"No," Ingrid screamed, letting go of the others' hands.

"There's no time," Raina said firmly, grabbing her hand again.

"But it's Eli," Ingrid said.

"It's too late," Shaneesha said as Eli mechanically walked into the skirmish.

"Let's hope this works," Raina said, resuming her chant.

As Willow began to chant with them, the wind, which had been kicked up by the other witches, quadrupled in strength. Dirt seared into their skin, and Sagely struggled to keep her eyes open. The four elemental witches circled her, their hands locked together so she couldn't step through to join Viziri. Their chant seemed to hypnotize her.

"Four is the perfect number. Four is whole and complete, the square of a square. Four directions, four seasons, four elements. Join to protect our sister who is without element, without season, without direction. Make us five, a circle instead of square, as our earth mother is a circle, the true perfection and union of all."

A bolt of lightning seared from the sky, blinding white as it ripped the trees and fried the road at the end of the drive. Several witches screamed. The wind ceased, except for around the circle of chanting witches, where it began to spin like a cyclone. Something inside Sagely cracked, and she screamed, too.

From what seemed far away, Quill's panicked voice asked if she was okay. Her body was under her control again, collapsed to one knee on the ground. Inside her, she could feel the void magic loosening, stretching out into every limb, every pore. She stood, blackness swirling around her, radiating from her in every direction. For one moment, the power of it surged through her, and she almost choked on it. She felt invincible, as if she could squash everyone on the planet like a bug. Giddy laughter threatened to bubble from her lips.

Her friends gasped and dropped their hands from the circle as she stepped forward. The sea of hypnotized witches parted, and a figure stepped through to meet her. Not only were his eyes void and black, but his entire figure was, just as she remembered. Even in broad daylight, he was so dark that she could see nothing but his shape and the black cloak whipping behind him in the wind. He wasn't radiating power, as she was. He had consumed it, and it had all turned inwards.

Dark clouds roiled overhead and thunder cracked, shaking the ground beneath their feet.

"So you're the one with the void magic," he said, his voice a leathery hiss. "I've come for what's mine."

"Come and get it, you coward." Sagely spit the words at him. "You killed my pregnant mother to get the magic that she possessed. Now you turn my coven into your sheep and send them to the slaughter instead of fighting one small woman by yourself. What kind of warlock are you?"

She was yanked forward by a vortex of blackness, as if he would vacuum her into the void of himself. But she ground her heels in and remembered the words of the Wise One. Remembering her elemental magic training, she called upon the earth to hold her firm.

"You won't even show your face," she snarled at Viziri.

"You want to see my face?" he asked, sounding amused.

Around him, all the witches in Sagely's coven had gone preternaturally still. He had stopped using them as puppets so he could focus on her. But she was not alone in this fight. Behind her, she could still feel the swirling, buzzing magic of her friends, her sisters, her coven. Her family.

Suddenly and without warning, the blackness that enveloped Viziri flickered. Then it began to melt away, and he came into view like a Polaroid photo. He looked... familiar.

He was aged, but she recognized the square jaw and dark blond hair combed back into a widow's peak. She'd seen him kill her parents. That was why. A wash of red fury flashed across her field of magic.

A ball of pure black emptiness shot from Viziri's hand and crashed into Quill's chest, and he fell to his knees. With a squeal, Maude fell to the ground, limp as death. Quill's magic went completely dark, as if a light had been extinguished. Not like the void magic the others had, but the darkness of a dark warlock full of shock and hatred and murderous intent.

"What's the matter?" Viziri sneered. "Stand up and fight your father like a real man."

Quill didn't move. He had fallen to one knee, his head bowed, shaking slowly back and forth. Sagely could see the muscles in his arms straining against what he wanted to do. She could feel the infinite depths of his rage and shame. And she could see the ball of void magic searing into his chest, towards his heart, like a coal burning through his flesh. Blood seeped from the wound.

Sagely crouched beside him. "Quill," she said, taking his face between her hands. His magic only flickered towards hers. His eyes were still green, though. He was still himself. He hadn't been controlled, just injured.

"Oh, this is just too pathetic," Viziri snarled. "Give me your magic and I'll go. You're not worth it."

"What's happening to him?" Willow cried, hovering with her hand over her heart. "His magic is dark. He's completely consumed."

"He's not consumed," Sagely said firmly. "He's still himself."

Himself, but without magic that could help them.

"Go," Quill said through clenched teeth. "You're a fighter, Sagely. You have the void magic to defeat him. You're the only one who can."

"But you're hurt."

"Don't stay for me," he said, his fingers straining until they cracked the dirt apart under his feet and crumbled the hard-packed soil. Pitch black smoke swirled from the symbols on his ring. "I can't protect you. My magic can only destroy something now."

"So help me destroy him."

He clutched the dirt swallowing his hands like it was the only thing saving him right now. "If I failed, I'd destroy you instead."

"Then don't fail."

"I don't have void magic to fight him with. If I kill my own father, I'm no better than he is. Maybe worse." He tipped sideways, clutching at the black nothingness eating into him. Raina and Shaneesha rushed to hold him up.

"Go," he said again, wincing above the pain. "I'll never forgive myself if you don't at least try. But don't you dare die on me."

"Then you can't either," Sagely said, tears streaming down her cheeks. "You better not. Promise."

"I'll hold on."

Without another word, Sagely stood to face the father of the man she loved. "All right, old man," she said. "It's me you're after. So fight me."

FORTY

Viziri's magic wrenched her forward, and this time, she waved the other witches back when they reached out their magic.

"That's more like it," he said. "I knew you must have a little faerie in you. They're always…what do you kids say nowadays? *Ready to rumble.*"

"Less talk," she growled, raising her fists and getting into fighting stance. "More action."

"That's cute," he said. "Just like a faery. For a minute, I thought the daughter of that bitch I married might be the fae-witch who had it. But I should have known she could never raise a warrior with all that peace, love, and happiness bullshit. Even my own son cowers like a beaten dog before me."

"Stop hurting my friends," she said. "Now you deal with me."

Striking out with faerie swiftness, she slammed her

fist into his jaw. He stumbled back, shock crossing his face. Apparently, warlocks weren't used to physical attacks. He expected her to fight with only magic.

"And now look at him," Viziri said, spitting blood in the dirt at her feet. "He's a dark warlock, just like his father. What is it they say about apples falling far from the tree?"

"He's nothing like you," she growled, striking out again. This time, Viziri was ready, and he grabbed her arm and slammed her to the ground. Suddenly, she was back on the roadside where he'd first attacked her. Completely bewildered and injured, expecting help, not an attack. She was not that naïve anymore.

She leapt to her feet, but he hurled her down again, his magic crushing her into the dirt. Squirming and then kicking in fury, she tried to rise, but she couldn't. He held his hand over her, pressing her into the dirt with some invisible force. She was a butterfly, trapped under the pin of his magic.

All around them, the witches and warlocks of her coven stood motionless, silent witnesses. Shifters, including Willow, were nursing the wounded. The fae stood guard, knowing they couldn't help in a battle of magic. And Quill. Quill had collapsed into the dirt. Raina was kneeling over him, trying to bring him back.

Fury boiled through Sagely.

"You killed my parents," she said. "And for what? You didn't even get their magic, because they'd already had a child. You're nothing but a sick, power-starved psychopath."

Something flashed across Viziri's face, but she couldn't read the expression before it was replaced by a sneer. "Power is everything, foolish child," he said. "Don't you feel it? When the void magic was unlocked within you, didn't you want to use it? That's power. Your coven may simper on about love and peace, but the reality is, power runs this world. The powerful have always risen to the top, and they always will."

Viziri leaned over her and grasped her throat, his grip crushing. He was right. He was powerful, and he was going to kill her. All the love on earth couldn't save her now. Sucking in a deep breath, he flickered to pitch blackness again. In answer, the blackness swirling around her streamed into his mouth. He was literally consuming her magic. Though she tried to hold back, after a minute, she couldn't. She screamed.

Just as she thought she'd lose her mind, something dark and urgent pressed into her. Instantly, she recognized it. Fox's energy. She grasped at it, opening herself to their connection while trying to stay closed to Viziri. A rush of Fox's naughty, playful, fierce energy washed over her, and she found a dark hole in it. One of the bound magic parcels. She pulled it into herself. But just as quickly, something ripped a hole inside her, and the parcel was gone. She screamed again.

"That's a neat little trick," Viziri said, his voice echoing from inside the swirling blackness of his form. "Where'd that magic come from?"

She shook her head, grasping at his iron hand, but his fingers tightened further. She was losing consciousness. The words from the book came back to her, floated through her head along with what little else she knew about this magic.

Void magic can be battled with all magic and no magic.

Every magic can be defeated by its opposite.
The opposite of nothing is something.
The opposite of struggle is surrender.
The opposite of dark is light.

Suddenly, she knew what he was doing. He was trying to piss her off, to make her void magic dark like his. Like he'd made Quill.

Quill. Her magic pulsed weakly in his direction, searching for his familiar, comforting presence. His strength that could save her, like she'd saved him once, when he'd become her intended. Could he send her some of his magic now?

Raina's words were faint, faraway. "It's not working," she cried, panicked. "He has no magic left that responds to mine. It's all dark."

"Help him," Ingrid cried.

"I can't." Sagely heard the sadness, the finality, in Raina's voice, and she knew this battle was over.

Summoning the last bits of her strength, she gathered all the void inside her. Swirling emptiness swam through her veins, centering in her heart, where a black hole opened. Viziri's fingers tightened, and blackness overtook her vision. With the last bit of energy she possessed, she turned the black hole inside out and blasted it into Viziri's face.

FORTY-ONE

It was only a few seconds before her vision cleared. Viziri was gone. So was the coven. And so was all the void magic she'd had inside. He'd gotten what he came for.

Sobbing, she rolled onto her side. Around her, a handful of witches were left—the ones that had arrived late and had never been under Viziri's control. The ones who hadn't drank the brew with her magic. A few of them ran to loved ones who had been injured or killed in the fight. The cries of fallen fighters sounded all over the yard.

But Sagely hadn't given up for them. Forcing herself to her knees, she began to crawl across the dirt.

Ingrid ran across her path, nearly stepping on her hand. "Eli," she called desperately, though it was obvious he was gone.

But Quill was still there.

Sagely crawled forward another pace. Suddenly, strong arms circled her waist and lifted her off her feet as if she were weightless. She struck out, but she was no match for Fox's faerie strength. He shifted around to cradle her in his arms.

"Someday, when it's you and I who need each other, I hope he will return this favor," Fox said. With that, he sprang across the yard in a single bound and knelt at Quill's side. Gently, he lowered Sagely to the ground.

"Thank you," she breathed.

Fox bent and pressed his lips to her forehead, then stood and leapt back to his people, giving her and Quill a moment together.

Quill glared at her with undisguised anger. "Why didn't you kiss him while he was here, maybe rub it in my face a little more."

Stunned, Sagely opened her mouth to defend herself. But then she stopped. She wouldn't react the way he wanted, the way his magic wanted. That would only feed his anger.

The opposite of fighting was peace. And the opposite of dark was light. She'd only been a witch for a few months, and her magic had always been tainted with darkness. It didn't bother her, because she didn't know anything else. And now, it let her slip into her bond with Quill, although his magic was all hard and bitter.

"Come on," she said, taking his face between her hands. "You told me how to make dark magic light. Creation. Love. Being my intended." With those words, she kissed him.

At first he resisted, bitterness and shame and hatred coloring even this. After a moment, though, his lips responded, his kiss demanding and forceful. He rolled over onto her and pressed her to the hard ground. A flicker of fear shivered through her when she felt his unrelenting, hard body crushing hers. She couldn't get away. If she tried, he could stop her. His lips crushed hers so violently she tasted blood. A spasm of panic wracked her body.

But she didn't break the kiss. She knew Quill. Deep, deep down, he was good, no matter what shade of darkness had cast a shadow across his magic. His magic may have gotten twisted, but he wasn't. Quill would never hurt her. He couldn't. It was not in his nature, not anywhere in his makeup. He was incapable of harming her.

Relaxing away from her instinctual fear, she ran her hands down his taut muscles, relishing the strength of him, letting it thrill her with excitement rather than fear. Softening her lips against his, she surrendered for the second time that hour, giving herself up completely to his control. Trusting that no matter what he did to her, it was out of love.

At last, she felt a trace of tenderness slip into his embrace.

Slowly, she pulled away. "I love you, you big, beautiful warlock," she said, forcing his green eyes to meet hers, to see her sincerity. "And I'm never going to stop. So you better just get that doubt off your face and show me some of that superior warlock skill you've been talking about for months."

"We're going to need some privacy for that," he said, his lips twisting into the slightest smile. A bit of light filtered through that darkness.

"Just like a man," she said, rolling her eyes. "The thought of sex can literally cure anything."

"No, but the act can," he said, his eyes growing warmer, sparkling again.

"When we tell our kids about this, I'll say my love brought you back."

"Okay," he said, a dimple sinking into his stubbly cheek. "You do that."

FORTY-TWO

A few days later, they met in the big cavern, which felt empty with only a dozen witches and their familiars in it. Most of them weren't students, and Sagely hardly knew them.

"I still don't understand how everyone disappeared," Quill said. "It doesn't make sense. It's…it's impossible."

"I'm telling you, he just went…*poof!* Sucked up into a black hole," Shaneesha said.

"Along with your magic," Quill grumbled to Sagely, a deep frown creasing his brow.

"But why us?" asked an older man. "Why didn't we get taken over?"

"I don't know," Quill said, his shoulders hunched. He stared miserably at the table where they'd measured their magic that first day. Sagely wondered how much he'd have now, if he placed his hands on the table.

But it measured capacity, and he'd still have just as

large a capacity for magic. Whatever he'd spent, it would eventually come back to him. He just needed time to recharge.

So did she, but she knew she wouldn't get it. Not yet.

"I know," she said quietly.

"What? You do?" Raina asked, her eyes narrowing.

Sagely nodded, knowing this confession was not going to win her any points with Raina. "I think…it's my fault."

"Figures," Raina said, but she didn't look like she wanted to murder Sagely, so that was an improvement. Though she'd expected Raina to be an enemy from the start, she'd turned out to be a friend who could always be counted on to have her back. She was a sister to Sagely—and to Quill. Like sisters, they didn't always agree. But knowing she could trust Raina let her use her energies where they were needed.

"It's not your fault," Quill said.

Sagely had heard that too many times from him. He always wanted to protect her, but sometimes, it really was her fault.

"They were taken over because I made them susceptible to void magic," she said. "That's how he was able to control them. Because he had similar magic, but stronger. Like calls to like, right?"

"Willow took your blood at the initiation," Quill pointed out.

"And she started to be taken over," Shaneesha reminded him.

"Maybe she could resist because of her faerie blood, the same way I'm immune to their venom," Sagely said.

"I like that answer," Fox said with a grin. "And

285

you're not immune to the venom. It just affects you differently."

Sagely ignored him, but she could feel her face warming at the memory of exactly how much she'd enjoyed that venom. It had made her stronger, though. Maybe that's how she'd resisted Viziri, though he'd gotten control of her until she fought it. But she hadn't been devoured like the other witches. She'd come back to herself.

"Maybe it was her shifter blood," Quill suggested, glowering at Fox.

Unlike Quill, Fox had been unharmed in the fight. While Quill was still recovering, Fox was as spry and irritating as ever.

"Did anyone here drink the brew that had Sagely's blood?" Raina asked. As they surveyed the witches, one by one, the others shook their heads.

"She's right," Shaneesha said. "That's got to be it."

"It's my fault they're gone," Sagely said. "So I'm going to bring them back."

"Like hell you are," Quill said, jumping to his feet. "You are not fighting Viziri again."

"I won't fight him," she said, holding up her hands. "But I'm going to get the coven back. I can't leave them to be his puppets."

"And Eli," Ingrid said softly. Sagely gave her a reassuring smile.

"You don't even know where they went," Quill said. "Or if...they're alive." He muttered the last words, wincing as he said it.

"But she can look," Fox said. "Because of the stone I gave her."

"About that…" Sagely darted a glance at Raina. "Actually, I kind of…gave it away."

"You what?" Fox barked, spinning on her. "I gave you that as a…a…"

While he spluttered, Sagely shrugged. "I know it's rare, but Raina needed it."

"You have it?" Fox demanded of Raina.

"Yes, but——."

"Give it back."

"There's no need to fight over it," Quill said hurriedly. "It's still here. Raina, why do you need it?"

"I used it to see my brother," Raina said quietly.

"Your brother?" Quill asked. "What brother?"

A tiny part of Sagely was pleased that he didn't know everything about Raina.

"I had a brother," Raina said. "He was kidnapped by faeries when I was a kid. I wanted to see if he was alive."

Sagely found herself holding her breath as she waited for Raina to go on. She hadn't wanted to pry after giving her the stone, so she hadn't asked.

"And?" Shaneesha said at last.

"And he's alive," Raina said, biting her lip as a smile began to form.

Sagely let out a breath. "That's great."

"I was thinking…maybe I'd go and find him. I'm a water witch. I don't belong here. I never belonged here. I stayed for you, Quill. But you don't need me now."

"We do need you," Quill said quietly. "You're part of the coven."

"I never meant to join an earth coven," Raina said. "And honestly, I can't watch you two together anymore. It's too hard. You're in a collective. There's no more reason to stay."

"I can think of one reason," Shaneesha said. "Who's going to balance my fire?"

"Where's your brother?" Sagely cut in.

Raina's eyes went misty, a faraway look falling across her face. "He's at the sea."

"Fine, we'll help you find him," Sagely said. "It should be easy with the stone. You can join his coven, and we'll take the stone and use it to find our coven. Is everyone agreeable to that?"

Quill sank back onto his stool, fixing his eyes on the table again. Sagely could feel the magic he'd given her, the only magic she had left. She could feel the dark, muddled hue of it. It had yet to recover. But she could also feel Quill's resistance to the idea of going after the coven.

"They'll come back," he said at last.

"Look, I know it's your father," she said softly, sliding in across from him. "You don't have to go."

"It's not that," he said. "It's…Willow. I promised my mother I'd always protect her. And I failed."

"And now she's with those shifters, and you don't trust them."

His shoulders slumped in defeat. "Not after seeing how they changed her. And my mother is gone, with the others…"

"And you made a promise to her."

He raised his eyes, misery pooling there. "I can't leave Willow now."

"And what about us?" asked another warlock. "What about the coven that's still here?"

"I'll go with Sagely," Fox said with a wink. "I'll take good care of her."

"The four of us will go," Sagely said. "We'll look out for each other. Stronger together, right?"

"And I'm supposed to sit on my ass while you go off into danger?"

"Yes," she said, leaning across the table to kiss him. "You said witches are matriarchal. So it should be fine for me to go off on a dangerous quest while you protect the coven at home."

"Not funny," he growled, slipping a hand around the back of her neck. He pulled her in for a rough kiss.

"Let's talk more in private," she whispered. "I think we should be alone for this."

Back in Quill's room, he sank down onto the edge of the bed and dropped his head into his hands. "I can't let you go," he said miserably. "I'll find a way to come with you. I'll bring my sister along."

"Willow's not going to leave the shifters," Sagely pointed out, resting a hand on his shoulder. "She won't even come back here. How are you going to make her leave the state?"

"I'll make her," he growled. "She's not old enough to make that decision."

"You can't kidnap your sister," Sagely said gently. "I'll be careful, I promise. I'll call you from the road. And I'll see you with the stone. How about every night at ten, I'll look and see what you're doing, and you can talk to me?"

"I won't be able to see you," he said, lifting his head. "I can't let you put yourself in danger because of me."

"Not because of you," she said. "Because of your father. You're not your father, remember? He would have come after me for the void magic with or without your interference. It was me he was after all along. All you did was save my life. No big deal, right?" She smiled, hoping to lighten the mood.

Quill answered with a half-hearted smile. "And you repay me by running off with your other fiancé."

Sagely put a hand on his chest to push him back and straddled his lap. "Is that what you're worried about?"

"No," he said, leaning back on his elbows. His warm hands rested on her knees, and this time, his smile was more genuine.

She let her red hair cascade over her shoulder as she leaned forward and kissed him. "Liar."

"Hmm, maybe a little," he said, stretching up to kiss her again.

Lacing her hands around his neck, she sank down against him, pressing deeper into the kiss. His magic was still chaotic and darker than it should be, but instead of making her wary, it excited her. She couldn't read him so well now, but their connection buzzed across her skin, down her back, up her thighs.

"Then you better give me something worth remembering when I'm on the road," she said, pulling away at last. She reached for the hem of her shirt and peeled it off over her head.

Quill's eyes went muzzy with desire as his fingers traced over her hips, up her sides. His ring put off a slight vibration as it grazed her skin. "Now? Tonight?"

"What are we waiting for?"

For a second, he ran his fingertips over her skin, watching as if transfixed. Tracers lit up along every nerve ending as his fingers skimmed over her back. But then he met her eyes, and she saw a resolve there she hadn't expected. "It feels too much like a goodbye," he said. "Like a final farewell."

"It's a promise," she said. She thought she might scream if she couldn't have him. She was finally ready. "A promise I'll be back."

"I've waited this long," he said. "I can wait until you're back."

"Then I better make it a short trip," she said. "I don't know how long I can wait."

His expression darkened, and he worked to swallow. "You'll have Fox there."

"Don't even say that," she said, giving his shoulders a shove. But a part of her knew that it would be even harder to resist Fox, with his faerie blood calling to her. And he wouldn't be so gentlemanly and patient as Quill had been.

"It's okay," Quill said. "I know it's going to happen eventually. You're going marry him, too."

"I'm going to marry you first," she said. "You'll always be my first love, Quill. My first husband."

"You don't have to do that."

"I want to." She leaned down and kissed him again, this time with the same resolve he had. "You'll be my first. I promise. I want you to. You've waited for me all this time. I can wait for you while we're apart."

He swallowed hard, his hands tightening on her hips. "I'm honored."

"You should be."

"I do have one request for tonight, though," he said, smiling up at her.

"What's that?" she asked, unbuttoning his jeans.

He caught her wrists in his hand. "We can save that one thing until we're married, but tonight, we'll do everything else. You're not leaving this room until morning."

She smiled coyly at him. "That sounds more like a command than a request."

He sat up, his arm circling her waist. When he pulled her body against his, the explosion of sparkles through her blood almost made her cry out. "Tomorrow you get to lead your troops off on your mission," he growled. "Tonight, I'm the boss."

FORTY-THREE

The morning came too soon. As they loaded up Raina's car, Sagely lingered, trying to catch moments alone with Quill.

"Are you sure you have to do this now?" he asked. "Couldn't you wait until my sister's gotten over this craziness?"

"I'm responsible for what happened to them," she said. "And it's my coven now, too. You can take care of what's left here. The precious few members left need your protection."

"I want to protect you," he said, taking her hand.

"That's what I'm here for," Fox said, stepping up behind Sagely.

She sighed. "Exactly. He's disposable. I'll just use him as a shield."

Quill looked pleased by this answer. "And you'll have two of our most powerful witches to guard you."

"Exactly," she said. "You're the one we should be worrying about."

Quill walked her to the car, and after the others had gotten in, he pulled her into a long, tight embrace. She stood on tiptoes, her arms circling his neck, and kissed him with all the passion and pain and uncertainty of the moment. When she finally let him go, he pressed his fist to his heart. "If you need me, I'll feel it in your magic."

She climbed in the car, trying not to cry in front of him. "Take good care of Rizzo," she said, and closed the door. Her cat didn't even bother to look up from where she was sunning herself on the porch.

"I will," Quill said. "I'll treat her like my own familiar." Maude bared her teeth at that, and Quill gave her head a little pet. "Almost like my own," he amended.

As the car pulled away, Sagely could feel their magic stretching thin. An almost unbearable pain thrummed through her, along the channel of their shared bond. How could she do this? How could she leave him? She doubled over, fighting for breath. She had to go back. She couldn't do it. She wasn't strong enough.

But when she opened her mouth, no words came out. She bit her lips together and clenched her fists in her lap. She would not turn back. Quill needed her to be strong. He needed to fulfill his promise to his mother, to take care of his sister. And he needed her to bring back his coven.

And she needed to do this on her own. To know that their bond wasn't just proximity and shared magic. That their love was real and lasting. That it would stand the test of time and separation.

So she turned forward, and steeled herself for the

journey ahead. She would get her coven back from that dark-magic wielding bastard, and she'd bring them home. And though she'd told Quill otherwise, she knew that she would fight Viziri before she returned. The world needed to be safe from him. She might have given him her void magic, but she still had her internal flame, the one that would rekindle her magic. It would lead her to Viziri, and this time, only one of them would walk away from the fight.

And her boots were made for walking.

ABOUT THE AUTHOR

Lena Mae Hill still hasn't outgrown her love of fairy tales and never intends to. She is the two-time USA Today Bestselling author of more than twenty young adult and new adult books, including The Winslow Witch Chronicles and the Young Witch series, an upcoming series of fairy tales about the next generation of witches in the First Valley. Girl Among Wolves trilogy is a set of fairy tales also set in the Three Valleys. Lena Mae enjoys the challenge of finding new ways to tell classic tales, twisting them together with other tales, and interweaving her own stories together.

You can find her online at lenamaehill.com and most social media channels.

www.ingramcontent.com/pod-product-compliance
Lightning Source LLC
Chambersburg PA
CBHW020230260626
47156CB00002B/613

* 9 7 8 1 9 4 5 7 8 0 3 2 5 *